The
PAYMENT

S.G. MimLance

iUniverse, Inc.
Bloomington

The Payment

iUniverse books may be ordered through booksellers or by contacting:

iUniverse
1663 Liberty Drive
Bloomington, IN 47403
www.iuniverse.com
1-800-Authors (1-800-288-4677)

ISBN: 978-1-4620-0132-3 (pbk)
ISBN: 978-1-4620-0133-0 (ebk)

Printed in the United States of America

iUniverse rev. date: 3/15/2011

ONE

THERE WERE sixty-seven applicants for two job offers. All women except for two men, competing for the position offered: house cleaner. The waiting room of the employment agency was small and dark, the carpet on the floor showed a few bald spots and the plastic flowers in the vase on the wobbly table had known better and straighter days. The receptionist was smoking and chewing gum at the same time and when the phone rang, she pulled the gum out of her mouth to speak into the receiver. She wore a very mini skirt and a very tight blouse; her make-up made one think of an untidy painter's canvas.

"Next" she called after an applicant left the office. A man entered a room bearing the sign "Interview" on the door. Soon he too left.

"Next" the receptionist called. It was my turn; I gathered my folder and handbag and went in. Two very blue and very tired eyes X-rayed me from head to toe, then their owner invited me to sit down.

"You are Raphaëlle Luens?" the interviewer asked.

"Yes I am." She looked through my file and lingered longer on my résumé. Suddenly I felt insecure...I may not get this job...I will be rejected...She doesn't like me...

"Do you know that you are over qualified? You have excellent schooling, you could aim higher than housecleaning, what are you doing here?"

"Applying for the house cleaner position." The blue X-ray machine met my green eyes head on. I held the gaze.

"You could work in a nice office and a nice building, you know. Why housecleaning?"

"I enjoy cleaning. Especially in a house that really needs cleaning; and I do a very good job if I may say so myself."

"Are you sure this is what you want? I know a company that is looking for a receptionist and if you wish, I could recommend you, the pay is much better than housecleaning."

"Thank you very much, you are very kind, but I still choose housecleaning. I could start any time."

"So be it then. How would you like to work for a rich widow who lives in St.Thomas? Will it be too far from your home?"

1

"No, it is not too far, the drive doesn't scare me and I guarantee you the lady will be satisfied with my work. When do I start?"

"The first of June at nine a.m. Go see Murielle the receptionist, she will give you documents to sign. Good luck."

"Thank you, Ma'am."

"Call me Francesca, and let me know how you are doing."

'Over qualified' she said...I only showed high school on my résumé. I am glad I didn't disclose the rest, she probably would have screamed at me and shown me the door. My work paper showed that my new employer was a woman named Mrs. Betty-Ann Jahe, widowed, who lived alone in a large mansion located on the border between St.Thomas and Windoaks. That's a long drive from home and I hoped the road would be well plowed in the winter. I took the subway home and stopped at the grocery store to buy a bag of apples as my aunt Sumika asked this morning.

"I got it, Aunt Sumi, I got it! The job, I mean. I start on June first," I said as I entered our house through the side door.

"Don't tell me it's the housecleaning... oh Raffee, how could you? Why did you? You could teach high school, what are you doing cleaning people's houses?" Aunt Sumi almost yelled at me. I closed my eyes, raised my eyebrows and smiled, nodding on and on. But she wouldn't let go.

"Some universities would also welcome you, teaching runs in the family, why all of a sudden housecleaning?"

"All right, Auntie, I'll tell you why. In those days when you were teaching, students were respectful and looked up to their teachers and academia thrived. Today students insult their teachers or kill them. They get an F on their paper and you need a bodyguard. There is too much administrative paperwork for teachers and less pure teaching. Physical education has become extinct, children are obese and sick and parents wonder why. Do you really want me to teach in these conditions? I hold teaching way above other professions, in my opinion teaching is a calling, not just a job. It is sacred and accepts no compromise."

"Your thinking would make you a superior teacher, but the conditions you describe are unfortunately very true. The profession is losing ground, society has become weak and too lenient and in this society children no longer have a model to look up to and follow, they grow up like wild weeds blown around by wild and uncontrolled winds. Whichever way the wind blows, the child goes. It is a very sad situation. But, Raffee, *housecleaning*?"

"Why not, Auntie? Look how easy it is: I arrive at work at nine a.m., don my smock and start chatting with feather duster, broom, mop, sponges and rags...all things quiet and obedient. There are no documents or papers to read or to initial, no bell to scream in my ears, no recess duty, no report cards, etc…It is plain and straightforward work until noon when I am done and come flying home. I hope my employer is not too demanding and will let me do my job in peace."

"What if she is and keeps ordering you around?"

"Then it will be Ciao Signora! and I am gone" I said with a very military salute.

Aunt Sumi laughs heartily, I laugh with her as I go to my bedroom to change my clothes. The kitchen clock chimes to let us know it is tea time. I always like tea time with Aunt, we take the tray to the patio and enjoy the beverage and little treats; she always surprises me with new mini cakes of various colors. I especially like the red ones with a mungbean centre; the recipe comes from Thailand where Aunt Sumika has lived a great many years. These are small cakes the size of a mouthful, tasty and easy to eat.

The garden is in full bloom, the shy spring flowers have become bolder and are now showing their true shades of blue, pink and yellow. They are unashamedly flirting with the many butterflies that are busy visiting each cluster of colors. When the gardener came last week, he brought a small bag of seeds to plant in the backyard.

"Wait till they grow…you'll have delicious herbs for cooking and for drinks," he said.

"Thanks, Ramon, but please don't use the whole backyard," Aunt told him.

"No. And I won't touch Raffee's corner either."

"That's good, I'll tell her you said that."

My 'corner' is a tiny little shallow pond reserved for frogs; I have also built a few frog houses around for them. My friends think I am insane because I love owls, mice and frogs. They don't think I am insane when I tell them that I loathe snakes, caterpillars and leeches.

"Aunt Sumi, did you have leeches in Thailand?"

"Oh yes, millions of them. I hate them and fear them. I used to call them 'creatures from hell'. I am glad we don't see many around here."

A red-wing black bird landed in the garden and we held our breath in admiration. He looked very proud hopping around in search of insects. A blue jay arrived and within minutes the garden was empty of visitors. This majestic bird is loud and so aggressive, even squirrels stand at a safe distance, ready to flee. Sometimes we leave peanuts outside for them and once or twice I saw Auntie put out crackers spread with peanut butter for the squirrels. In the winter, only squirrels, sparrows and starlings come begging for food; we always have seed for the birds and nuts for the squirrels.

"Raffee, did you see this morning's headlines in the paper? They caught the pedophile who killed that little girl. Finally he will be brought to justice."

"What justice, Aunt Sumi? He lives but she is dead. You call that justice? In my opinion there will be justice if he too dies."

"That's impossible, Canada has abolished the death penalty a decade or two ago."

"Then they removed justice when they removed capital punishment."

"Why kill the killer, Raffee? It won't bring back the dead. And in today's world I don't think it will even be a deterrent."

"It's true, the victim won't be back and it is not a deterrent."

"Then, why a second killing? Revenge?"

"No, Auntie, not revenge. It is much simpler than that. It is called *guarantee*. Society desperately needs the guarantee that the killer will never, ever, kill again. The name of this guarantee is Capital Punishment. There is no other solution. Whoever abolished the death penalty was a coward and a criminal. Coward because he did not have the guts to send a killer to the electric chair. Criminal because he allowed the killer the opportunity to kill again. The whole so-called justice system spends huge amounts of money to save the life of the killer. And you and I are required to pay for this parody of justice; all of us must pay. You call this justice, Auntie?"

"Still, Raffee, we are talking about a human life here; why not send the killer to prison for life? That would be punishment, don't you think?"

"Yes, punishment for all of us, rich and poor, because we will be forced to pay for all his needs in prison, I mean everything, every breath he takes, we will have to pay until he stops breathing. The burden will be on us, like it or not. What have we ever done to deserve such treatment?"

"Still, we are part of this society, we don't live on a desert island, we must help."

"I will never, ever, help a pedophile. Pedophiles are on top of my 'execution list'. I hope the killer of this little girl gets killed by the inmates in his prison. At least inmates are not coward, they practice capital punishment."

"Oooh, Raffee, you *are* virulent!"

"Yes. On the other hand, look what I love: owls, mice, frogs, animals!"

"You are quite a mixture, you know that?"

"Yes, love and hatred. If someone I love is threatened or hurt by somebody, I pity that somebody because my hatred won't subside until the culprit is severely punished and pays for his action. Then, and only then, will peace and satisfaction return to me. I remember when Uncle Chris was still with us, he used to tell me, "I see both blue sky and dark storm in those green eyes." I wonder how he is doing these days."

"He is doing fine in his Buddhist temple. We communicate through spirits. I miss him but I fully understand his decision. Some day, maybe, we'll be together again. In the meantime I cannot tell him that his favorite niece has decided to be a housecleaner!"

"If I could communicate through spirits, I would tell him myself…but I do not possess your exceptional power. Next time you talk to him, tell him I miss him too. How about getting busy in the kitchen for dinner? Did Maria say when she'll be back?"

"Another week and she'll be all good again. Let's play in the kitchen, what would you like for dinner?"

Aunt Sumika is an excellent cook and performs culinary miracles with almost nothing and in almost no time. I have told her many times that she was doing magic and she would say, "That's because you are so easy to please, you never complain." Maria's cooking is good too, but I find it a bit too greasy and heavy.

Our house is not very large, not at all a mansion, it has only three bedrooms, but it is comfortable and Aunt and I are very happy here. Since Uncle Chris left for the Buddhist monastery in Thailand years ago, I have joined Aunt Sumi and we keep each other's company. She is such a peaceful and utterly quiet person, almost ethereal in many ways. Her spiritual life is beautiful, deep and rich and her heart is pure gold. Sometimes the light in her eyes is focused far away, she is then absent from earth, traveling I know not where, and I never interrupt her inner journey. Instinctively I feel that there is a part of my aunt's life where pain and regrets and longing seem to dwell. I respect her inner life and love her more because I know for certain that there is a huge empty spot in her heart. When she is not traveling beyond earth, she is a wonderful person full of energy and joie de vivre, with an intellect clear as crystal and lips with many quick repartees. When we talk about current events, our conversation may go on for two hours, the intelligent exchange is that prolific and enlightening; she is a well of knowledge and I a thirsty sponge drinking in her input and experience. She listens to me, I listen to her and together we have on many occasions come very near to finding a universal remedy for all the aches and pains of this pathetic world! And each time we have rewarded ourselves with a glass or two of our favorite liqueur, Curaçao.

I have often wanted to ask Aunt Sumika about what I strongly feel is missing in her life, but when I look at her so gentle and kind and ready to spoil me like a princess, I keep my mouth shut, I don't want to rock the boat. I don't wish to see a look of hurt on her face. And so, her inner life remains a mystery to me. Some day perhaps she will open up and I will welcome her secrets with open arms. I will want to know why Uncle Chris went back to Thailand to join the monastery; how long will it be till he returns home to

Aunt and their life together; I know – from my cousins and other relatives - that they were a couple very much in love, they married many years after they met, their life before they married had been shattered by many incredible upheavals and trials; they have no children and when my parents died six years ago in a horrible accident in Argentina, Aunt Sumika immediately opened her home to me. I became a daughter to her. It was the year I turned sixteen and each year since, we celebrate my birthday with a visit to my parents' grave followed by a dinner at a chic restaurant and a party at home with a few close friends. I never liked large gatherings and our parties rarely had more than a half dozen guests. Aunt does not observe her birthday but rather the anniversary of her becoming a Buddhist, this was very important to her. In her bedroom there is an altar to Lord Buddha and a deep dish where she burns triangular prayer sticks whose fragrance dispenses a feeling of peace and serenity not experienced anywhere else. At least that's how I feel when I am in that room and she burns the sticks. She buys these at an Oriental products store downtown.

When my brother Peter died of intestinal hemorrhage three years ago, Aunt Sumi wore white and stayed indoors for an entire week. Many prayer sticks were burned and I often found her sitting on the floor in front of the altar in deep meditation during that week. I didn't ask but I was sure it was her way of grieving the loss of her 'little Peter dear' and of communicating with spirits in the beyond. The house was very quiet during that week and I, despite my limited knowledge of Buddhism, was more than willing to welcome the overall feeling of deep respect for the dead in addition to my own sorrow at the loss of my brother. I was grieving the loss in two ways: the Buddhist way of Aunt Sumi, and my non-Buddhist way. In the end the result was the same: we both grieved the same loss.

As I look at Aunt Sumika now busy preparing dinner, I feel a wave of affection leave my heart and reach toward her. I want so much for her to be together again with Uncle Chris and happy as she has been before. When will he return? Have they had an agreement on this? But most of all, why did he leave? These questions I do not dare ask Aunt. Besides there is no guarantee that, if I knew the answers, I could change anything. All I can do then is accept the mystery and pray for his return.

"Let's eat on the patio, shall we, Raffee?"

"Good idea. Let me take the tray and you bring the wine. Oh it smells so good!"

"It's rabbit stew with the shallots that you like better than onions."

"No wonder it smells so good, I am suddenly very hungry. Let's have a good strong red wine with this feast."

"Bread or potatoes?"

"Bread, please."

While we enjoy this delectable dinner, night tiptoes in and crickets begin rehearsing for their nocturnal concert. I close the screened door to keep night insects outside. Our next door neighbor, Eileen, does the same and we wave to each other.

"It's so lovely to have dinner outside, I like it, we should do this more often now that the weather allows it. You didn't have fierce winters in Thailand, did you, Auntie?"

"No. Winter in the tropics is never like what we have here. Thai people have never seen snow and we never had to wear heavy coats. I tell you, what I hate most here is winter."

"Do you miss Thailand? Would you go back there some time?"

"I miss Thailand when winter hits us here. That's when I want to go back there. But, spring, summer, and especially fall are such lovely seasons in this part of the world, I want to stay to enjoy them."

"What kind of weather did you have on your native island?"

"Ah, in Vanuatu the sun is bright and warm year round. Plants, fruits and flowers thrive. In Thailand we have the same flora, so for me living there was almost like home. I would very much like to go back to the island for a long visit some day."

"If and when you go, would you take me with you?"

"That's a deal. How about dessert now?"

It must run in the family this love affair with ice cream... Aunt and I are having huge helpings of coconut ice cream with coconut finger cookies. A taste of paradise.

Night is well established now and we are treated to a concert by invisible but very loud crickets. Stars are whispering ever so softly in the immense dark sky, I wonder what they are saying to each other as they slowly travel on their nocturnal journey. I miss my brother Peter, I am thinking of my parents, I want Uncle Chris to come home to Aunt Sumika and place smiles back on her lips. I wonder what kind of boss my new employer will be. And I am praying that some day the right man will show up on my path.

As Aunt herself often does in the privacy of her bedroom, I thank Lord Buddha for keeping me alive and in good health. I don't know Lord Buddha very well but I thank him because I have an excellent model to look up to: my Aunt Sumika who has special connections to the world beyond.

TWO

WHEN AUNT Sumika asked me what kind of smock I wanted for my new job as a house cleaner, I winked and said I wanted one bright red and one lime green. She raised her eyebrows and I hastily explained,

"I am not *any* house cleaner, Auntie, I am a unique house cleaner who will dress as she pleases. And if it shocks the employer – or anybody else – all the better. It is such fun to shock people!"

"Oh my, I hope you'll do a good job in that mansion and not break anything. I hope the lady won't have a heart attack at the sight of a red smock. It's a good thing that we don't live in Spain or Mexico, or you'd be trampled by ferocious bulls within minutes. They react to the color red."

"I am glad we are not living in those countries. I find their matadors and bullfights rather primitive and very cruel indeed. When I see a matador gored by a bull, I applaud."

"With you it is always white or black, there is no gray, is there, Raffee?"

"No. Gray is for weaklings, the hesitant, the lenient, the liars and sometimes the cowards."

"Can you elaborate?"

"It's simple, Auntie. When a murderer is sent to jail 'for life' and he is released only a few years later, that is a lie. Society has been lied to by what it holds almost sacred: the law. This happens all the time. When a judge says 'for life' it should mean the entire life of the criminal, until he takes his last breath. Mark my words, the pedophile who killed that little girl will be out of jail and free in a few months. Unless his inmates kill him first."

"All right, young lady, I agree with you on this one. Where do you get all this deep thinking and strong opinion?"

"It runs in the family, you know that. Sometimes I wish I had some of your special connection with the spirits; can it be taught?"

"It can be acquired but each one of us has to find it in our own way. It takes time, sincerity, faith and patience. In return it brings us peace, serenity and a deep love for Lord Buddha; not to mention the special connection and contact with the spirits who live beyond earth. Through this medium I am often in contact with Uncle Chris and other beloved beings gone from earth but not from heart. If you are interested, start with meditation. As you progress, I will tell you more about Lord Buddha. Remember, this is not a hobby, this is life. When you achieve what I have, you will be like me: you will have two lives."

"It sounds very extraterrestrial and I am very interested. Living with you all these years I have often felt that there was another life in this house, not just the two of us. I do hope that some day I'll be able to join you on the many inner journeys that you take. You will teach me Buddhism, won't you, Aunt Sumi?"

"Yes if that's what you want. You will discover how beautiful and peaceful this religion is. It will show you that 'to give is to receive', that after a storm – even the worst storm – the sun always rises; where there is darkness, somehow, some way, light will find its way there, and most of..." The phone rang and interrupted our conversation.

"Hi, Raffee, this is Fred. Am I disturbing?"

"No, not at all, what's up?"

"Do you remember the "Group of Three" we met last year at Stephie's party? They are back and I am invited, would you like to come with me?"

"Oooh, that'll be nice. When and where? Thanks for asking me, Fred."

"Friday next week, I'll pick you up at eight in the evening, all right with you?"

"Hold on a second, Fred, let me ask my aunt something." With Aunt Sumi's approval, I returned to Fred.

"How about dinner here before we go? All right with you?"

"Oooh, that'll be nice! Thank you, what should I bring?"

"A good appetite. See you then, have a nice week."

Fred is a good friend, we are the same age but for precision's sake I often remind him that I was born twenty-one hours before him, which makes me his senior. We joke about this of course but only because I know that he has never heard of the Oriental belief that one day, one hour, makes a big difference in many things; in the Orient he would have to address me as 'older sister'. All this I learned from Aunt Sumika and Uncle Chris before he left for the monastery. I do wish he would come back soon.

Maria, our maid and cook, resumed work yesterday after a bad bout with the summer flu. She is an excellent worker; a widow raising three children. When she and her family arrived from Mexico some ten years ago, they had nothing and spoke very little English. Today the three children speak fluent English and almost no Spanish; they are good students and the grades they bring home make Maria beam with pride.

"The boys in school very good, Madame," she would tell Aunt. We also hear of their success in sports, but we never mention bullfights. In my book bullfighting is not a sport, it is a killing; the name should be bullkill, not bullfight, and it should be banned all together.

When Alfredo, Maria's husband, was killed in a car accident, we took the boys in with us so Maria would have enough room in her house to accommodate relatives who came from Mexico for the funeral. It was a very sad affair, Maria was disconsolate and very emotional. The boys kept very quiet, as quiet as the tears we saw on their faces. Aunt Sumika talked to them and gently tried to explain that death was not an end but the beginning of another life, that their father had now started that life out in the beyond where he was watching over his beloved wife and children. We on earth should continue to live until life leaves us.

"Can we find out when life will decide to leave us?" Raul, the youngest, asked.

"No, nobody can. It is written in the Book of Life and no human can know in advance."

"Then, how can we prepare so we don't go to hell?"

"We prepare by living a clean and honest life. In your religion you believe in hell; not in my religion."

"Can we know more about your religion?" Roberto, the eldest, asked.

"If and when you have your mother's approval, I will be happy to tell you about Buddhism."

While they were talking, I went to the kitchen and prepared a tray of sandwiches, cookies and pop drinks; these were much appreciated by three young and hungry stomachs. We treated them every day to excellent meals; we tried to make them laugh with funny stories and jokes; we rented a few cheer-me-up movies. Every day we drove them to their home early afternoon to be with their family in their time of grief and one of the relatives drove them back to our place around dinner time. One evening as we were on the patio ready to attack our crossword puzzles, Alejandro, the middle boy, suddenly asked,

"Mrs. Luens (that's Aunt Sumi) why are you alone here with Raphaëlle? Where is your husband?"

"Oh Alex, be quiet!" Roberto ordered his brother.

"It's all right, Roberto, I don't mind answering," Aunt Sumi said. At this point my eyes were riveted on her lips, I was hoping to learn more from her, I almost didn't dare breathe in anticipation.

"My husband is away but not for ever, he will be back some day. Raffee and I look forward to his return." Utter disappointment, I wanted more. Once again Uncle Chris' absence kept its secrets from me.

With time Maria and the boys conquered the tears of grief and resumed their regular routine. Aunt returned to wearing colors after the white robe reserved for mourning. Tomorrow I will start my job as a housecleaner, a job that does not make Aunt Sumika happy at all. I am not in seventh heaven myself but something mysterious and very insistent pushes me to do it. Although, as I have already mentioned, I do not have contact with the spirits, I feel a presence near me telling me to be a housecleaner for this Mrs. Betty-Ann Jahe. Of course I can't mention any of this to Aunt for fear of being teased, I am still such an embryo in this world of spirits. If and when Roberto starts learning about Buddhism, I want to be present, I need to learn, I want to go deep into the yet unknowns of this religion. I don't know much about it but I feel something, someone, a presence near me, and I know that there is a being invisible and intangible waiting for me and watching over me. Perhaps more will be revealed to me as I progress in my daily meditation.

My mother was a devout Catholic who believed in God almighty, in heaven and in hell. She used to tell me that God loved all his creatures, his children, the good and the bad. It was confusing to me, I did not understand how a god who loved his children could send them to the fires of hell; how, if he loved his creation so much, he could create hell and purgatory, there to send his children. It did not make sense and I never embraced my mother's religion, to her great disappointment and threats of hell fire for me.

My father, John-Peter Luens, brother of Uncle Chris and a Buddhist at heart, was very much in love with my mother and allowed her Catholic faith to pervade every nook and cranny of our home. "For the sake of peace and harmony" I often heard him say. There were then two religions under one roof, but I grew up without a religion of my own. That is until I moved in with Aunt Sumika and gradually felt the serenity that emanates from her. I was sixteen then but already I sensed that something or someone not of this world lived with us in the house. When Uncle Chris left for the monastery a few years ago, I was lost, not comprehending and extremely sad. Aunt Sumi only said that "It was necessary for now for the both of us; not to worry, he will come back some day." Crushed as I was, I bowed and accepted the fact. I will meditate, I will learn and I will find my way to reach the spirits so I can communicate with him and beg him to return. How can they be apart so long? They love each other so much. Something must have happened, something horrible… but how can I ever find out? Could I even help if I knew? Knowing, or rather feeling, all this, I can only love my aunt more and I pledge to stay with her for ever.

Last Friday at Stephie's house the party was a great success. The "Group of Three" performed to perfection, there was dancing, singing, joking, lots of food and punch, also Champagne offered by Stephie's father. Walter could not resist clowning around and we helped him by spreading cake icing all over his face from ear to ear while Fred and Rhys were holding him down. We demanded more clowning, he obliged, and satisfied we pushed him in the swimming pool with his clothes and cake icing on. Later we rewarded him by officially crowning him King of the evening. After a delicious dinner, we all sat out on the large patio for conversation, mini cream puffs and tea or coffee.

"Are you relieved that the pedophile is now behind bars?" Mr. Rowlands asked.

"Dad, I would be happier to see him sitting tight on the electric chair," Stephie answered.

"Hear, hear, I agree," Rhys said.

"What about the group of 'homos' who wanted to demonstrate in front of City Hall? Should we give them a voice?" Walter asked.

"That's plain disgusting; homosexuals should hide and never show up, they belong in prehistoric caves," Kevin said.

"They are indeed very disgusting and they behave so indecently during their annual parade; they make people want to puke," Andrew added.

"Oh yuck, they jump and gyrate half naked on their floats, I wonder what they want to accomplish. They must be blind not to see the imbecility of their action. In my book they are abnormal beings and should be shunned by society," Rhys said with disgust. I was surprised at the controlled anger in his voice. He must really hate them.

"Nah, come on, don't be so judgmental, these people are…" I started to say but was interrupted.

"What! You, Raffee? You defend homosexuals? That beats all, I can't believe what I am hearing!" Fred barked out holding his head in his hands. A brouhaha ensued, I looked at each one of them with raised eyebrows and a half smile on my face. When they calmed down, I jumped in.

"No, I do not and will never defend homosexuals, they make me sick. However I believe in freedom of choice. These people choose to live a life that is counter-nature, they enjoy it; let them. If a man wants to marry a man, and a woman a woman, let them. If…" I was interrupted again.

"That's it, Raffee, you *are* defending society's garbage, yuck!" Andrew hissed.

"No, please, let me finish. If these people are happy living against the rule of Nature, let them. Sooner or later Nature will turn around and punish them with horrible diseases. They are doing everything they can think of to attract the world's attention, they feel insecure, they are begging the world to acknowledge and accept them, because they know they are abnormal people; they know that the Creator created Man and Woman, He did not create Man and Man. They are sinking deeper and deeper in the muck of their lifestyle. The more they scream, beg and demand, the less they will receive. Where I put my foot down vehemently is when homosexuals demonstrate and demand that the government and society treat them as normal people; they demand to be married by priests whose religion condemns homosexuality; they demand normal marital status, benefits and pensions. They demand the right to adopt children – this makes me shudder and retch – In one word they *demand* all that is normal while they themselves are not normal. So, my friends, don't believe that I defend homosexuals, because I don't. And I repeat, all these things they do not ask, they demand. In my opinion they cannot be part of society."

"They really have forfeited their title of 'humans', they have become inferior even to animals. A male dog does not mate with a male dog, it mates with a bitch, a female dog; there is no homosexuality in the animal world," Rhys said.

"Yes, 'homos' are hopelessly doomed," Fred added.

"Serve them right!" Kevin concluded hotly.

Following this very hot conversation, we unanimously voted in favor of a dive into the pool. Later, Stephie's father threw in a ball and the men started a game of water polo. The ladies returned to the patio and, unanimously, gave the coup de grâce to all the remaining mini cream puffs; we left no survivors..

Around one a.m. Fred drove me home in his gorgeous sports car. I felt good and happy to have such wonderful friends.

"That was a lovely evening, Fred. Thank you for inviting me."

"My pleasure. I must apologize for barking out at you and triggering that brouhaha."

"Don't apologize. I like energetic talks and lively exchanges. Stephie's parents are really amazing and her father is champion at steering us toward intelligent conversation. He started the whole thing, remember?"

"Yes, he is a superior brain. Here you are, Raffee, safely home; good night and see you soon," he said as he parked the car in front of my house.

"Thanks, Fred, and good night to you too." As he opened the gate for me, he took both my hands to his lips. I looked deep in his brown eyes for a second and with a wink said,

"Here's looking at you, kid!"

"Raffee you are terrible, but I love you anyway."

"Love is a huge word, Fred, be careful when you use it because it is known to break hearts and I am not ready yet to pick up pieces of a broken heart. See you soon, you romantic Homo Sapiens."

Before I left for my first day of work this morning, Aunt Sumika served me a succulent breakfast; I told her it was going to be a red smock day and she laughed her gentle laugh that I like so much.

"Watch your tongue today, Raffee, it's only the first day, don't go and scare your employer off. If you need any tip while you work, you can always call me. As Maria would say, 'Vaya con Dios!' and come home for a good lunch."

On my way to St.Thomas where the lady lived, I sang Beethoven's Ninth Symphony entirely in German and remembered that Aunt Sumi used to be an opera singer many years ago. I don't think I have what it takes to be an opera singer but I love all classical music. I also wondered what kind of person my employer will be; kind and fair? Or nasty and demanding? I have no fear whatsoever because I am a quick decision-maker; what I like, I keep; what I don't, I discard at once. I can't wait to see her reaction at the sight of my vivid red smock.

The mansion looks beautiful and imposing from the outside; a gate opens onto a long and circular driveway that turns around green bushes, passes the massive entrance door and continues on to a second gate that leads to the street. The lawn is so trim and smooth, it looks like a green carpet freshly cleaned. There are rosebushes showing many colorful blooms and a dozen tall and gorgeous Oriental poppies bursting red. A round and white fountain in the center of the lawn is hugged all around by the soft purple blue of Forget-me-nots. The contrast is a delight to the eyes. There are lace sheers on all the windows. Curiously I see no front patio, no verandah or swimming pool. Life must be rather lonely in this magnificent home.

I end my appraisal of the mansion and approach the entrance, ready for the job at hand. After my two knocks on the massive oak door, the lady opens and invites me in. She is tall, slim, wears thick eyeglasses, has gray hair and I notice a slight limp as she takes a few steps back to let me in.

"Good morning, Madame, I am Raphaëlle Luens reporting for work," I say.

"Good morning and thank you for coming. I am Mrs. Betty-Ann Jahe. Would you like a cup of tea or coffee before you start?"

"Thank you very much, but I think I'd like to see where you want me to start first, this being my first day and I don't know my way around."

"Right. You speak good English, I like that."

"Thank you."

If the outside of the mansion looks beautiful, the inside leaves me speechless and in awe. It is rich from floor to ceiling and looks like an art museum complete with displays and special lighting for special effects. I thought to myself, 'in the middle of all this opulence lives one person, one woman'… I do not envy her, life must be very lonely here; how lucky I am to have my aunt, my many friends, and specially Fred. There are four bedrooms, two bathrooms, a large kitchen, two dining rooms and one huge living room. The lady takes me to the back and, voilà! the secret is revealed and I see a large, covered patio, a swimming pool with an adjacent shower room, a table and chairs, and on the left side further back, a carport big enough to accommodate four cars; at the moment there is only one black Mercedes parked there. Then reality hits me: how can I ever clean this castle in one morning? So I ask the lady.

"Right. I forgot to tell you that you don't need to clean the entire place in one visit. Since you come twice a week, why don't you divide the work in two and start with any section you wish. I only ask that the living room be cleaned on Fridays because I entertain every Friday evening. If you need anything, please don't hesitate to ask; I am usually on the patio."

"Thank you. I shall start right away then."

The corps de ballet showed up then with broom and mop and sponges; vacuum cleaner and chamois cloth joined in, and the show started. I did all sorts of jetés and pirouettes to reach unreachable corners, sneezed a couple of times when dust teased my nose and did not stop turning and dancing until one look at my wristwatch sent me the message 'lunch time!' After putting away all the tools of the trade in the closet that the lady showed me earlier, I went to the patio to take my leave and say goodbye.

"Right. Thank you, see you Friday. I will pay you every Friday if it's all right with you."

"It's all right with me, goodbye Mrs. Jahe." I was tempted to say "Right" at the beginning of my sentence, but thought it wiser to keep quiet. Aunt Sumika told me to 'watch my tongue' this morning. I laughed silently to myself as I walked to my car.

A delicious lunch welcomed me home. I was famished and very thirsty and decided right away to take a snack and a bottle of water with me on my next work day. Aunt watched me devour the food speedily and silently, I was too hungry to talk. When speech returned to me, I smiled at her and nodded a few times.

"This is so good, Auntie, thank you. I was really hungry, why didn't I think of taking a snack along with me? First time, first mistake, won't happen again."

"Did your boss push you around? You look exhausted."

"No, she did not push me; after showing me around, she went out to the patio and stayed there until I was done. The house is huge, she lives alone in that castle; she told me I could divide my work in two as I didn't have to clean the whole place in one visit. And she'll pay me every Friday."

"Did she faint at the color of your smock?"

"No, she did not. Actually I don't think she even noticed it. So much for my wanting to shock the world!" We both laughed.

"What's your first impression? Are you going to keep the job?"

"The mansion is gorgeous, extremely rich, opulent; easy to clean too as there are no children and no pets to soil it and so far, the lady has been pleasant. I think I'll continue for a while. Remember not to tell anybody the kind of job I have, my friends would faint in utter disbelief! And Fred won't 'love' me anymore."

"Fred loves you? Since when? Do you love him, Raffee?"

"Slow down, Auntie. When Fred told me he loved me, I told him to use that word very carefully, that it was known to break hearts, and that I was not ready to pick up pieces of a broken heart. I like all my friends and perhaps Fred a little more than the rest. But there is no hurry to change things, is there?"

"That's for you to decide, honey. You know I am always all ears and all heart where you are concerned."

"And you know that I love you and admire you no end. Did Maria bring good news about her sons' summer school?"

"They are doing very well, Maria is a proud mother. The boys will be together in high school this September. How fast they have grown."

"And they are polite too, which is an extra laurel in Maria's crown. Today's teenagers are so bad and disrespectful. I was a teenager not that long ago but I sure don't like what I see today. When I hear 'children are the future of our country', I am afraid and wonder about that future…"

"True, it doesn't look very promising, but out of the bad masses I am sure some good ones will emerge and become good leaders."

"You are a confirmed optimist, Aunt Sumi."

Later, when night whispered soft words to beckon the first stars to come out, Aunt and I settled on the patio with our after-dinner liqueur. A gentle breeze embraced us with whiffs of rose and honeysuckle scents from the garden. The moment was so peaceful, I seemed to be breathing serenity in and out with nothing to hinder the feeling of oneness with Nature.

"Auntie, this night is so beautiful and gentle, it makes me feel like flying away to the nirvana that you have mentioned so many times and of which I know almost nothing. Would you like to tell me more?"

"Every time one asks to know more proves that one is ready to know more. This night is perfect and I will tell you more. I have learned that nirvana is a dimension only attained by, and granted to devout Buddhists. In nirvana, all pains, worries, concerns and suffering are erased. The temporal body remains on earth while the soul travels and soars towards the perfection of nirvana. It is only in nirvana that I am able to reach the only true love of my life: Neil, whose life was taken away too soon, leaving me alone on earth where I became an utterly empty shell. It is in nirvana that Neil and I reunite, talk to each other, renew our perfect love and pledge to, some day, be together again for eternity. The love between Neil and me was perfect, so perfect that Life became jealous of our happiness and took Neil away from me. It is only in nirvana that I can again be with him. Lord Buddha is kind, compassionate and generous, he grants me the power to reach nirvana when I need to be with Neil. When I am on earth, everything imperfect clings to me and I live the life of an imperfect human being. When I reach nirvana, my whole being is permeated with the divine and perfect happiness of the world beyond. Need to know more, Raffee?"

"Oh, Aunt Sumi, I am so grateful and so happy that you have explained nirvana and confided in me. When your heart is heavy with sad memories, remember that I am near you and will always support you. Neil is a very lucky man to be loved by you and, although he lives in the beyond, I know that he is watching over you and protecting you. I will master the art of meditation. I will "breathe" Buddhism and maybe some day I will be allowed to meet your beloved Neil. What is his full name, and when did he leave?"

"He left a great many years ago, his name is Neil Jahe."

THREE

THE NAME hit me like a rocket and left me speechless with a racing heart and difficult breathing. I wanted to scream but no sound came. I wanted to talk but no word left my lips. No wonder my heart didn't know which way to beat and chose to race. I was stunned by the enormity of the coincidence. Mrs. Betty-Ann Jahe…Neil Jahe…Could it be? How could it be? It's a small world, they say… Slowly, very slowly, brains that I wasn't sure I had, began talking and I listened. I must not ask more about Neil Jahe, at least not now. I must remember the name, inquire to see if it is related to my employer, the lady in the mansion; little by little I must find out from Aunt Sumi what happened in her life, why she lost her perfect love, who made it happen. I must tell her again and again how much I love her and how I will always be by her side when she needs me. Then, when I know more about what or – especially – who hurt her so much, I will find a way to inflict punishment, direct and harsh. But reasoning with myself, I thought perhaps this was just a coincidence, surely there must be many people named Jahe around here, I must not jump to conclusion; that's right, take it slowly, breathe slowly, act slowly but surely.

Later when we said goodnight, I felt the need to repeat, "I love you, Aunt Sumi". Sleep was not kind to me, I tossed and turned, the name Neil Jahe kept dancing in my head, always followed by a question mark. Who was he? Where was he? Why did he die? And most painfully, why did Aunt and Neil not marry? I will need to have all these answers before I can see clearly and decide what to do. Drifting finally into sleep, I remembered what I told Fred, 'love is known to break hearts'. Handle with care. Won't happen to me, I swear.

Next morning Maria woke me up with sounds of pots and pans and the aroma of coffee. Aunt Sumika was already on the patio with the morning papers. I kissed her good day and joined her for breakfast. My eyes kept wanting to scrutinize her face and I had to force them to concentrate on and stare at the croissants and orange marmalade instead.

"How did you sleep, Raffee?"

"Not very well, but I did sleep some. What's on the agenda today? Can we talk again tonight as we did yesterday? I want to know many things, everything…only because I love you very much, Auntie. I want to feel what you feel; what hurts you, I want it to hurt me too. This way I will be sharing *life* with you, not just a home and everyday things."

"Oh my, Raffee, you can talk! So much like your mother. I like it and I love you. I am only a few years your senior, but my life's age is three times that long if not more, because of what I had to endure. We can talk tonight again if the weather allows us to stay here on the patio. And if you really want to hear more."

"I do, Auntie, very much so. Let's keep our date here tonight then. Are you going out this morning?"

"Only to the Asian market; want to come?"

"Yes, yes, I do. I always enjoy that part of town, the colors, the smells, the foreign languages and I find it very amusing to see how insistent vendors are, almost clinging to the visitors. I may find something to buy for myself."

"Like what?"

"I've been thinking of a statue of Lord Buddha and books on Buddhism, and incense sticks to burn in my room. I want to learn and master meditation."

"And if you are a good and sincere student, I'll take you with me next time I go to Bentre Pagoda."

"I am very sincere, Auntie, and very eager. I don't know why or how, but there is an overall feeling of 'hurry, hurry, or else'. You see how badly I want to share your other life? I can hardly wait to go to the pagoda with you."

"I am happy to hear that. Remember, to feel one with the world beyond and have a connection with it requires more time, silence and thinking than books, even the best of them, can bring you. It all comes from the inside, the other you, the spirit of you. Is this too deep? Or too unreachable?"

"Very deep, but I want to reach this depth. I really want to be able to talk with spirits and ask them a thousand things."

"You can come to me any time, Raffee."

"Careful what you ask for, Auntie!" I said this almost in a whisper.

"Oh my, aren't you mysterious! What goes on behind that sweet face of yours? Don't answer if you feel I am prying, I don't want to make you feel uncomfortable."

"There are a thousand things running and jumping in my head; they are like horses that I cannot control, horses that don't obey my commands. But I am strong, I almost always end up winning and the horses lower their heads, obey, and I lead them home to the stable. That's why by just looking at me nobody can guess the presence of these horses in my head. Do you like horses, Aunt Sumi?"

"Raffee, you are impossible! How easily you can change the subject and steer clear of what is on your mind. I will respect that. To answer your out-of-context question, yes I like horses, they are majestic, intelligent and loyal animals. Shall we get ready to go out now?"

At the Golden Dragon store, Aunt Sumika bought conical incense sticks of many colors, sheets of thin gold paper, a string of white lotus flowers and a wooden bead rosary. She helped me choose a statue of Lord Buddha, a box of long and brown incense sticks and a special bowl to be filled with sand where the long sticks would be placed. As I approached the book display, she pointed to a brown bookcase near the altar.

"You will find what you need there. The other books here are superficial, they deal with Buddhism the Western way, not sincere. Those over there are the real thing; is this what you want, Raffee?"

"Yes, absolutely. I want deep, not shallow."

"Bless you, child. Would you like to first meet Lord Buddha?"

"Ye…yes… How do I do that?"

"We'll take this large book, it tells you about the life of Siddhartha Gautama, founder of Buddhism; you will meet him there and you will learn a lot from the book. If you want it, let me have the pleasure of buying it for you as a welcome present to my world." I felt my eyes burn and accepted the gift with gratitude.

"It is wonderful, thank you from the bottom of my heart. Now, let me treat you to lunch at a Vietnamese restaurant just three stores away, shall we?"

"That's very sweet of you; how do you know about Vietnamese food? I must call home and let Maria know."

"My friend Arielle's mother is Eurasian, she knows everything Vietnamese. The food is very good and much lighter than Chinese food. Are you game, Auntie?"

"Of course, let's go. My first Vietnamese meal! Do I need chopsticks?"

"If you want them, you can have them; if not, you'll use fork and knife and spoon, nobody would mind."

The Mekong Restaurant was small, busy and noisy. Round tables with red tablecloths and four chairs each occupied the entire room, leaving very little space for guests to move around. Only three tables were unoccupied, I chose the one by the window and we sat down for Aunt Sumika's first Vietnamese meal and my nth. Two seconds after we touched the seat of our chairs, a waitress appeared by magic holding a pad and a pen. She smiled, we smiled back and got busy with the menu. I helped Auntie, we selected two delicious-looking dishes and ordered ginger tea. Chopsticks were declined, we opted for forks and spoons. Aunt Sumi looked around the room from the entrance door to the long counter that separated the dining area from the kitchen; she looked at every table and at the decorations on the walls; then she noticed in a corner near the cash register an altar to Lord Buddha with incense sticks and offerings of fruits.

"These people are Buddhists, I feel at home here," she said in a whisper.

"I have been here many times and I've always seen the incense and the offerings. These people must be very religious. This place is always clean if a bit noisy, what do you think?"

"I like a clean restaurant and I am sure the good food we ordered will compensate well for the noise."

The waitress arrived with our orders; she smiled, we smiled back, and I wished Aunt Sumi bon appétit. The fried cuttlefish with lemongrass and the sautéed mushrooms with angel hair noodles were succulent. We were happy to have forks and spoons – not chopsticks – to grapple with the fine and slippery noodles. Hot ginger tea and small moon cakes soon turned this simple meal into a feast.

When evening began to whisper gentle secrets to the purple sky, we took our after-dinner drinks to the patio and prepared to eavesdrop on Nature's conversation. This has always been my favorite time of the entire day; it brought peace to my heart and kindness to a world that was not always kind. Would evening help a hurt soul to pick up the pieces of her broken heart? I was sure Aunt Sumika's heart was broken; I must find out who caused it to break, and I must punish the culprit. It can't be Uncle Chris because they are married and love each other deeply. It can't be Neil Jahe because he left this world a long time ago – I think even before I was born. Whoever the evil person is, I will find out and I will make him pay. This, then, shall become the quest of my life from this day forward. Having found a goal to pursue, I let out a deep sigh.

"Was it a good sigh or a bad one?" asked my aunt.

"Oh it was a good one I think, time will tell. Did you like the Vietnamese food we had today?"

"Everything was very good and tasty."

"And very noisy!"

"No, not too noisy, we were able to chat and hear each other. The little moon cakes are not new to me, we had them in Thailand and I've always liked them. Your Uncle Chris likes them too." It was not often that Aunt Sumi mentioned Uncle; I wondered what triggered her confiding mood; should I seize the opportunity? Should I probe further or let her take the lead? How to gently steer her toward opening up to me? I so wanted to know more, and understand more, and help more. This woman has suffered much, holds heavy secrets and, behind her everyday serene mask, I knew she was still grieving.

"Aunt Sumi, does Buddhism heal all wounds?" I asked, breaking the silence. She stared at me for a second and, though the evening had become much darker, I saw her eyes fill, which made mine follow suit oh so silently. She sighed and with resignation – or was it strength? – regained her composure.

"Only Time heals all wounds. Buddhism helps one to accept the duration of Time and to walk serenely along one's predesigned path. Acceptance, Raffee, is what we must master; it is not always easy. But we must conquer it."

"If accepting keeps us suffering, where is the joy of living? When suffering, how can we offer the gods a pure and total gift? A gift untainted by tears and grief and regrets? Surely the gods are entitled to perfect gifts?"

"Yes, but the gods also know that we are imperfect human beings and thus cannot offer perfect gifts. They do not expect perfection from us, they expect our acceptance and they help us to achieve it with a powerful and magnificent tool: Buddhism. This is what helps me as I try to forget the past, to forget Neil Jahe my perfect love, to forget why we are not together today. There are so many things to be forgotten and only one brain – mine – to do the job. That's why I need both Time and Buddhism. Is this too heavy for you, honey?"

"It is heavy, but you know me, I like heavy and deep, I hate shallow… Let me go refill our glasses and when I come back I'd like you to tell me more about Neil Jahe."

Night was fully established now, yet we chose not to turn the light on. I thought to myself, 'It is better this way, I won't see her embarrassment and she won't see my tears, if… Because Aunt Sumi continued to keep silent, I hesitantly decided to take a baby step toward the revelations that I was sure would burst forth from her lips with just a sign of encouragement. How long has she kept her pain hidden from the world? Does Uncle Chris know? Will I be able to help her? She will need help because once she starts talking, the wound will reopen and drown her in unthinkable sadness all over again. But talk she must; this will clean the wound and rid her heart of all the hurt that someone had inflicted on her so many years ago. She had to heal and I was more than willing to be the physician who would heal her.

"Did you love Neil Jahe very much, Aunt Sumi?"

"I adored him, he worshipped me."

"It was true love then?"

"It was perfect love. They say there is no perfection on earth. They are wrong or they are lying. We had perfection."

"Where did perfection go, Auntie?" She was silent and, in the darkness of night, I felt her eyes on me. In the same darkness, I knew I was holding her gaze.

"Life was jealous of our perfection and took Neil away from me. We parted in utter despair; we *had* to part, but not until we made a pledge in the presence of a Life Counsellor at a Buddhist temple in Thailand. We pledged to reunite after the imposed thirty-five-year trial. Neil was an idealist and in the end his ideal became his killer. His ideal has a name, I'll tell you her name later. After Neil left Thailand, my life began to unravel, I lost my memory, I sank into deep depression, I did not recognize my friends and I lived cloistered in my little house. Only Lord Buddha and my orphanage work kept a shred of sanity in me. I became an empty shell wondering if it wouldn't after all be better to end my life. Thirty-five years to wait, remember? That was the pledge and we would honor it, come what may."

"It is a very long time to wait. How did you do it and what took place at the end of the trial?"

"When I recovered from the long depression, I resumed teaching and increased my volunteer work at the orphanage. A nun at the temple befriended me, talked to me, supported me and encouraged me to look Life in the eye. And that's when inside of Buddhism, I found profound peace, healing, acceptance and the courage to go on living. I was counting the days, the years until my reunion with Neil. Lord Buddha showed me the way and I followed it with gratitude."

"Where was Neil all that time, and how did he fare?"

"He was back in his country. Through my contacts with the spirit world I knew that he was not happy; his wife made his emotional life pure hell; he missed me and he missed the perfection that was ours; she never gave him what I've given him. And so, year in, year out, Neil and I lived our separate lives counting the days until the end of the pledge and our reunion. I went to the pagoda very often, there to replenish my supply of serenity and courage to accept what we could not change. Whenever depression clawed back at me, the nuns at the temple helped me to push it away. When I had doubts about the possibility of our reunion, Lord Buddha stepped in and showed me the way to walk toward that reunion."

"So you had help. But I know that it must have been horribly difficult; I admire you, Aunt Sumi. When did the pledge end, and how was the reunion?" She sighed deeply and kept quiet. I did not want to push, I just waited. It was her life she was talking about, a life heavy with sadness and suffering, I had no say in the telling of it.

"The day the pledge ended was the day I learned that my beloved Neil had died of pancreatic cancer. He didn't make it to our reunion; we could not, as planned, forsake them all and together fly into our sunset cycle to be happy for ever. Neil had left this world, he had left me a second time. Now my life had really come to an end, there was no more reason for me to live and I prayed for Hades to come and take me away. I so fiercely wanted to die that Lord Buddha sent me a Spirit – I call it my Spirit – to stay with me every hour of every day until my name is called. It is very hard to accept. But, Raffee, acceptance is what we, I, must master."

"Pancreatic cancer does not forgive, there is no cure. I believe that it is linked to certain dietary factors; nutrition then plays a major role here; at least I read about it in a medical magazine. And it hits mostly people over fifty. Was Neil over fifty?"

"Yes, he was. Within four months of the diagnosis, he was dead. And when I learned about it, I wanted to die too. Through harmful foods and nutrition, that woman slowly but surely killed Neil. As long as I live I will not forgive. As long as I live, the wound will live with me and within me. I am afraid it will eat me and eventually destroy me. Life is unfair: she lives and Neil is dead."

"Life has indeed dealt you a cruel blow. Because it hurts you, it is hurting me too. I want so much to change things for you, Aunt Sumi. I want to help you accept each day that is placed at your doorstep; think of it as a present from Lord Buddha and, with support from your Spirit, try to make the most of it. Good people will be rewarded. Evil ones will be punished. What's the name of that wicked woman?"

"Wicked, yes, Betty-Ann is wicked and life is not fair: she lives and Neil is dead."

That name! Oh my God, the name…I closed my eyes, bit my lips to stop the rising scream, and bowed my head low, very low, as if to contain the sudden shiver that was running through my entire body. I was stunned and at the same time grateful that it was pitch dark on our patio because Aunt Sumika could not see my emotion. After a while I knew I had to say something or Aunt would think I had fallen asleep.

"As you know, Auntie, the bad will be punished and the good rewarded. I strongly believe it. It may not help much considering the magnitude of your sorrow, it may not bring closure, but I think it will bring a flash of victory and your heart will feel somewhat lighter. What wouldn't I do to see a flash of victory in your eyes!"

Later, as we wished each other good night, my head was already spinning with ideas for punishment. As if I had any power or say in this matter. It was my love for my aunt that made me feel powerful and gave my imagination the wings to fly away.

It was a heavy and very busy night. I slept, woke up, wondered where I was, slept again and finally woke at seven a.m., totally exhausted. I felt as if I had run a night marathon or gotten myself into a boxing match with an invisible pugilist. Did I win any medal? Why was the crowd not applauding? An unusual silence enveloped the house. Maria not coming today? Maria not making coffee? I always loved that coffee aroma first thing in the morning. Where was everybody? Then, as the sun touched the sheers on my bedroom window, it hit me: this was Sunday, Maria was off, it was still early, Auntie still in her bedroom.

Collecting my wandering thoughts together, I decided to make coffee and treat Aunt Sumi to a delicious and special breakfast. She deserved to be cherished, she deserved all the good things in life. As long as Uncle Chris was away, I will make it my duty to bring joy and sunshine to her every day. Last night's revelations were powerful and still held me under their might. Aunt Sumika has loved Neil very deeply, she called their love 'perfect'. And I wondered, 'Is it humanly possible to reach perfection on earth? Isn't loving somebody that deeply and perfectly too close to God? When we humans dare to come that close to deity, are we not punished and pushed back to where we belong: earth? Did Aunt Sumi exaggerate a little in the heat of the revelations? Why would she exaggerate? No, she did not, her emotion and her voice told the truth; it was her suffering coming out from her soul, she opened up to me, she needed no overstatement, her story was poignant enough. I wondered again, 'Is it humanly possible to suffer what she has suffered and remain human? She is all that is best in a human being, gentle, sincere, thoughtful, peaceful, generous. In my opinion she is close to perfection. If only I knew what to do to soothe her pain and erase the dark imprints of it that I sometimes see in her eyes.

She opened her door and I hurried back to earth to greet her.

"It is a good morning, Auntie. Shall I bring breakfast to the patio?"

"Oh it's very sweet of you, Raffee. What are you feeding me this morning?"

"How about pancakes with strawberry jam and light cream? And the superior coffee from Brazil, of course."

"It sounds delicious. At what time did you get up?"

"Around seven, it was the sun on my window that woke me up. I forgot that it was Sunday and when I found no Maria in the kitchen, decided to get busy and do something useful around the house for a change." I went and kissed her on both cheeks before carrying the tray to the patio.

"What are the lovely kisses for?" she asked.

"For trusting me enough to confide in me last night. Everything you told me is now part of me, I am living a part of your life. What hurts you is hurting me; what you hope, I will hope; what you ask Lord Buddha, I will ask. I want to do everything I can to bring smiles and laughter in your life. And since I live part of your life, we will smile and laugh together at the same things. Right?"

"You are too much, Raffee, you wonderful being. I am blessed to have you in my life. And your friend Fred is lucky to be in love with you."

"He didn't say he was in love with me, Auntie, he only said, "Raffee you are impossible but I love you anyway. Subtle difference."

"It means the same thing to me. Perhaps you heard with your ears but not yet with your heart. Give it time."

"Aunt Sumi, I am not ready for commitment; maybe not until I am thirty." She opened yesterday's unread newspaper and exclaimed,

"My goodness, a bear… a bear found its way into the backyard of this house where a woman was picking weeds. She screamed so much, neighbors came and… and…"

"And what? Did she die?"

"She was saved, but a man with a rifle killed the bear on the spot. The woman was taken to the hospital."

"They killed the bear, did they? They could not just injure it, they had to kill it. I am sick in my stomach, sick and tired of this injustice."

"Injustice, Raffee?"

"Yes, injustice. Think about it: we steal and destroy the bear's habitat and sources of food, we victimize him, he puts up with our stupidity. But when the bear is hungry and searches for food, when he finds it, anywhere he finds it, he grabs it because he is so desperately hungry…What do we do? We take a gun and kill him. He can't speak for himself because the Creator forgot to give him speech, so Man, feeling all powerful with a rifle in his hands, shoots and kills the bear. Applaud, applaud. We call this man Homo Sapiens. Where is sapiens in man, Auntie?"

"You are almost vitriolic in your opinion, honey. But now, *you* think: If the man hadn't killed the bear, the woman would have died for sure. Don't you think a human life is more precious than a bear's?"

"It depends what you mean by 'human'. If 'human' means you have the right to steal and destroy animals' habitats, then kill the animals when they search for food and shelter, then the word 'human' is improperly used. Human becomes beast. And the beasts in the forests should, in return, kill the human who steals their food and habitat. Because we have guns and can speak by no means makes us superior creatures. I would say it makes us inferior in many, many cases. The bear in question could have been wounded and rendered incapacitated until the proper authorities arrived to anesthetize it and carry it away to a zoo's veterinarian. That would have justified 'sapiens'. But, oh no, "have gun will kill" is man's motto. Why are humans like that, Auntie?"

"I think we have kept our prehistoric instincts. Under the disguise of high technology, doctorates and supersonic rockets, we cannot dismiss what we are: primitive Homo."

"Next time I see Fred I'll call him Neanderthal and watch his reaction!"

"If he laughs, he is intelligent. If he doesn't, well…"

"I'll tell him to go back to his cave!"

We both laughed and returned to our pancakes and coffee.

FOUR

WHEN I started my job as a housecleaner three months ago, I was supposed to only clean the mansion on Mondays and Fridays. That was the idea. The lady must have liked the work I've done so far and appreciated my punctuality and unassumingness because she has asked me to do a couple of extra things for her such as bringing her a glass of juice from the fridge, starting the coffee machine before the end of my shift, and changing the water in the flower vases. I did not mind as long as I left in time to have lunch at home with Aunt Sumi. The lady calls me Raphaëlle and I call her Madame. Each time I enter the mansion my heart starts to pound, I relive everything Aunt told me, my heart aches and I grind my teeth in anger. And each time I tell myself, 'Wait, don't rush. Observe her carefully, look for the weaknesses, search for a solution and when you are sure you have found it, start your mission'. So I observe like a snake watching its prey, silent and motionless, in full control. When the time comes, the conclusion will be swift and final. Only then will I be able to reconstruct a life for my beloved Aunt, a life free of the past and of suffering. This is my quest. The mission is dangerous and demands thorough and careful preparation, development and completion. Nobody, absolutely nobody should ever have an inkling about it; this is my personal and private pursuit. When I know where her weakness lies, I will know what to use, how and when to use it. Regardless of how long it may take, it is the culmination that I am focusing on, the payment, the retribution fair and long overdue.

Meditation comes easily to me now, I am discovering its benefits and am more and more in tune with the other world, with the thoughts and philosophy of Lord Buddha. A yet small window is beginning to open for me to glimpse into the other life that Aunt Sumika mentions so often. I am still a neophyte in the teachings of Buddhism, but a very eager student. Something or someone is nudging me, hurrying me, I hear, 'Hurry, hurry, or else'; I am not sure what it is and why I must hurry but I hope that deeper meditation will bring me the answer. For now I must concentrate on my double mission: make the culprit pay, and change Aunt Sumi's life into a garden of many joys and much happiness.

As I slowly return to earth after this early morning meditation, I remember our visit to Bentre Pagoda last week. Aunt Sumi kept her promise and took me with her, it was my first time ever visiting a Buddhist temple. At the entrance of the small pagoda, we removed our shoes, Aunt placed two fingers on her lips signaling 'total silence' from this moment on. I nodded and followed her closely. She bowed toward the altar where Lord Buddha was, I did the same; she put six incense sticks in a special dish, gave me six to do the same, and together we lighted them; then Aunt placed our offerings on a table nearby. Turning to me, she pointed to a far corner of the temple; I nodded and followed. Everything was so new and alien to me, I literally became Aunt Sumi's shadow, I didn't want to do anything wrong or to attract attention. The place was small but so beautiful. I saw sheets of gold paper, red ribbons, candles, lotus flowers, and tapestries; I noticed how clean and tidy the place was. When I finally stopped my silent inspection and appreciation, I took one furtive look at Aunt Sumi and almost didn't recognize her. Her head was slightly bowed, her hands were joined, she was sitting straight on the straw mat looking at the altar. But it was what I saw in her eyes that drew one muffled gasp from me: the look in them was not of this world, Aunt was far, very far away; I knew not where she went, but she was gone from here. Transfiguration? Could she have left earth and soared to nirvana? Was she in conversation with Neil Jahe? With Uncle Chris? Oh, why can't I reach that dimension? I must meditate more and ask Lord Buddha to grant me this wish. Suddenly in the back of my head I heard it again, 'Hurry, hurry, or else'. Tears burned my eyes because I still did not understand the message. If it comes from you, Lord, please make it clear to me and direct my steps; if it comes from you, then I will obey, I want so much to be accepted by you and allowed in your realm. Please help me with my mission, I desperately want to remove all pains and regrets from my Aunt's life. I know, I want many things and I am but an imperfect human. But you are kind and generous, you can help me; I want to be and remain your obedient servant. Thank you for listening to me.

I bowed deeply and got up to leave. Aunt Sumika had disappeared, I was all alone and felt panic taking hold of me. How could she vanish like this? Mere moments ago she was by my side while I was talking to Lord Buddha... Where did she go? My panic intensified, but then I saw her standing near the door. With relief I opened my mouth to speak, but she placed two fingers on her lips and I remembered, 'total silence'. I nodded; we both bowed once more to Lord Buddha and left. I seemed to be walking on air, light headed; a feeling of accomplishment and satisfaction was taking hold of me, there was a need to sigh deeply as if I had just performed a very important task. A new experience; I had never known this before in my life. Was it discovery? Was it revelation? Who was I?

Outside, the late August sun greeted us with softness under a gentle and blue sky. We walked to the parking lot and Aunt Sumi slipped her arm under mine.

"I like what I saw and now I know," she said.

"Oh, unfathomable words… what did you see and what do you know, Auntie?"

"I saw you in conversation with Lord Buddha and I know that you have established contact with him. This is a very important day to remember. If you keep the link with his world, you will progress very quickly in your meditation and eventually you will be able to connect with spirits and the world beyond. You are a fast learner, Raffee."

"That's because I have an excellent model to follow."

"You are a sweetheart. Let's have lunch at a Thai restaurant I know very well, shall we?"

"Did you say restaurant? That means food…I am suddenly very hungry, let's go!" She chuckled, I liked the sound of it and thought to myself, 'later when chuckles become outright laughter, I will be much happier. It will take time but, by George! I will make it happen. This woman deserves the very best, I will help to heal the wounds that are in her heart; by any means, by all means.'

Aunt Sumika was very comfortable in the restaurant, I could see she had been there before; when it was time to order our food, she pointed to dishes with incredible names such as Moon light, Daydream, etc. I couldn't help smiling at the names. The food was delicious and very light; I was glad Aunt didn't order anything spicy, I had heard about the famous Thai chili pepper that could in half a second trigger spontaneous combustion in one's mouth. For dessert, Aunt chose custard apples, green fruits with an out-of-this-world taste. I had to ask,

"Do they sell these fruits at the Asian market?"

"Yes, in season. They come directly from Asia, do you like them?"

"Oh yes, the taste is close to divine, never mind that it takes some work to reach the flesh inside the fruit."

"That's right, because of all the seeds. I will introduce you to other tropical fruits, it will be like an adventure for you with me as your guide."

"I'd like that very much. Thank you for this succulent lunch."

That evening, settled comfortably on the patio with Aunt Sumi, I could no longer hold my burning question.

"Auntie, when we do something bad in order to help someone we love dearly who desperately needs to be helped, are we punished?"

"We may not be punished by humans, but our conscience will chastise us for a long time. Therefore, it is our responsibility to choose our action: do we, or don't we do something bad? How bad is the something? And bad in whose eyes? Are we strong enough to endure the chastisement from our conscience day in, day out?"

"I see. It is not as clear and simple as I thought. What's your opinion?"

"If the game is worth the candle, I'd say 'Go for it'. But with extreme caution, of course."

"Of course. You are a wise woman, Auntie."

"Do you have something bad in mind, young lady?"

"Oh no, not me. I was just curious." Curious and without a clue about the something bad that had to be done to someone who did much worse to my Aunt. To be revisited later in the privacy of my room.

Around nine p.m. the phone buzzed and I answered.

"Raffee? This is Rhys, I hope I am not disturbing; if it weren't so important, I wouldn't call this late and…"

"To the point, Rhys, don't waste time, what is it?"

"It's Gosh Josh, he had an accident, he is in the ER, unconscious."

"Can you pick me up in two minutes? Are we allowed to see him? Which hospital?"

"Get ready, we're coming, Fred is with me." I turned to Aunt Sumi; she had guessed it all and signaled to me to be ready, not to worry about anything else. Wonderful woman, so understanding.

On the way to Windoaks General, Rhys filled me in.

"A truck hit his car on Highway 12, he was thrown out and landed head first on the graveled shoulder. He was still unconscious when he arrived at the hospital. His dad called my dad who phoned me at the Lab just as I was about to take away a tray with all the blood samples. I hope to God he's regained consciousness, I am thinking of serious brain injury."

"Please don't think, just pray. You too, Fred," I said.

"I'll go to the synagogue tomorrow morning and will pray my heart out for his recovery; I want to hear many more 'gosh!' from him". At this point I felt much burning in my eyes and looked out the car's window to hide my face from my friends. We all loved Josh, he got his nickname because the word 'gosh' seemed to mean everything in his vocabulary: surprise, excuse, excitement, shock… Sometimes he would also say 'my gosh!' and we would ask him who his gosh was. Yes, Joshua McMahon has always been the life of our group, we will all pray for his recovery.

At the hospital we were told that Josh was resting in a private room in the East Wing; his parents were with him.

"Is he conscious? May we see him?" Fred asked.

"He is conscious but very weak. Five minutes is all we can give you, he needs to rest."

"Thank you," we said in unison as we flew to the East Wing.

At the nurses station we were told, "One visitor at a time, please." Rhys went in first. Then Fred. I followed five minutes later, said hello to Josh's parents and turned to my friend. His head was one big bandage. And in this bandage I saw two bright eyes that seemed to be laughing as he blinked in lieu of speech. I knew right then and there that Gosh Josh was going to continue joining us for each party and each picnic. With much joy and relief, I bent down to kiss the bandage and whisper in an invisible ear, "See you soon, kid!" His hand, the one without the perfusion needle and tube, touched mine ever so lightly and very quickly fell back on the sheet.

Outside in the waiting area, Rhys and Fred stood up from their chairs the moment they saw me. Three pairs of eyes talked to each other before our lips joined in.

"He seemed ok despite the bandage," Rhys said.

"And I heard him sigh," Fred added.

"He touched my hand briefly and weakly."

"So, what's your opinion?" Rhys asked. I looked at Fred, he raised his thumb. Rhys looked at me and I said, "It looks good."

"Now we are going to drive you home, it's late. It was good to see him together, he knows he can count on his friends. Shall we go?" Rhys said.

At my gate, I thanked them and hurried inside. I had no jacket on and it was chilly outside, the kind of 'chilly' that never failed to remind us that winter was not that far away.

Eleven days later Gosh Josh was released from the hospital and back home with his parents, not in his own apartment as yet; he needed more rest and more TLC from his folks. The head injury was bad, but there was no brain injury, Josh would be back to normal in no time. It was a close call. The truck driver was found guilty of impaired driving, fined an enormous amount of money, received numerous demerit points and had his license revoked for a number of weeks.

It is Friday and I am expected at the mansion at nine sharp this morning; it's going to be a lime-green smock day. Aunt Sumi asked me to buy a large chunk of Brie cheese on my way home from work. We both love Brie and Camembert. Aunt says the older the Camembert, the better it tastes. True, but I don't like to see the greenish ring around the top of the old cheese… so I remove the crust and eat the creamy inside.

On my way to St. Thomas I hum the beautiful theme from The Gadfly; marvelous music by Shostakovich, it always fills my head with pictures of a dance floor hidden in a forest and a prince dancing with a princess. Each time I play the CD at home, the same image returns and takes me away to dreamland.

"Good morning, Madame," I say as Mrs. Jahe opens the door. She is limping more today, what happened?

"Right. Come in, Raphaëlle; looks like rain for today," she says.

"That's what the weatherman said on the radio this morning, but weathermen have been known to lie. Do you have to go out?"

"Yes, and I think I should take my umbrella, you never know just in case the weatherman told the truth this morning."

"I always leave one in my car."

"That's very wise. I'll be off now. If I am not back before noon, just slam the door shut when you leave. Your pay is already on the kitchen table."

"Thank you."

I am alone in a beautiful mansion overflowing with objets d'art and marvelous paintings. There are a few photographs on one of the dressers in one of the smaller bedrooms, I have noticed them before and today I am going to look in their backs to see if there are any names and dates. One photo shows a woman with very white hair holding a cat in her arms; on another there are two couples leaning against an enormous tree on a background of mountains and hills, the date says 1968; that's old! The third photo is a black and white print showing a smiling man whose eyes show unlimited kindness; I look on the back of it and my heart jumps to my throat, the name is Neil Jahe and the year is 1972. Such a long time ago, I wasn't even conceived yet. So, this man, this Neil Jahe… he was Aunt Sumi's perfect love, the idealist whose ideal became his killer… You fool, you blind. Other epithets burn my lips but I don't pronounce them out of respect for Aunt. Neil Jahe, you left my aunt to follow your ideal; you hurt her and you hurt yourself, you are sadist and masochist, but worst of all, you are a fool. In the end, what did your *ideal* – represented by the woman who lives here – do for you? She killed you by inches with patience and determination. You have left this world and you have left my aunt a second time. Wherever you are, Neil Jahe, I hope you see her unending sorrow and I hope it makes you regret and suffer as much as she is regretting and suffering. Since you are no longer here to contend with my anger, your *ideal* will pay the price, full price, full payment, or my name is not Raphaëlle, Jenna Luens.

It was a monologue but I knew Neil Jahe was there and heard me. I felt his presence; probably a sign from the world beyond in which I believe more and more. Now there remains the task of finding the appropriate mode of payment. Time is a good counselor, I shall not hurry; with time, the right retribution will show and I will execute.

I resume my cleaning of the manor and just before leaving, I go back to the bedroom with the photographs and say to Neil Jahe, "Not to worry, Sir, she will pay the amount owing in full!" Then, slamming the door shut, I drive home and stop at the dairy products store to buy a large chunk of Brie cheese. There is not the shadow of a doubt in my mind that I will fulfil this mission of retribution. What I need is careful planning and extra careful execution.

My encounter with Neil Jahe left me with many new feelings and thoughts. He was a good looking man with light color eyes so full of kindness and gentleness. You see, Neil, when you are that kind and gentle, you are easy prey to someone as evil and cold as Betty-Ann; you don't see the killer, you never think of the killer being your own wife, not even on your deathbed; no, you are an idealist and you stuck to your ideal until your last breath. What good did it do? It sure didn't make you happy all those years when you missed Aunt Sumi so much and wanted her so much; you missed the perfection that the two of you were blessed to have. Was your death at the hand of your wife some sort of punishment for what you have done to my beloved aunt? I wonder. I am twenty-two years old, my eyes see only the misery and sorrow inflicted on my aunt by Mrs. Betty-Ann Jahe and I can think of only one thing: retribution. So help me, God.

"Honey, you are talking so much to yourself, I can almost hear the conversation," Aunt Sumika says as she pours Curaçao in our little glasses. We are on the patio, it is dark and the first stars have just arrived in the night sky, glimmering shyly as they wait for their nocturnal friends to join them.

"There is a horse race and competition in my head, Auntie, but I know Curaçao will soon bring law and order in there."

"Would your head feel lighter if you threw some of the thoughts out? I am ready to catch them before they touch the floor, if you wish."

"Oh, thank you wonderful lady; right now the thoughts look like a spaghetti factory, I wouldn't know what to tell you. So, let's enjoy this divine liqueur instead."

"How is your friend Josh?"

"Fred told me Gosh Josh went back to his apartment. That's a very good sign. Maybe he'll go back to his laboratory soon. That was a close call, wasn't it? We were all so worried."

"A close call, yes. What would you say if we had a party here for all your friends? Good food, good fun, no worries and no concerns. We don't need to have a birthday to have a party, and we want to show Josh that we all love him."

"You have done a lot of thinking, Auntie, and it's all good thinking. I am in favor if you'll let me help you and Maria prepare the food. What a wonderful idea! Thank you a zillion, Aunt Sumi, you're the best."

"Since the weather is so fickle these days, how about a buffet indoors?"

"Another good idea, Auntie. How about Saturday next week? This will give us plenty of time to get ready. I can get on the phone tomorrow to invite my friends. Do I have a 'Go', Auntie?"

"Go!" she says. That's all I needed to forget my troubling thoughts and look forward to a good party.

Ramon the gardener arrives and gives Aunt Sumi a brown canvas bag.

"Time to plant for next spring, Señora; these are bulbs that will work slowly during the winter to give you beautiful and fragrant flowers as early as March. Where would you like me to plant them?"

"How nice of you, Ramon; plant them in the best spots and you know better than I do where these are. It is getting chillier now, don't hesitate to ask Maria for hot coffee or tea. And thank you for the bulbs, how much do I owe you?"

"Nothing, Señora, it is my pleasure. Is Raphaëlle home? I have something I would like to ask her opinion about; if she has time, that is."

"She is here, I'll let her know right away."

I stop Ramon as he is about to dig the first hole for the bulbs.

"Hi, Ramon, how are you? Aunt tells me you want to ask me something? Shoot! I am all ears."

"Hello Raphaëlle, and thank you for your time."

We sit at the round table near the garage door and I lend Ramon my two ears.

"It's my daughter Mayra. She spoils her little boy Jaime and lets him do everything he wants. He is four years old and thinks he is the last emperor. He screams and refuses to eat what my daughter feeds him. And what does she do? She throws away the good food, gives him a cookie or two and promises to buy him a bag of junk food; says 'it's more fun to eat' and Jaime will eat it. I tell her junk is no food; junk is junk; the boy needs food, not junk."

"And?"

"She ignores me totally and feeds the boy those awful greasy and salty fries. We didn't raise our children that way. Our children ate what we ate and everything was fine. I think it's her husband's bad influence."

"You see, Ramon, in most households in North America, children are the dictators and parents are the obedient subjects. It is frowned upon when parents discipline their children. Food has to be fun to eat or children won't eat it. I ask you, do you eat for fun or for keeping alive? When somebody is very hungry, on the brink of starvation, ask him if he wants food that is fun to eat. I tell you, if he has one ounce of energy left in him, he will kill you before he answers that question. I'll tell you some more and you can do whatever you want with it: when a child refuses his food because it is not fun to eat, remove the food, give him nothing until the next meal. When he gets hungry later and wants to eat, tell him it's not dinner time yet, he'll have to wait, he should have eaten earlier. Stick to your gun, do this a few times. Unless the child is a total idiot, he'll quickly get the message and eat what is in his plate, fun or no fun."

"Ooooh, Mayra will never go for that!"

"Too bad, because it is the best way. The responsibility is with the parents, either they teach or they don't. Every child is ready to learn the moment it is born. Why, it even learns when to give its first wailing! The bulbs you are going to plant will start working the moment you put them in the ground, right? Have a nice day, Ramon. Are you going to cover the frog's pond for me? It is getting colder by the hour."

"Of course I will; thank you Raphaëlle; I feel lighter for having talked to you about this, it's been on my mind for some time."

"Any time, Ramon, any time."

The pond is covered, the bulbs planted and Ramon gone home. In a couple of weeks he will cover the less sturdy plants, remove the faded annuals, and our garden will stand ready for winter. It is not my favorite season only because there is often black ice on the roads, which petrifies me. I will have to be extra careful when I drive to St. Thomas every Monday and Friday. All my friends go skating and always invite me to join them. When I go with them, I bring a book to read and wait for them in the warm and comfortable lounge at the club. Skating is not for me ever since I hurt my back a few years ago. But hiking in the snow on sunny days and throwing snowballs are things we always enjoy. Two winters ago there was so much snow, our garden looked like a ghost place shrouded in all that white. Birds and squirrels came by the dozen to beg for food and Ramon – with his truck turned snowplow – came to clear our driveway every day. Without him we would have been snowbound. Each winter I wonder 'why can't it be summer all year?'

Aunt Sumi is already sipping a liqueur on the patio; I take two cardigans out and join her with a glass of Grand Marnier.

"Thank you for the cardigan, Raffee; it is getting unpleasantly chilly in the evening now. Did you have a nice chat with Ramon this morning? He is such a hard working man."

"We talked about his grandson Jaime who refuses to eat his food because it is not fun to eat. Can you believe children today! Food has to be fun to eat or they won't eat it…and parents kowtow to them. I told Ramon to tell his daughter that you eat not to have fun but to remain alive. What an absurd notion that food has to be fun for children to eat it. Beyond my comprehension."

"It is utterly silly, I agree. You were never that silly when you were growing up, you always ate what was in your plate, even broccoli and spinach. Speaking of food, any idea what we'll prepare for the party?"

"Things tasty and easy to eat, maybe? Those Thai spring rolls that you make so well will be a big success; tacos from Maria, a Lasagna from me, a huge salad, a couple of cheeses, a sinfully good dessert smothered in chocolate, and very important: superb wines. The party will be a resounding success and Josh will say' 'Oh my gosh!' and we'll ask him who his gosh is!"

We both laugh heartily at this mention of dear Gosh Josh.

FIVE

THERE WERE a few flakes of timid snow last nigh; it all cleared this morning and a gorgeous sun is trying hard to warm things up a bit down on earth; I am grateful for its effort and wink my thanks to El Sol up there. We are having our party this evening; my friends Walter, Josh and Rhys are coming with Arielle, Stephie and Alexa. Fred is coming alone as my special guest. Andrew is on call at the hospital but may be able to join us later, especially when he heard about a cake smothered in chocolate.

"We need much *comida* for all the young people," Maria says and I nod my agreement. To her, we are all 'young people', even Rhys who is twenty-five and the senior in our group.

Aunt Sumi ordered the cake from the best bakery in town and I know the boys will go to heaven when they taste it, especially Andrew. An intern is almost never rich but always needs much good food to keep up with his maddening schedule. Whenever we can steal Andrew away from the hospital, we serve him the best food and pack a bag for him to take back to his dorm. When he hesitates to accept, we tell him, "That's what friends are for, Doctor!" His parents live so far away, they can never visit; so Aunt Sumi has taken him under her wing. Last Spring I taught Andrew how to sew buttons back on his lab coats and shirts. It wasn't easy for him to do, but he was grateful for the lessons.

It is lunch time and Aunt and I are having sautéed shrimps on farmer's bread; it is tasty, light and always a treat.

"Funny, our food is always fun to eat," I say.

"And we never refuse it," Aunt Sumi adds and we chuckle as we remember Ramon's story.

"I don't know why parents allow such behavior with their children. Even if they are filthy rich and eat caviar at breakfast, lunch and dinner, they shouldn't teach their offspring that it is all right to throw away food because it is not fun to eat. It is not because we live in a rich country that has never known war that it is all right to waste food just because our children don't find it fun to eat. You will tell me I am a disciplinarian, but I can't help it. When I see a child refuse food because 'it is not fun to eat', I want to slap and spank that kid till my hands burn."

"Corporal punishment has been banished, you don't spank children any more. If you do, your children can sue you and you'll be found guilty of child abuse. Discipline is now called child abuse."

"That's why we have what we have today: the plague of an entire generation of indisciplined children. I don't want children of my own, they are a mega headache!"

"Oh, Raffee, don't say that. They are not all bad, they are what their parents make them. Good parents make good children and I know a few good parents out there, beginning with Maria."

"Yes, she must be a good parent because her three boys are polite and well-behaved. I will accept them as three exceptions. But there are thousands of bad ones out there, imposing their law on their parents. Makes me sick."

"At least you and your peers are out of that sphere; I like all your friends, they are wonderful people and I look forward to seeing them tonight. I hope Andrew can slip away from the hospital and join us."

"I know he'll do his best, he heard me mention a cake smothered in chocolate and he can't resist that, no, not Andrew!" It is so good to hear Aunt Sumi laugh, I'll have to make her laugh more often. When she laughs, it means her heart is light; and this makes my heart lighter too. I want to fill her days with laughter; this way, her sadness will – I hope – fade away gradually until her memory is free of hurt and regrets. A very ambitious project, but I am determined to work hard on it. I will eliminate the source of Aunt Sumi's suffering; whichever way, by any means, every means, all means. This quest of mine occupies my mind every single day, I toss and turn it in every direction trying to find the answer to my question, 'How?' I must find not *a* way, but *the* way to realize it, bring it to final conclusion without incriminating myself. The perpetrator, Mrs. Betty-Ann Jahe, has never been punished. The victim, Aunt Sumika, has lived a life of sorrow and regrets, silently and resignedly. I am not the angel of divine justice, I am not seeking kudos for a job well done, I don't even want approval from anybody. I just want to eliminate all pain from my Aunt's memory, remove the woman who has done her so much wrong, who has killed her perfect love and erased all hope from her life. The bad must be punished and the good rewarded. I make it my duty to fulfil this commitment.

Perhaps I should go to my room and sit before the altar, meditate and search for the answer, a means, (a weapon?), a time frame; but most of all I must find enough courage to carry out the mission. Time and patience, calm and observation…the snake watching its prey.

Rhys and Stephie arrive first, soon followed by Gosh Josh and Arielle, then Walter and Alexa. Aunt Sumi and I greet them with joy and hugs. They give Aunt an enormous bouquet of purple orchid in cello wrap with a golden bow, absolutely gorgeous.

"Thank you so much, they are beautiful, but you shouldn't have," Aunt says.

"It's our pleasure, Mrs. Luens," Walter declares. We hear a car door slam, Fred is here.

"Hello you all. Good evening, Mrs. Luens, Raffee, thank you for inviting us."

"And welcome to you all; let's relax in the living-room where you'll find bottles and glasses and canapés. Be at home, help yourselves," Aunt Sumi tells them before walking toward the kitchen. It's my turn to be hostess.

"The flowers are out of this world, thanks all of you. How have you all been? How are you, Josh?"

"Oh gosh, it was bad but I am tough, ready to live it up again. I think the idiot truck driver should have been more severely punished… but let's not go there, it's past history. I want to enjoy this evening with my best friends."

"Who wants a kitten? My cat has just had five little ones, cute as can be. Do I hear a taker? Two? Come on, friends, raise your hands," Arielle says, but no hand is raised.

"Sorry, Ari, no takers. They don't allow pets in most apartment buildings. It's unfair but that's the rule," Rhys answers.

"Is Andrew coming?" asks Walter.

"If he can slip out of the hospital later, he'll join us. I don't understand why doctors make life such hell for interns," I say.

"It's their power trip, it makes them feel very superior and important. They also have a very short memory: they were interns once. I keep bombarding my father on this subject," Alexa says.

"And?" Fred asks.

"He says not all doctors are like that, not all doctors need power trips, etc."

"But in this hospital they do and Andrew and his peers have to put up with it," Fred continues.

"I hope he can come tonight. Are you hungry yet?" I ask.

"And I hope you are, because dinner is ready; come and help yourselves," Aunt Sumi announces.

"Auntie, let me serve you; why don't you sit in the living-room and I'll bring you a large plate well filled," I offer.

"Ah, child with a golden heart! Thank you, Raffee; see you in the living-room."

As we sit and are about to start eating, we hear a knock on the door; Andrew enters and we greet him with one loud cheer, "To Andrew!" I quickly leave my plate on the coffee table and take him to the main table where I order him to fill his plate to the brim.

"It's so good to see you, Andrew, so good you can join us. I hope you can stay till the end, enjoy the food; there are two or three wines to accompany everything."

When you are hungry and there is good food, speech is not needed; all we hear now is the sound of forks against plates. It is a lovely sound and the busier we get with eating, the lovelier the sound. As I look around and see my good friends in my home with my dear Aunt Sumi, I feel warm all over. It is good to have a home and such true friends. Without thinking of any other god, I say to myself, 'Thank you Lord Buddha.' Rhys goes back to the table for salad and cheese; he winks at me; I wink back and smile. Aunt Sumika takes her plate to the kitchen; I hear more plates coming out of the cupboard, the fridge door opening and closing, and I know the cake will soon make its entrance.

"Fill your glasses, my friends, King Cake is about to enter," I announce. Wine is quickly poured, Fred fills my glass and his, we clink and he whispers, "This is a wonderful evening, Raffee, and you are wonderful."

"Thank you, Fred, you're wonderful too; I am glad you are having a good time."

Aunt Sumi arrives with the star of the evening placed on a silver tray with a silver knife.

"Here is the cake smothered in chocolate that Raffee talked about. Take your plates and fill them up," she says. I serve her a large chunk and as I pick up a plate for myself, Fred brings me one already filled.

"Thanks, Fred. Where is your plate?"

"Right here on my chair."

"Mm, Mm, Gosh this is good!" Josh – who else? – sighs. That's all we hear for a while, every mouth much too busy to utter a word. The cake is a huge success, but it is too big and we can't finish all of it. At least for now. I know my friends and their sweet teeth. Before we go out to the patio with blankets, Alexa steals another piece of cake and rolls her eyes, she is in heaven.

"Not to worry, we'll finish all of it later, I promise," I say in her ear.

It is my turn to serve the after-dinner drinks. Aunt Sumi joins my friends, I ask them to make room on the low table for cups or glasses and liqueurs. Nobody wants tea or coffee, they are making my job easier. In the dining room I prepare the large tray and discover that I need help to carry everything outside, so I ask for a volunteer. Andrew jumps up and comes to rescue the damsel in distress.

"Thanks, Andrew, you are a dear."

"Are you calling me Bambi?"

"Ooooh, you are good! All I want to say is that you are a wonderful man, it is so good to see you. Are you having a good time?"

"Are you kidding? The company, the food, the drinks… this is paradise, I'll dream of it tonight in the dorm."

We bring the glasses and bottles out and Andrew offers to be the barman. Curaçao for Auntie and me; they choose their drinks among the bottles. Stephie asks for an ice cube in her Cream of Cocoa and I bring her a small bowl with four cubes.

"Mrs. Luens, everything is perfect to make this a perfect day for us," Fred says.

"Thank you for having us over," Arielle adds.

"The pleasure is all mine, I mean it. As I was telling Raffee, we don't need to wait for a birthday to have a party."

"Hear, hear!" and glasses are clinked all around.

"Santé! as they say in some countries. I learned this from Gustav who immigrated from Kazakhstan not long ago," says Josh.

"An immigrant from Central Asia? There aren't too many of them around, we usually see people from the Far East, Africa and the Caribbean. Is he a legal immigrant?" Rhys asks.

"He is working, so he must be."

"Not necessarily. Most immigrants – most, not all – are here illegally. Do you have proof that Gustav is legit?"

"I took his word for fact. What if he turns out to be here illegally?"

"He will be found out and probably sent flying back to his country."

"Not necessarily. Look around. Illegal immigrants are everywhere, tens of thousands of them here. How do we know? Why, they have become so numerous, they no longer need to hide; in fact, they feel so strong in number that they now demonstrate en masse in the open; they shout, they brandish banners, etc…and,"

"Wow! Raffee, you *have* been watching them! What do they want now that they have the nerve to show themselves?" Fred interrupts me. Aunt Sumi now joins the debate.

"They demand their *rights*! Yes, I said the word 'rights'. These parasites think they have rights; they crawl into this country like a pest, a plague; they hide like a disease and now they demand rights. They have never heard the word 'duty' or 'legality', their language probably does not contain these words. But, oh yes, they congregate, they march and protest and demand rights. My friends, what rights are you willing to give these outlaws?" I can see Aunt Sumi is very keen on the subject but I'll let my friends answer.

"I personally will give them, all of them, one right: deportation, immediate and final," Walter almost shouts his reply. He is always hot in his opinion when something hits his interest.

"What if they have married here and have children?" Rhys asks.

"My answer remains the same: Get out, and when the children reach the age of eighteen, they can choose to come back since they were born here," Walter again.

"But what if their spouse is from here?" Rhys continues.

"The family gets out together, we don't break up families," Walter says. I decide to put in my two cents.

"What if they really like it here and want to stay for good? Do we close our door?"

Aunt Sumi steps in.

"We don't close our door to legal immigrants. But those who arrived here illegally, must leave; they must go through the legal process of application, investigation, et cetera, and wait the required number of years, which incidentally has been shortened not long ago."

"And what does our country do about this plague?" Josh asks.

"As you know, our country lost its backbone about two or three decades ago. It has become very lethargic and lenient, and blind. We have all heard about some confirmed terrorists living here, free and comfortable. The people want them out, but the government lets them stay. Sometimes it looks as if we are cupping our hands to receive the world's vomit with words like, 'come, come here, we'll welcome you, our door is open, come, come, come'. And so they come, all shapes and colors and backgrounds, the good, the bad and the ugliest. We are the world's melting pot – chamber pot is more appropriate. – When you hear 'children are the future of our country' does it not scare you?" Aunt Sumi answers to Josh, but speaks to us all. Walter jumps in as if something had just spiked him.

"They have become so bold that now they want to eliminate our 'Merry Christmas' and replace it with 'Happy Holidays'; they insert their customs into our own calendars, imposing on us their religious and civil festivals and celebrations. What the hell are they trying to accomplish?"

Everybody is getting so hot on the subject, I go to the kitchen and bring out four bottles of Evian water and glasses for all. I do this quietly and quickly so as not to break the general train of thought and miss anything said.

"They are so desperate to be like us and accepted by us, they think they are doing the right thing forcing their customs on us. I cross these out on my calendars when I see them. Why don't they print their own calendars for crying out loud?" Alexa says, rolling her magnificent blue eyes.

"Remember, they are parasites, they need a host to cling on and live off, that's the life of parasites. And they are so uneducated, they may not even know how to print a calendar!" Fred adds, sniggering in disgust. Do I detect a trace of vitriol here?

"And what does our Prime Minister do about all this?" Arielle asks, shrugging her shoulders.

"Nothing. He lets his underlings handle everything, he is too busy fighting for his political life; the illegal immigrants know this and use it well with the help of rotten lawyers," Josh says.

"In conclusion, we are plagued with a disease called illegal immigration. There is a cure called deportation, but our government does not want to use it. Our country is ill but the cure is rejected. Any more cake, ladies and gentlemen?" Aunt Sumi offers.

We fold our blankets and head back inside. Andrew and Josh bring in the bottles and glasses and place them on the dining table. A last round of chocolate cake finds all of us savoring the sinfully good dessert. It is one a.m.

"Thank you, Mrs. Luens, Raffee, the whole evening has been wonderful, you have spoiled us," Andrew speaks for the group.

"Oh gosh, yes, more than wonderful, thank you a zillion!" Joshua adds.

"Thank you for coming and for the flowers. See you soon. Now drive carefully, good night all," Aunt Sumi says. Stephie starts whistling the 1812 Overture but Arielle stops her, "Shh, it's one in the morning!" Aunt and I chuckle as we close the front and back doors and turn on the night light in the driveway.

Maria is off on Sundays. I tiptoe to the kitchen to start tidying up a bit before I can converse with the coffee pot and fix something for breakfast. The dining table needs clearing, so does the coffee table. I'll do it a little at a time. My first cup of coffee always seems to be sent to me from heaven it tastes that good and wakes me up in a wink. The party was a success, everybody enjoyed it and I was happy to see that Josh had fully recovered from that horrific accident. He is right, the impaired truck driver should have been much more severely punished and his license removed for a full year, not just a few weeks. We have some lasagna and rolls left over and I am thinking of Andrew…but we couldn't give him anything to take away last night, it would have embarrassed him. We can only do this when we invite him alone. Eight more months and he'll be a resident. Soon we'll see on his door a plaque with 'Andrew Kozell, MD'. It sounds good! I wonder where he'll establish his practice after his residency.

The coffee is hot and good, I add dark toast with orange marmalade to my breakfast. Last night we had a lively and very interesting conversation and

I am glad each one of us took part. The exchange was mature and intelligent and, as Josh would say, 'Gosh, it couldn't be more up-to-the-minute stuff'. Bless you, Josh. I hear a door open and see Aunt Sumika stretch her arms.

"I am in the kitchen, Auntie. Good morning, how did you sleep?"

"Ah there you are, little princess. The coffee smells divine, can I have some? I slept soundly. You?"

"As soundly as you; here's some coffee, there is also toast and marmalade. Don't look around yet, we'll take our sweet time to clear everything, there is no rush. Last night was marvelous, thank you for everything. It was a brilliant idea, Auntie."

"Your friends are really nice, I like them all. It was good that Andrew could get away and join us. When will he be a resident?"

"Eight more months, we hope; he works so hard, he'll make it. I wonder when he sleeps, if he sleeps at all."

"Sometimes they fall asleep in the linen room between calls. What a life!"

"But it's all worth it in the end. Soon he'll have his own practice somewhere."

"Or he'll join other doctors to form a group practice."

"I think he is a very deserving man."

"Doesn't this make Fred jealous?"

"Whatever for, Auntie? I like Fred as I like all of them, they are all dear to me. If Fred decides to be jealous, that's his business, but he will look ridiculous in my eyes."

"Love is almost always accompanied by jealousy."

"That's Fred's business, not mine. I am not yet interested in falling in love. Life is a bit complicated at the moment, so I'll leave love somewhere else. Besides, Aunt Sumi, I am Buddhist and Fred is Jewish…can you see the insurmountable obstacle? It makes me shudder and I don't want to deal with it just now; there are a few important things I must take care of in the near future."

"There's my mysterious niece again. Oh, look at the orchid! How gorgeous, breathtaking. And put in a vase with cool water, they'll last for days. We had them everywhere in Thailand. One of my students once called them 'the picture of perfect creation'; isn't it a beautiful description?"

"Yes it is, and very appropriate; I can imagine whole forests of them… pity they have no scent."

"Their beauty speaks for everything, they don't need fragrance."

I see the Saturday's papers in a corner, untouched because we were too busy preparing the food for the party last night. On the front page there is the picture of a cute looking dog on a leash, without its owner. The caption is not so cute, it announces that the Attorney General has decided to have all pit bull dogs put down as there have been many complaints of attacks by these dogs. Owners of pit bulls are directed to have their dogs euthanized within one week or face heavy fines. No pit bulls will be allowed in this province. I read this aloud so Aunt Sumi can share the news with me. And the news infuriates me, I fly into incredible anger.

"You see, Auntie, once again it's the animal that gets killed, not the stupid humans. Dogs can't speak in their defense, so let's kill them by the dozen. If they attack it's because they are provoked or annoyed and their owners have taught them to attack; they were not born that way, we made them that way, we taught them to kill. And when somebody higher up decides that they have attacked more than once, they receive the lethal injection. The Attorney General may have high education in law, but when it comes to common sense, he has none; he points the finger at the dog, not at the owner who has trained his dog to kill and is proud of it. Perhaps the A.G. is also a coward and doesn't dare antagonize people, it is easier to abuse one's power on an animal. He may look good in the eyes of a few people, a minority to be sure, but he does look a bit dumb to have come up with such a dumb decision. I am utterly disgusted."

"So am I, Raffee, but the A.G. dictates and we are expected to obey. What can you do?"

"I'll tell you what I can do. And on Monday I'll show *him* what I can do. I will buy a pit bull puppy. So, Mr. A.G., bring it on! Alexa had a pit bull once, she was so cute and adorable, the Vet called her 'you silly goose!' That's a pit bull in my book. And my pit bull will not be trained to attack anybody – except maybe our Attorney General – " And I wink at Aunt Sumi who smiles and shakes her head.

"Raffee, you are impossible, yet so strong and sincere in your feelings. I can see why Fred feels the way he does toward you."

"Hush, we are talking about pit bulls here. Fred is not a pit bull, Auntie." Now she laughs out loud and a feeling of warmth accompanies every beating of my heart. That's the magic of Aunt Sumi's laughter.

SIX

ON MY WAY to St. Thomas this morning I can't help noticing the change of color among the trees that parade along the highway as I speed toward the mansion. Dressed in yellow, rust, orange and vivid red, they don't want to be late for the grand party: the upcoming summer's finale. The sun is already up but still shy, it is only humming whereas I want it to burst into strong notes of warm gold. Why do seasons fly so fast one after the other? Is summer doomed to be just a short interlude before the agonizingly long winter? Can a magician reverse the roles and make winter very short and summer very long? Soon the small pond that I always admire on my way to work will turn into solid ice and children will go skating on its surface. Ducks and geese won't come in search of food any more, they will hide somewhere till the first signs of spring and I will miss seeing them. All these colorful and magnificent trees will soon be naked, they will probably shiver for the next five or six months and only silence will keep them company. Winter has many beauties; one is silence, another is its costume of brilliant white satin sprinkled here and there with the shiny red and green of holly. And winter offers the meditative soul a gift of pure magic: peace so deep that only the beating of one's heart can be heard.

However, before winter surprises us one cool morning, there is fall. Ah, fall is the in-between season half linked to summer and half to winter. There are people who choose to think it is still summer and continue to wear summer clothes; others decide to get ready to greet old man winter; they prepare their gardens, put away sandals and shorts, and bring out warmer clothes and shoes and boots. Animals feel the change of season and they, too, prepare for the cold winter. Colorful birds of summer disappear, groundhogs and dormice hibernate in their winter homes. Earth gets ready for a long sleep, I can almost hear it sigh and yawn.

Ahead of me the mansion looms, it is time to return to reality and face the work at hand, the world, and my boss – the woman who caused so much pain and sorrow in my Aunt's life. Every time I arrive at the gate, my bitter feelings resurface, I see the regrets in Aunt Sumi's eyes, her seemingly acceptance of her fate; and my non-acceptance of it grows stronger. I have always believed in the bad being punished and the good rewarded. Look at the woman who lives in this mansion. She has taken Neil Jahe away from Aunt Sumika, she has killed him slowly over the years, she has inherited everything and now lives like a queen in this opulent home. Her eyes are devoid of sadness, or longing, or guilt; she has accomplished everything she had planned from the start, she is Machiavelli resurrected. I shudder at the thought that in a few minutes I will be under the same roof as this master schemer. She succeeded without incriminating herself. I must do the same in my quest, I must watch before I act. Let the watching begin!

"Good morning, Madame," I say as she opens the front door.

"Right. Hello Raphaëlle, is it very cold outside?"

"Not yet, but the trees are telling us to be ready, they are already changing their colors."

"Are you a poet?"

"Oh no, Madame, I am just a house cleaner." She looks at me from head to toe, my eyes follow hers down to my shoes. I hope I didn't go overboard with my description of the trees… quick, I have to say something more down to earth or else she will think I am a poet.

"It is not cold now but summer is going away, you can feel it in the air."

"Right. Soon there'll be snow and ice. Well, don't let me keep you. I'll be on the patio."

Phew! I scold myself, no more poetic description from now on. Concentrate on the work and the mission. I don't waste a minute, don my vivid red smock and begin my three-hour conversation with cleaning tools and products. The feather duster looks pathetically emaciated, I take it outside to show the lady.

"Right. It does look rather skinny, I'll get you a new one next time I go downtown. If you need anything else, let me know."

"Thank you."

How can she be so comfortable and at peace when she knows that she has killed a man? Doesn't it disturb her conscience? It was not *any* man that she killed, it was Neil Jahe, Aunt Sumika's perfect love; Neil who with Aunt made the sacred pledge of reuniting after their long trial but who, at the hand of this woman, met his death prematurely. Why has she not been prosecuted and punished? What magic did she use? How am I going to fulfil my mission? Visions of arsenic powder and cyanide waive at my brains and frighten me the moment I realize the direction my thoughts are taking. Now I am really scared and begin to tremble. Will it take such a drastic measure? Where will I find the products? Is this the only way to take her out of the picture? If I do it and she dies, won't I become like her, a killer? Won't I become 'the bad' that must be punished? My whole being rebels against this thought. I will not be another her, she killed for personal gain, out of greed. If I kill, it will be payback fair and simple… Who am I? A new generation law enforcer?

All this cerebration mixed with the motion of the broom followed by the mop has given me a headache, and I am no closer to a solution. Before my head explodes under the pressure, I take one gulp of water from my small plastic bottle and two deep breaths. A look at my wristwatch tells me it is twenty minutes before the end of my shift. Hurriedly I go upstairs to inspect the master bedroom, then the hallway, then back in the kitchen downstairs; I make sure everything is where it is supposed to be and, after returning all the tools and products to their closet, I step outside to say goodbye to the lady.

"Right. Thank you Raphaëlle. See you on Friday and I'll have a new feather duster for you."

"Thank you Madame."

Lucky her, she can stay on her patio all winter if she wishes, it is covered and there is a portable heater in one corner. Our patio at home is open and we already need a blanket to stay out there, though this is only early October. Whenever I speak to Mrs. Jahe and look in her eyes searching for one speck of sadness or regret, I never succeed and never see that speck. The woman has no regrets, she is pleased and satisfied with what she has done, and I want to scream my anger, my thirst for revenge. I also feel much sadness for Aunt Sumika. Surely, if there is a god out there, he can see that there is no justice here. Betty-Ann Jahe has committed two crimes: she killed one person physically and the other emotionally. One killer, two victims. Neil now rests peacefully in the beyond. Aunt Sumi lives, suffers and grieves her loss every single day. If there is a god out there, in the name of this god am I supposed to close my eyes and not seek retribution? Somehow, somewhere I have to find a way. I must, or else I'll be the one living in deep sorrow, witnessing the deep sorrow in my Aunt's eyes day after day.

Lost in my thoughts I almost don't see the resplendent colors that greeted me this morning. My eyes burn because I feel so ignorant and helpless in the art of retribution and because at the same time I am very intent on finding a solution that would lift the veil of sadness away from Aunt Sumi's eyes. There must be a way and I must find it on my own. In this mission there can be only one person involved. A fleeting thought of Fred nudges my mind… but, no, absolutely not, never. Don't even go there. Aunt Sumi is my dearest aunt, she took me in when my parents died, she loves me as her own child, she has given me everything I ever needed. She and Uncle Chris have become my parents. It behooves me to remove all sorrow and that far-away look from her eyes, to help her to accept life without Neil Jahe. It's been such a long time for her, surely if I offered her the final result of a successful mission, she would find peace and acceptance… What should I do? Where do I turn? Who will help?

As I leave the highway and enter our street, I need to clear my head of this monologue and these thoughts. Somehow, some way, one day the solution will come to me. In the meantime I must remain in control of my feelings and refuse clouds of doubt access to my eyes lest Auntie should notice and start asking questions. It is going to be difficult to keep such a gigantic secret. It makes me feel like somebody on a small boat out at sea and a storm is looming near; I stretch my arms out and try to grasp invisible hands to help take me back to shore; the hands are slippery, I see no face and hear no voice; the storm comes closer and I need those hands more than ever. Whose hands are they? Andrew's? Fred's? Is it my way of asking for help with my mission, I wonder. But I know that nobody can be part of my quest, not even Fred who says he loves me. I have never had to face something of this magnitude, still I accept the fact: I am on my own in this. Succeed or fail, I'll have no help.

I stop at the grocery store and buy a basket of apples, the green ones that Aunt likes best. The tarter the fruit, the more she likes it and sometimes she eats it with salt and chili pepper. It reminds her of some fruits she ate when she lived in Thailand. Except for a few anecdotes, her life in Thailand is another unknown to me. Perhaps one day she will tell me more; I want to know, but I don't want to push. As I park my car in our driveway, I hear the phone buzzing inside; Aunt will take it. I linger outside and look at the garden: Ramon did a good job, annuals are removed, perennials are partially covered with protective canvas, and small mounds of soil are covering the seeds newly planted. The garden is ready to welcome winter and a deep sleep. I am not sure I am ready to welcome snow and ice. The other day Aunt reminded me how often I used to catch cold when I was growing up and how my mother insisted on stuffing me with extra vitamins as soon as September came around. Come to think of it, perhaps that's what makes me dislike winter so much. As much as having to swallow those huge vitamin tablets.

"Hello Raffee, ready for lunch?"

"Oh yes, Auntie, I am very hungry. I got you some apples, the green ones."

"You're a dear. Everything all right at work?" Did she say 'work'? Mrs. Jahe?...

"Er, yes, all's fine. Did somebody just call?"

"Yes, that was Rhys. He'll call again later. He has such a beautiful baritone voice, why doesn't he join the opera?"

"I guess he prefers the company of his many vials of blood and other things to check every day. But you're right, I've heard him hum a few times, his voice is very beautiful with a perfect pitch that doesn't hurt your ears or make your teeth grind. When you were performing, Aunt Sumi, were you a soprano?"

"Yes, but also an alto when the conductor needed one."

"Did Uncle Chris attend?"

"Oh yes, he did. Rehearsals and performances. Those were glorious days and nights. Someone else also attended long before your uncle came on the scene."

From nowhere a cloud arrives and covers Aunt's eyes. I stop breathing, she has gone far away beyond earth, beyond this meal here with me and I'd rather die than interrupt her voyage. I know she is with Neil Jahe this very instant. If it takes pain to cure her sorrow, I will respect her pain in silence and try to heal the sorrow. If it takes time to relieve the hurt, I will give her all of my time. It is beyond my comprehension how that woman in the mansion can enjoy all of life's pleasures while this woman here dies a thousand deaths each time she thinks of her perfect love taken away too soon. Once again I tell myself that there is no justice. If the world belonged to me, I would give it whole to the gods in return for happiness in my aunt's life. Perhaps we should go to the pagoda again soon and converse with Lord Buddha in his own home. I have learned through my meditations that if I am willing to accept the outcome of my actions, I am ready to take action. I was shown the way where Fred is concerned. He loves me but he doesn't know that there exists an insurmountable obstacle between us: I will never ask him to leave Judaism and embrace my religion. And I will not leave Buddhism to adopt his religion. There is no way out, we must remain just friends, very good friends. The spirits also whispered that Uncle Chris was in good health; a little longer and he will end his self-imposed retreat and return to his family. And I wonder if his return can – or will – bring joy and sunshine and laughter to Aunt Sumika. In our family we've always heard of the great love between my Uncle and Aunt. So, why did he take such a long retreat away from her? Can such a great love die over the years? If it does die, can it be resurrected? Lord, please show me the way as I feel very inadequate and useless; I have the will but not the know-how. In your limitless wisdom, please direct my steps.

As I wait for Maria in the kitchen, the phone buzzes loud and clear in the quiet morning.

"Hello Raffee, this is Rhys, did I wake you up?"

"Hi Rhys, you didn't wake me up, I am in the kitchen. What's up?"

"I was wondering if we, all of us, should take our first walk in the first snow of the season. The weatherman is calling for heavy snow on Saturday, we all need to get out of the city and breathe the forest air. What do you think?"

"Superb idea! You sure there'll be no ice?"

"No ice, just snow. Let me get our gang together and I'll call you back. It'll be wonderful again this year, I know it. Talk to you soon."

As long as there is no ice, I am game. The forest is always quiet when heavy snow falls; it seems there is a pact between forest and snow, and it is the early walker that enjoys the peace to the fullest. If I were braver, I would go to the forest early in the morning, alone. Because I am not brave, I gladly go with my group of friends. Alexa always brings mini chocolate bars with raisins or almonds. And at the end of our walk we treat her to coffee and cakes at the Coffee Palace, a mere fifteen minutes drive away. This has become a cherished ritual on each first snowfall of the season. I think it was Andrew who suggested it the first time a few years back. We have never succeeded in persuading Aunt Sumi to join us, she abhors winter and all things related to it. Winter is not my favorite season either, but a walk in the pure snow of the first fall is something to be treasured. We don't talk, just walk on and on with the only sound that of our boots swooshing in and out of the brilliant white powder. I feel one with the forest and my surrounding. I hold conversations with my inner self, talks which nothing and nobody can interrupt. It is always this way when I walk with my friends in the forest at the first snowfall of the season. After about an hour of utter silence, one of us would sigh deeply and, as if on cue, all of us would speak at the same time, thus ending each private monologue. Games and races follow and soon we walk back to our cars and head to the coffee place, our faces red with cool air, exercise and delight. Aunt Sumi never fails to admire my red cheeks when I come home and I never fail to invite her to our next hike, although her answer never changes, "Not on your life!"

Maria comes in with a bag of fresh bread and pots of strawberry yogurt, and I am back to reality from my recollection of walks in the snow. I hear a door open and signal to Aunt Sumika to join me for a late breakfast in the kitchen while Maria attends to her other chores.

"Did you sleep well, Auntie?"

"Yes, I did, and you? Did the phone wake you up?"

"I slept like a log and was awake when the phone rang. It was Rhys setting things in motion for our walk in the snow. I wish you would join us, Auntie."

"Not on your life, Raffee. I heard the weatherman announce much snow for Saturday. I can't believe winter is already here and we'll have to endure the torture for at least five months. It's like being in a dark prison waiting for the first light of spring."

"But when we see that first light, oh the joy and promises of spring! Worth waiting for, don't you agree?"

"You, eternal optimist, you are the light in my sometimes dark moments. You are the best niece an aunt can have."

"And you are the best aunt a niece can have. What wouldn't I do to take away for good those dark moments. I am sure with time and reflection I'll find the way. Let's enjoy our delicious breakfast. Do you have anything special planned for today?"

"Nothing special, just a letter to write to my friend Arlene in Pennsylvania. And you?"

"I thought it would be nice to go to the pagoda and converse with Lord Buddha. It is cold outside, so I'll drive if you agree to come." For a fraction of a second I see surprise in her eyes, as if she couldn't believe I was the one wanting to go to the pagoda.

"You've come a long way, sweetheart; I am so very happy that you have welcomed Buddhism into your life. We'll go to the pagoda and then have lunch in the Asian market area."

We tell Maria not to expect us for lunch and I add that I have not forgotten what her son Raul wanted from the Thai store.

"Thank you Raffee, but don't buy the large model kite, the small one will do just fine and, if possible, nothing over ten dollars. Raul will be in heaven!"

At eleven o'clock we leave; traffic is not too heavy for a change, we can look at the almost naked trees along the road. The beautiful fall colors are no more and, except for a few tall evergreens, all else looks gray or black, giving the scenery a rather foreboding picture, one that will remain unaltered for many months.

"I hope all the birds and other animals have found a place to stay," I say, looking at the vast emptiness.

"I am sure they have. The Creator takes good care of his creatures. He feeds them, clothes them, shelters them and shows them the safe way to live their animal lives. But for humans with guns, Earth would be a paradise."

"What is it with humans and guns? They can't seem to be able to live without the awful weapons. Don't they see what cowards they are when they shoot and kill an innocent animal? Does it make them feel "superior" because they have taken the life of a fox or a squirrel? You know, Aunt Sumi, I would like to be given the free use of a gun for a couple of days."

"What for, Raffee? You hate guns!"

"True. But just for two special days I will delight in using one. And I promise you that many humans will fall just like the animals they kill for sport fall and die."

"Here you go again. It's all black or all white with you, there is no gray in-between. Life is not like that, Raffee, it has three colors: black, white and gray."

"You mean in the gray area it is all right to kill innocent animals? I'll never go for that, I love animals too much. Why, even an earthworm that tries to cross from one side of a lawn to the other at great risk of being trampled to death, I stop to pick him up on a twig and deposit him where he wanted to go, safe and sound."

"And you talk of killing humans if given the chance?"

"Yes, Auntie. Humans who kill innocent animals and humans who kill the spirit and happiness of other humans do not deserve to enjoy life. I may never be able to dispatch the former, but it is different with the latter. I have no gray area for such killers." Aunt's eyes pierce mine and I hold the gaze with a faint smile. I cannot disclose more.

After I park the car at the back of the pagoda, we enter the home of Lord Buddha. From this moment on silence will be absolute for all the soul needs to hear is the beating of one's heart and one's conversation with Lord. Immediately I feel the presence of spirits, friendly and welcoming. They will direct my steps toward deep meditation, close connection with Lord Buddha and – I hope with all my heart – my first entrance to nirvana. Time in earthly terms is now non-existent, Aunt and I have left this world for one of pure meditation where spirits dwell. A stream of thoughts and images takes hold of my mind; there is good and bad, sunshine and shadow, light and darkness. I am winning and I am losing an invisible battle. I question and receive suggestions in lieu of clear answers. And I understand that the fight and the search must go on until I find the solution. My mission is not as yet totally defined, I must continue to look for the key to its success.

Hours later, happy with this visit to the pagoda though I was not granted nirvana, I take Aunt Sumi to an exquisite little Thai restaurant for a late lunch. She orders her favorite seafood with hot chili and I enjoy a dish of fried rice with curried shrimps. For dessert we both have fresh pineapple with dark rum, a divine combination.

"Thank you Auntie for coming with me. I like the quiet atmosphere of the pagoda very much, it is very inspiring and soothing. No matter how uncertain or preoccupied one can be, peace is always there ready to cover us and heal wounds of all sorts."

"Buddhism is a religion of peace, Raffee. It will always give you peace. I hope you are not presently burdened by uncertainty or preoccupation. At your age everything should be bright and clear. But whenever you feel downhearted, you know you can always count on me, I am a good listener and you are my favorite niece."

"Of course I am your favorite niece. There are only boys in the family, you have only one niece!" We both laugh heartily and order our coffee.

"After coffee let's go to the store, I want to buy a kite for Raul. Did Maria tell you he got an A in poetry writing? Superb English writing by a Mexican boy…that's a feat Maria can be proud of."

"And she is, believe me, bless her heart! What a deserving woman she is, raising three sons on her own and never complaining. Have you noticed that she no longer mentions Alfredo her husband?"

"That's because she understands that the past must remain in the past and not interfere with the present. She has taught herself to let go of the pain and sadness Alfredo's death has brought her. It is not easy, but with willpower and strength it can be accomplished. Oh, don't get me wrong, she has not forgotten and will not forget him, but her daily life belongs to the present and to her three sons. Yes, she is an admirable woman."

"Where did you get such strength yourself, my favorite niece? Has something really dreadful happened to you that I don't know about and can't help you with? It would sadden me to know that I've let you down somewhere when you needed help and support. You know I am here for you."

"You have never let me down, Auntie. On the contrary you have always been the shield that protected me from evil since my parents died, and I will always be grateful. I confess, there are puzzles in my present life that need to be solved, of which I cannot talk. I am confident that with time and meditation I'll find the solution. Then, and only then, will the sun truly flood our home with a happiness free of shadows. That's all I am asking from the spirits who live near Lord Buddha."

"It all sounds rather mysterious to me and I can't help but worry about you. However I will respect your private world and not ask for details. Just remember that you are not alone, I am here entirely for you."

"Thank you Aunt Sumi, you are the best. Shall we go buy the kite?"

At the intersection three streets from our lane, a great crowd is marching toward City Hall holding large "On Strike" signs.

"Who are these people, Auntie? Can you find out who they are?"

"Let's see… Ah, here is the main banner, it is the local school board. Teachers are on strike for crying out loud! What a disgrace, they've brought education down to sewage level. How dare they? The poor children missing classes so close to first quarter's exams. Total lack of professionalism. I'll ask again, 'how dare they?' " Aunt Sumi is fuming mad and I'd better concentrate on driving slowly and carefully until I reach the first side street where I can turn in and get away from the waves of demented and shouting creatures.

"Phew! We are safe now. Yes, how disgraceful this generation's teachers are, I am embarrassed to witness this circus. To answer your question, they dare because they have the right to strike. Look at postal workers, auto workers, medical workers, etc. they all have the right to strike. And when they do strike, the population complains, everything is perturbed, nobody is happy, public transportation workers join in and the city turns into sheer chaos. Yet the solution is simple."

"Oh my, are you so sure there is a solution?"

"Yes Aunt Sumi, and it is simple: if we don't want them to strike, why did we give them the right to strike in the first place? These people are only doing what they have the right to do. And all of them, not just these teachers, will continue to do so until the right is removed, taken away."

"But who will remove the right to strike? I've never heard of such a thing, at least not here."

"The right may never be removed because we live under dictatorship, that of the labor unions, they call all the shots. As a great newsman used to say, "And that's the way it is"."

"So we're back to square one, workers will continue to strike; where is the solution?"

"It is here but nobody has the courage to use it. The right to strike is a self-inflicted disease that will not go away on its own. Potent medication is needed to eradicate it."

Maria is beaming at the sight of the red and blue kite we bought for Raul. Under ten dollars she said, we paid nine ninety-five! She is laughing silly and we join her.

"I hope Raul likes it," I say to Maria.

"Oh, he will be overwhelmed and will want to fly it right away, I am sure. Thank you so much."

"It is our pleasure. When you get home, tell Raul to go fly a kite and to be careful of the fishing line that connects the wings to keep them solidly and invisibly attached to the body of the kite."

"It looks very solid. Fishing line is so strong it's been known to decapitate an animal in the blink of an eye. Raul will be careful not to cut himself with it or trip on it and break his neck in his haste to see this bird fly."

A little boy will be happy and will dream tonight of a limitless sky and white clouds opening their doors to welcome a red and blue kite.

My night was unpleasantly disturbed by visions of dead rabbits whose decapitated heads were stringed on a long and straight row ending with the string tied into a bow.

The string was fishing line.

SEVEN

A GORGEOUS sun greets me. It is Friday, the day before our walk in the first snow of the season. Rhys was able to get our group together and the men will fetch the ladies at their homes Saturday at nine a.m. because we want to hit the forest before the neighborhood wakes up. The entire white immensity will be ours to enjoy to the fullest. I always like to stop at the forest entrance to look everywhere around, inhale the cool air deeply, hear the silence and, when every beautiful detail has delighted my inner feelings, I leap for joy and dig my boots into the brilliant powder before running to catch up with my friends. This little pause is my way of greeting the forest on a perfect winter morning and I can hear myself whisper to this vastness, 'I am with you forest, with you trees, I love you, have a good winter.'

I look forward to this outing as I get ready to go to work wearing a lime green smock under my coat. What awaits me at the mansion? Will I look at the photographs again? How I wish I knew what Aunt Sumi feels each day, each night. I know there is a great sadness in her, but with my outsider eyes I can only perceive a blurred image of her inner feelings, a picture with no details. A great sadness that I pledge to erase from her eyes before my uncle returns. When Aunt laughs, my heart feels warm. When she looks far away to a world unknown to me, my heart wants to break and I want to penetrate that world where I would do another type of cleaning: that of throwing away all remaining tears and sorrows, regrets and longings and, in the end, give her a world without the shadow of pain or suffering. It is a tall order, but I want to try my best and succeed. And when Uncle comes back, I want to see happiness in my aunt's eyes, a happiness without the shadow of her painful past. I owe her and Uncle so much, that's the least I can do. Perhaps I am exaggerating, wanting too much, thinking of myself as the world's saviour... Who am I to aim so high? On the one hand I feel weak and inadequate, on the verge of calling it off; on the other, the pain in my aunt's eyes gnaws at my young happiness and pushes me toward action. Success is not guaranteed, I do not have the key. More thinking, more meditation and more visits to the beyond are needed. I made this decision the night Aunt Sumika confided in me and I realized that Mrs. Jahe was the person responsible for the sheer hell that has become my aunt's life. I will not change my mind, I must proceed and succeed.

The mansion is looming in the gray distance. Except for the majestic evergreens along the road, all other trees are now bare naked and, I am sure, already asleep for the winter. There is a light powder on the ground, heralding the first serious snowfall of the season. Tomorrow we will take our first walk in the forest and have our first snowball fight. Today I must face Mrs. Jahe and I grit my teeth so I won't spit venom in my car. This is an exercise in willpower and control; patience and observation; my eyes must look everywhere and see everything lest I miss an important detail, the telltale sign of a potential solution. And I must, all the while, show her a pleasant personality, the carefree happiness of youth, a sweet and gentle me.

"Good morning, Madame."

"Right, good morning Raphaëlle. Looks like winter is here to stay. Are the roads slippery?"

"Winter has arrived, but the roads are still good, there is no black ice."

"Black ice is the worst, nobody likes it. It has been called the silent killer, it is that dangerous. I never go out when the weatherman mentions it."

'Silent killer'… oh how well you should know it, lady, I think but do not say.

"Yes, black ice is very dangerous and very silent. It takes away the life of the unaware and the over-confident. If black ice were a human being, it would deserve capital punishment; but it is not and we must be extremely cautious when driving on icy roads."

Her eyes are fixed on mine, I hold the gaze, she says not a word; I smile faintly and head to the broom cupboard. Did I overdo it? Did I resurrect memories? Let her chew on it, she has all the time in the world for chewing and remembering. I have a mansion to clean.

As I start up the stairs, Mrs. Jahe calls from the living-room.

"Right. Raphaëlle, I am going downtown, do you need anything?"

"Yes please, another jug of bleach if you don't mind. Thank you."

"I am writing it down. If I am not back before you leave, your money is on the kitchen table. Have a nice week-end, and thank you."

"Thank you, Ma'am."

'Silent killer' indeed. Wrong words for you to say, Madame, or is your memory fading? Ah, you don't know that I know. You have described not black ice but yourself; you silently took away the life of an honest and unsuspecting man, you killed Neil Jahe. And his death has brought unfathomable sadness to his true love, my Aunt Sumika. You live, he died. Somehow, somewhere, justice must be done and tears wiped away. Spirits, please show me the way, give me the key, take the burden away from my aunt and from me.

The purring of the vacuum cleaner takes me away from my silent monologue and I concentrate on the work at hand. At the top of the stairs there is a small tear in the carpeting and the vacuum cleaner always coughs when it goes over it. Why doesn't the lady have it repaired, it is such a small job? If the tear gets bigger, it could become a hazard and somebody could trip and fall. I must remember to mention it to Mrs. Jahe next time I come. The door to the second spare bedroom is open; I enter with my duster and the vacuum cleaner and walk straight to the dresser where there are several photographs displayed in beautiful frames. Only one photo has my attention. Neil Jahe was a very handsome man with a gentle smile. How tall was he? Highly educated as he was, why has he made such mistakes in his life? Aunt Sumi mentioned an ideal, a near non-existent ideal. Neil stuck to it and eventually paid with his life. It didn't have to be this way. I think this part of life is called destiny. And we are powerless prisoners of our destiny. Rich or poor, king or commoner, our destiny orders us around the many twists and turns of life on earth. It decides when we reach the end of the road and all we can do it bow and accept. It took Neil's life away too soon, and the pledge that he and Aunt Sumi made so many years ago did not have a chance to be honored. He took it with him to the beyond, but Aunt Sumi lives it day after day with all its promises and dreams unfulfilled. I shudder at the thought that the hand that helped destiny do its dirty job belongs to the woman who lives in this manor. I look again at the photo on the dresser and I see the same man with the same kind and gentle smile who died too young. With pain in my heart, I wish things were different.

The snow is falling a little thicker as I leave the mansion and drive home to have lunch with my aunt. Maria is making fresh enchiladas for us. Raul loved the kite and asked his mother to fix us a special lunch as a thank-you. Bless you, little Mexican poet! I wonder what presents to buy the three boys for Christmas; they are very religious and observe the anniversary of Christ's birth. It is time to think of a shopping spree. I must also send a card to Francesca who interviewed me for my cleaning job; better yet, I will bring her a box of fine chocolates. Last year Fred invited me to celebrate Chanukah with him, his parents and a few relatives. It was very pleasant, they all made me feel very welcome, the ambiance was warm and friendly and the little white cakes coated with honey were divine. Fred often caters to my sweet tooth, I wonder if he will bring something special tomorrow for our hike in the snow.

Evergreens look darker along the road now that the background is whiter than it was this morning. Sometimes I see a flash of red among them and I know cardinals are out looking for seeds inside the pine cones. An occasional squirrel darts in and out and I find myself silently scolding him and telling him to hurry back to the safety of his home. Nature is not totally asleep, it is only getting ready for its long rest. And during the many months of its slumber, the forest will keep quiet and remain a majestic sight for the appreciative eyes of one who is in tune with, and greets every season of life. It is the never-ending circle of life and its seasons that brings us the ingredients of our presence on earth: joy, beauty, gratitude, appreciation. Sometimes also tears, regrets, sorrow and despair. The mingling of joy and sorrow makes us what we are: earthly beings with a head and a heart. I am grateful to be among these earthly beings. Sometimes when Josh sees me this meditative during our stroll in the snow, he would wake me up with a cheerful, "Gosh, Raffee, where have you been? Your eyes are so far away, can I join you?"

I quickly return to earth and rejoin my friends with great pleasure. When I am with them and we talk about everything or nothing in particular, I don't feel the weight of my own life, the decision I made regarding my aunt, and the mission I must accomplish. I know they are my very good friends and I can trust them completely. I also know that my mission must remain hidden, not to be shared with anybody, not even Fred. This often makes me feel lonely and I say to myself, 'If only somebody, one of them, would accompany me on this quest…' But, of course, it is out of the question, why would I involve any of them in something as uncertain and risky as a personal settling of scores? Then I silently address Mrs. Jahe, 'See what you've done? Then and now? What you did was horrible. Don't you, as a human being, feel remorse? A life, Madame, a life. You took away a human life. Does it not disturb you? Here you are living in a mansion, happy and satisfied. Are you that shallow? That cold? Here I am living with much sadness witnessing my aunt's immeasurable sorrow caused by you. Do you believe you are above punishment? Do you think you are going to live happily ever after? Do you know there is something called revenge, retribution, payment? If you don't, it will hit you hard when it comes.

As I drive past the little pond, half frozen now, another voice talks to me, 'Don't go overboard, don't overdo it. You are not the almighty, you don't have all powers. What you are planning is unbelievable, will you be able to pull it off? You are not judge, not jury, not dispenser of justice. You are just you, Raffee, age twenty-two, an orphan living with your Aunt Sumika. Why do you want to turn the world upside down on account of Mrs. Betty-Ann Jahe?'

"Because I want her to pay for what she has done," I say out loud.

At the last intersection before entering our street, I see a small crowd and two men going at it with fists and feet. They have bleeding noses and blood runs down the front of their coats. What an ugly sight, I turn my eyes back to the steering wheel and concentrate on driving safely. There is much fighting and killing in our city, it is a daily occurrence and society has become blasé about it. Andrew said once very caustically, 'It's good business for the police, it keeps them busy and warrants their very high salaries.' To which Alexa quickly retorted, 'They are doing a good job though.'

"Yes, but why the absurdly high pay? Where's the limit?"

Hunger is sending signals to me and I hurry to get home. As if on cue, Maria welcomes me with, "Lunch's ready, Raffee, come and enjoy."

"Hi, Auntie, how was your morning?" I say to Aunt Sumi as she comes to the dining room wearing a beautiful light blue sarong made of Thai silk and a darker blue blouse. Even at home she looks elegant.

"All is well, honey. How was work? Are you hungry?"

"Work was routine and I am famished. You know, the scenery along the highway has changed totally; it is white everywhere your eye travels, except for the evergreen trees. I cant' wait for tomorrow's hike with my friends. You should join us, Auntie."

"Not on your life! Hiking in the snow is not for me, but I have a suggestion..."

"What is it? please tell me."

"How about going downtown to buy Christmas presents for our friends who observe the holiday? If we do it now, we'll avoid the lunatic crowds later. Are you game?"

"That's a wonderful idea. Your car or mine? Do you have a list? Which store do we hit first?"

"Slow down, Raffee, you're making me dizzy. After lunch we'll take my car and start with the Asian market, then we'll go to Wynmore Store. This should keep us busy the whole afternoon. Do you have your list?"

"Yes, it is in my head. I have a compartment there for each person who'll get a present from me. Maria's enchiladas are delicious, but we'll certainly be thirsty this afternoon. Refreshments will be my treat."

After dessert and coffee, Aunt and I leave to do what I simply love: shopping and buying presents.

It is night now and we are in the living room sipping a warm honey drink with rum. The spare bedroom has been divided in two: one side has all of Aunt's presents, the other is where I have stacked my packages. We will wrap our presents with the gorgeous papers we bought at Wynmore Store and use the colorful gift tags left over from last year. I treated ourselves to tea and Chinese cakes at the Mandarin Room. It was a very welcome stopover as our feet were beginning to feel the miles that have been forced on them.

"It was a wonderful idea, Aunt Sumi, I enjoyed every minute of our afternoon."

"Even when that man dropped his heavy books on your feet and you said a certain word to him?"

"Oh, that was rather funny. I don't think he even knows what "damn!" means. He looked a bit dumb to me. 'Damn' is not a bad word, I know many other interesting ones, Auntie."

"I have no doubt, honey. I have some too, believe me."

"You, Auntie? Oh no, I've never heard you say anything worse than 'shoot!'"

"'Shoot' is bad enough, it is a substitute for another word that is really bad."

"I see what you mean. Euphemisms to the rescue!" We both laugh and raise our cups of hot honey.

"I saw two men fighting today on my way home. There was a small crowd around, but no policeman," I say.

"Why waste a policeman's time? There are fights every day and it is almost always among the same people; these people are not from here, they come from other countries and islands in the sun; they bring with them their problems, their feuds and a thirst for revenge. You see, honey, these people don't have enough brains to settle matters with words, they have to use fists and weapons. They cannot talk intelligently but they can hit and kill easily. What can we do?"

"It's all because of our too lenient immigration laws; I mean, anybody at all is welcome here, even known terrorists. Where is our country headed?"

"Don't throw everything at immigrants, Raffee. There are many among our youths who also opt for fists and knives. The world seems to be suffering from a serious lack of intelligence, or a much reduced amount of it anyway. I hope Maria's children never find themselves in such a loathsome milieu."

"I don't think they will. All three of them show solid intelligence and Maria loves them intelligently. She does not spoil them, yet they have everything they need, even a red and blue kite for Raul!" We chuckle at the recollection and decide to retire for the night.

"Happy dreams, Auntie."

"You too, favorite niece. Rest well for your hike tomorrow."

Before turning the lights out, I take one look outside just to make sure: Yes, we'll have plenty of snow tomorrow.

There'll be no hiking today. During the night a severe storm hit the city and left debris of all sorts strewn over the entire area. Somebody's TV antenna is in our front yard with just its tip showing, the rest of it buried under a mound of snow. All our low plants have disappeared under a uniform white blanket. There must be at least three feet of snow on the ground and the wind must be extremely strong because our sole pine tree is swaying dangerously like a drunken man who can't stop moving erratically. There is snow piled up high against the screen of the front door. The wind is howling like a madman shaking his asylum's gate and each new gust deposits new debris on our driveway and shakes the pine tree even more. Mother Nature is very angry for some reason and gets full revenge with this show of destructive power. How long will it last and how much more snow? I wanted snow for our hike, but not this insane quantity.

My coffee has gone cold in my hand as I assess the damage, standing at the front window of our living room. With a sigh I walk to the kitchen for a fresh cup of piping hot mocha and wonder how the day will turn out. The morning news doesn't come on till nine o'clock, I must wait another hour to hear the weather report. Aunt Sumika is still in her bedroom and, today being Saturday, Maria won't come. For the moment I have the entire silent house to myself. With my new cup of coffee and a warm croissant, I settle on the sofa near the phone; if somebody calls, I'll pick it up before it rings a second time and wakes Aunt up. I wonder what my hiking friends are doing or thinking right now. Surely they must be as disappointed as I am that our walk in the first snow of the season has been so unceremoniously and unfairly cancelled. There is always the second snow... but it won't be the same, we all want to touch, walk, and roll in the very first snow; something like the opening of the season and the promise of many more walks.

Outside the storm is still vociferating at peak insanity, the wind tries to force its way in through loose doorknobs and keyholes, whistling madly as it does, and I am telling it to get lost and not come back. Fat snow flakes are still coming down from an obviously endless supply. I think of the birds, the squirrels and the raccoons out there and I say a prayer for their survival. The phone comes suddenly alive and makes me jump, I pick it up right away.

"Hello Raffee darling, it's me Fred."

"Hello Fred darling, what's up?"

"I am up; the storm kept me awake most of the night, so I decided to get up before the world even stirred. How are you doing?"

"I am disappointed because we have to cancel our hike, the first of the season; it's bad, bad, bad; if it were the second or the fifth, I wouldn't care, but Fred, this is our first. This storm has ruined everything. What are we going to do?"

"Oh my, you *are* upset! Tell you what, I am not sure if it is feasible but if we, all of us, could get together at my place, I promise a good time for all."

"In this weather? Have you lost your mind?"

"Not quite. You know I can borrow my father's SUV and pick you up one by one at your door. Late last night the weatherman said the storm was just passing by and the wind warning would be lifted this morning. The snow doesn't scare me, the wind does. With the wind on its way out, I won't mind a bit picking everybody up. We deserve a good time together to compensate for the cancelled hike. If you are game, let's divide the phone job, you call the ladies, I call the guys. Then I'll get back to you and hopefully we can get the ball rolling. What do you think, Raffee?"

"What a speech! You must be brilliant in your job. It sounds really nice and I do want us to be all together, but how do I get out of my house? There must be at least four feet of snow on the ground by now."

"Not to worry, it'll be my greatest pleasure to carry you in my arms from your door to my car. Do I get an 'all go'?"

"Your arms are very tempting… you've got my 'all go'. I will call the ladies in about half an hour. Get back to me soon, all right?"

"I will. You're super sweet."

This must be what they call youth's insanity. But because it is insane, I hope we all say yes and end up at Fred's large and beautiful home. He always has superb food and treats to offer. And his three Angora cats are the friendliest of felines. Suddenly this colorless day looks much brighter and I pull my address book out to call Alexa, Stephie and Arielle.

As Aunt Sumika steps out of her bedroom, the kitchen clock chimes the hour; it is ten and I am ready and waiting to be carried in Fred's arms to his car.

"Good morning Raffee. What a storm! Oh, you are all dressed… don't tell me the hike is still on with this weather."

"Good morning Auntie. The hike's been called off, but not the fun. Imagine what Fred came up with: a party at his place, he is taking his father's SUV and picking us up one by one!"

"Where do you get all that energy? He is going to drive in all that snow? Kind of dangerous, don't you think?"

"Fred is very careful, that's why his father trusts him with the SUV; he'll drive extra slowly, it won't be a problem because all the streets in Windoaks will be empty, we'll be the only souls out there. Auntie, his house is so beautiful and his fridge always filled with delicious goodies."

"This spur-of-the-moment party will surely compensate for the cancelled hike, I know how anxious you were to take that first walk. Call me the moment you are safe and sound at Fred's house, all right?"

"Of course I will. May I take a bottle of Dubonnet for Fred? I don't like going there empty handed."

"Absolutely. I think I just heard a car door."

"I'll be off then. You have Fred's phone number, call me if you need anything. Bye for now, favorite Aunt."

Fred arrives wearing snowshoes. The rascal knew better than attempting to walk without them.

"How do you like my stylish shoes, Raffee? Bet you didn't think of them and wondered how I was going to walk in all that snow, right?"

"Oh my, you smart, you. I don't have snowshoes and I weigh a hundred and ten pounds without my coat. Who is with you?"

"Andrew and Gosh. We'll pick up the two ladies now and head home. Alexa and Arielle are waiting for us, I couldn't reach the others. Let's hurry. In my arms now, princess Featherlight."

The drive was very slow, Fred was extra careful and in control. By the time we rushed into his living room, it was quarter to twelve, almost lunch time. I am now on the phone reassuring my aunt that we made it alive. Arielle is shivering.

"Fred, can you turn the heat up a bit, please, I am freezing."

"Right away, Ari. Do you want a shawl in the meantime? I don't want you to catch your death. There, the heat is up, it'll take just a few minutes. Anybody else need a blanket?"

"No, thank you. I'll put the kettle on for a hot drink. Fred, do you want to serve lunch now? We are all very hungry," I say.

"Yes, let's have lunch in the dining room. Later we'll play games."

Fred surprises us all with a succulent lunch and three desserts "au choix" he says. We are now having piping hot coffee in the living room. Nobody is talking, everybody is under the spell of a warm and comfortable home with a warm and comfortable feeling of satisfaction and peace. The snow has stopped falling and the wind is slowly dying down. Could it be that the storm has had enough with Windoaks and moved away? It was never welcome here in the first place, it ruined our first walk in the first snow of the season. What a waste of our hopes and expectations.

"I saw Stephie with our weatherman the other day" Alexa says, breaking the comfortable silence.

"With Barracuda?" we ask in one voice and in shock. Lukas Barrakovich is the six o'clock news weatherman; the nickname fits his personality like a glove.

"No, not him. She was with Cedric Peters, the week-end weatherman. They were having coffee at The Pallazio."

"Did she see you?"

"No, I don't think so."

"She wasn't home when I called this morning," Fred adds.

"Oh well, she'll tell us one of these days. How about a game of Monopoly? I feel like buying real estate today," Gosh Josh says.

"And I feel like blocking you all the way, my friend," Andrew teases.

Monopoly is a fun game and a long lasting one. After buying, selling and trading for hours, Andrew came out the winner with the most property bought; we congratulate him in the living room where Fred serves us hot drinks and small cakes of many sorts.

Around six p.m. Fred drives everybody home and then carries me to my door. It feels good and warm in his arms, I thank him with a kiss on the cheek. He wants more and I let him kiss me on the lips. To my surprise it feels even nicer than being in his arms and I don't want the kiss to end.

"Raffee, you know I love you. When will you love me back? There is life and there is happiness calling us, I want to share both with you. Will you share them with me?"

"Not in this storm I won't. A little more time, please? Why rush, Fred? You are special to me, that's why I need to be totally sure of my feelings before I speak. Will you wait?"

"Not too long, Raphaëlle. Life is passing by too quickly. I'll see you soon, darling. Good night."

"Good night, darling, and thank you for today."

In the warmth and quiet of our living room, I look outside at the remnants of that nasty storm. There is a new storm coming, it is within me. Looks like it will be a long lasting one until I am able to clear the mixed-up feelings that are assailing me now. Fred is in the middle of this storm, reaching out, offering me a life with him. I am a little outside the storm looking in, and I don't know what to do. On my horizon there are my aunt, my Buddhist faith, my spiritual life and, last but not least, my secret mission. I hold all of these dear. Yet I do feel something special for Fred. Time will tell, they say. So, for now I will trust time to show me the way.

EIGHT

A good night sleep is supposed to clear one's mind. So why did it not clear mine? Visions of Fred, Fred's love, Fred's offer to share his life are dancing round and round in my head and I am getting dizzy. I don't have a clear answer, there are too many things involved and I don't want one answer to destroy all these things. I am sure that my life will not be the same again, that a Yes to Fred will change everything, turn everything upside down, perhaps even hurt my Aunt Sumi who certainly doesn't need more hurt in her life. I know she wants me to be happily married, I know she likes Fred and she knows that Fred loves me. All clear, right? Then why do I hesitate? The road in front of me is suddenly branching off; a road that has been straight all my life now offers two directions; which way do I go? I am very fond of Fred, maybe I even love him, he has been present in my life ever since Grade Five, we grew up together, studied together, did a million things together. Perhaps we can live together? Is it time for me to decide?

Still unsure, I choose to wait a couple of days before calling Fred. When Aunt Sumi comes out for breakfast, we will talk about this, I will watch in her eyes the first reaction to my words. One tiniest sparkle is all I need to know how she feels. It is the sign that will show me where to direct my steps. Life with Fred or life with Aunt Sumika.

From the kitchen I hear pots and pans conversing and I know Maria has arrived and is fixing breakfast. Within three minutes I am in the dining room and grab today's newspaper.

"Hello Maria, how are you and how are the boys?"

"Hi Raffee, all is well considering the horrible storm we have just had."

"You're right, it was horrible, the roads are still so bad I am staying home today to clear some of the debris from the front yard."

"Would you like bacon and pancakes this morning?"

"No bacon please, just pancakes and that wonderful orange marmalade, thank you Maria."

Before I can unfold the newspaper, Aunt Sumi arrives and we start breakfast with our usual: first a cup of coffee; it warmly invites our taste buds to begin their indispensable job.

"How did you sleep, Raffee?" Aunt asks.

"I slept with two unwelcome visitors: Toss and Turn. And how did you sleep, favorite Aunt?"

"Soundly with no dreams. What was your unrest about, or would you rather not tell?"

"Well, er… you've just started breakfast… I am not sure…maybe after breakfast?" I say with a whisper of hesitation. She doesn't miss a thing.

"Out with it, young lady, I am all ears."

"All right but be careful not to drop your cup of coffee. Fred asked me to marry him."

She drops her fork, not the cup. Her eyes suddenly steal and hold all the light of day, they are limpid and beautiful and I see –oh, miracle!- a huge chunk of life in them. A faint smile forms on her lips. She remains silent for a while and then jumps up to come and hug me.

"How wonderful! My Raffee getting married! She will be Mrs. Silverman, she will have babies, she will stay in Windoaks so I can spoil the little ones, she.."

"Whoa, Auntie, not so fast. I am still Raphaëlle Luens, niece of Mrs. Sumika Luens. No ring on my finger… no reply from me as yet."

"Why not, sweetie? Fred obviously loves you, you have so much in common, you've known each other for decades; this is solid ground on which to build a life together. When will you let him know?"

"Sometime this week. Everything you say is true, this man loves me and is offering me a very good life; perhaps I should not hesitate anymore, perhaps I should accept the offer. Would you be happy, Auntie?"

"If you are happy, I am happy. This will never change, you know that."

"Then when I see Fred, I will say Yes and we'll set things in motion. There is still one thing on my mind…"

"What is it"

"I will never leave Buddhism for Judaism."

"Not to worry, sweetheart. Fred is intelligent, considerate and he loves you. I don't see an obstacle there."

"So, it's 'all aboard' the wedding train then?

"Looks like it, Raffee. A new life will welcome you with open arms, you will be the queen in his castle; great changes coming your way. Remember this: Love conquers all."

"Oooh, that's beautiful, Auntie. Back to reality: I am not going to work today, have a look at the roads, they are impassable."

"Then you should let your employer know as soon as possible."

"Yes, I am going to call her in a minute. Let's finish our breakfast. One request: let's keep this event under wraps for a while till we see only green lights everywhere, please?"

"Absolutely as you wish, honey."

While Aunt is busy in her bedroom, I call Mrs. Jahe to tell her I am not coming today because the roads are still unplowed and dangerous for driving.

"Right, Raphaëlle, I understand completely. Please don't take chances, come on Friday. It was a very nasty storm we had. Is everything all right in your home?"

"Yes Madame, everything is fine except for the mountain of debris that landed in the front yard. Thank you for asking, I will come on Friday then. Goodbye, Ma'am."

So solicitous, so caring... she doesn't know how much I hate her. Just wait and see, everything in due course. Never take revenge in the heat of the moment... this dish is best eaten cold, etc.

I dare brave the dangerous roads and drive to the pagoda. A very urgent message has been pounding in my head since I woke up; it urges me to go seek advice from Lord Buddha. I left a short note on the dining table telling my Aunt that I needed to go out, 'yes, even with these unplowed streets, so help me God'. The message from beyond was right, I do need to communicate with the other world, to seek advice and encouragement, to have my eyes opened on the way I must travel and to keep my steps on the right path. There is a new life coming to meet me, my present life will end the day I marry Fred. Am I prepared? Ready? Will I lose my beloved Aunt? My childhood friends? My secret mission? Do I accept this wedding wholeheartedly or with reservation? Why is there always this tiny pulling back sensation each time I want to say a total Yes? Something is there, what is it? I don't know and I don't understand. That's why I am here, Lord Buddha, confiding in you and asking for direction. Fred is Jewish, I am Buddhist. Isn't this an insurmountable obstacle? I will not leave you, Lord, and I will not ask Fred to leave his religion. Are we destined to be two roads that will never meet? Aunt Sumi says that Fred is intelligent and considerate... Yes he is, but will his entire Jewish family understand and accept this marriage? Especially his cousin Jerry Kaplan the Rabbi? I shudder at the thought. You see, Lord, I don't ask much from life; my aunt and uncle are my world, a secure and comfortable world; then there are my good friends from childhood, from school and college; there is my home where I am loved and protected; and there is you Lord, the light that always shows me the way. None of this should change, not even in the name of marriage.

Now I'll bow my head and listen to you, Lord Buddha, I am your obedient servant. Soon time stops. The peace and quiet of the pagoda now wraps around me, I feel my soul sigh and relax, I am leaving this world, I am ready to hear you Lord, please take me to the beyond, closer to you.

After a long while listening to words uttered by spirits, time and earth slowly return to me; I bow to Lord Buddha, place another incense stick in the bowl, and leave by the side door away from the main entrance. The overall sensation is the same each time I have spoken to Lord Buddha and to the spirits beyond: a deep feeling of peace, contentment and serenity. What a beautiful religion. It gives and gives and never stops giving. You offer your time, meditation and sincerity. It gives you a world of inner happiness, a gentle world, a world purified. No other religion can compare. I am blessed and very grateful to Aunt Sumi who introduced me to this world of infinite beauty and gentleness.

Instead of going home directly, I decide to visit Chinatown. Here the streets have been plowed and driving is less demanding. All the stores are open, business is swift and the horrible storm seems to be forgotten. Asian people are eager and energetic, they smile and their colorful stores always look ready for business. It shames us Westerners with many of our stores not opening until ten or eleven in the morning. We are closed on Sundays, Chinatown is open all week and the crowd never seems to diminish, there is much activity everywhere you look. It reminds me of an anthill where each member has an assigned work to do. It is no wonder that some of the more beautiful and expensive homes in town belong to Chinese people. They work hard and savour the fruit of their labor in their magnificent homes. Shop owners stand fiercely together and gangs of criminals rarely strike here. In each store there is an altar to Buddha with food offerings, fresh flowers and many incense sticks. When we enter these stores, Aunt Sumi always bows her head to Lord Buddha; if the owner notices, he in turn bows to Aunt and they smile, understanding the respect that links them to the same religion. True Buddhism is quiet, discreet and sincere; it needs none of the antics and absurd show-off of its westernized version. You will never see a Buddhist monk present a ring for you to kiss or wear sumptuous clothes embroidered with gold and silk from top to bottom. Less display, more depth.

After buying a bag of jamalacs and because the sky is beginning to turn gray, I slowly drive home on city streets that are just now being plowed. I will have to zigzag around to avoid the heavy snowplows and their most of the time blind operators. Main streets are plowed first; we live on a side street, I hope it won't take a month for the snow to be cleared as has happened many times before. Good Ramon always clears our driveway soon after a heavy snowfall; why, he even shakes the snow off our evergreen bushes. I teased him once asking him if he was afraid the trees would catch cold.

"No, Raphaëlle, it's because they need to breathe," he answered. That kept me quiet. Later that evening Aunt Sumi said Ramon was right, and the subject of trees catching cold was closed for good.

As I pull into the carport and park next to Aunt Sumi's car, I am once again submerged by thoughts and questions, uncertainties and hesitations about my engagement and wedding, new life and huge changes; I am also surprised that Fred is absent from all my silent deliberations. This wakes me up and, with a sigh, I leave the cocoon of my car. In the kitchen I hand over to Maria the bag of pink jamalacs and ask her to wash them thoroughly, we will have them after lunch.

"These are such unusual fruits, I am sure they don't grow here," she says.

"No, they are imported from Asia. We like them very much; feel free to try one and tell me what you think. How are your boys doing?"

"They are doing great. Raul says he wants to be a doctor… that's years of studies, where will I find the money?"

"There is help, there are scholarships, I am sure with Raul's straight A's he won't have a hard time obtaining all the help he'll need, don't worry yourself sick about it. He has always had A's; if he ever gets a B, let me know at once, will you?"

"He worships you, he'll never risk the B if he knows you're watching."

"Excellent, let's keep it that way! How long till lunch?"

"About an hour and a half. Your Aunt is trying to clear the snow from the deck, want to join her?"

"Absolutely, immediately, energetically."

While Maria giggles, I leave the kitchen and head to the deck where Aunt Sumi, all bundled up, is pushing the last of the snow off the last step of the deck.

"Well, my favorite Aunt, you've just done a man's job, thank you. Now it's my turn to do a niece's job; come inside and rest, I'll bring you a hot drink right away."

"Phew! So much snow. A hot drink will be most welcome; how was your expedition downtown?"

"It was an adventure in itself; the side roads were not plowed and it was not until I was on my way home that I saw the first snowplows moving towards the smaller streets at turtle speed. No speeding tickets for them."

While Aunt Sumi sips her hot chocolate, I toy with the idea of calling Fred. With a remnant of uncertainty fluttering about me, I want to hear one more time Aunt's thoughts about Fred's proposal and my wedding. Then I will call Fred and set the wheels of my destiny in motion. Images of our childhood and school days flock to my mind; memories of each little thing

Fred did for me and I for him through the years of our growing up, studying, playing, laughing and crying together wrap around me like a blanket that says Security. The feeling is tender, the heart is warm. What more do I want? I shall marry him and have his children, that's final.

"Thank you for the hot chocolate, Raffee, it hit the jackpot. Are you seeing Fred soon?" Aunt asks.

"Yes, I guess. Tell me again what you think of all this… you know, the proposal, my soon-to-come answer, the formal engagement, the wedding and life after the wedding…"

"Lots of things at once, it seems. But, relax, everything will be all right. Fred loves you and you love him; this alone spells success, the rest is only details which we will have great fun looking after. Don't worry about life after the wedding. You will not be abandoned, you will always have Uncle Chris and me near you, and this home will always remain your home. You will have two homes: one with Fred and one with us. Although with Fred it may very well be a castle!"

"I don't want a castle, Auntie. What I really want is the guarantee that our marriage will be a success and last for ever like your marriage to Uncle Chris. If I have this guarantee, then I can say a resounding Yes to Fred and the sooner, the better."

"My sweet niece, life gives no guarantees. We must accept life and what it brings us and do the best we can to attain AND keep happiness along our journey on earth. We are simple mortals and as such we have no right to demand guarantees. What we have is the potential to be happy and the duty to seek and find happiness. When you are happy with your life, life is happy with you. And, believe me, it is very important to be in perfect harmony with life."

"I like harmony, I feel it every time I sit on the floor of the pagoda and converse with Lord Buddha and the beyond. I know harmony and if I ever need it outside the pagoda, I will rush back inside to find it again. No problem. And so, Auntie, I shall now throw the dice and call sweet Fred. Promise me you'll help me with all the details you mentioned earlier."

"It will be my great pleasure. Now, call Fred. I am taking my cup to the kitchen and help Maria with lunch."

Fred is taking me to the renowned seafood restaurant where Stephie's parents invited us last year to celebrate their daughter's birthday. I remember the succulent food and the lovely and soft music playing in the background. We had a marvelous time and Stephie's mother asked for an extra dessert to take to Andrew who was on call all night at the hospital and could not join us. I thought it was awfully kind of her. I remember Josh's eyes when he saw that the cake was covered with chocolate.

"Oh gosh, will you look at the masterpiece!" he said to our merriment.

Tonight the masterpiece may very well be my engagement to Fred. We will probably also set a date for our wedding; I am thinking of a sunny day next Spring, a beautiful gown, my bridesmaids, Aunt Sumika in a gorgeous Thai silk outfit with, hopefully, Uncle Chris by her side. I know, I can feel it, the day will be a glorious ode to happiness.

"Yoo-hoo, Raffee... where have you gone, light of my life?" Fred asks and brings me back to earth.

"Sorry, sweetheart, I did indeed go away for a while. I couldn't remember the question you asked the other day...would you repeat, please?" I say teasingly.

"Raphaëlle Luens, my love, will you marry me? Have you got an answer for me today?"

"Yes, Fred Silverman, I will marry you. Shall we celebrate?"

"Absolutely, with good food and champagne, then we will take a walk by the lake, our first walk as a betrothed couple. You will be my wife and I will be at your feet adoring you. Suddenly life looks like a precious present sent from heavens just for the two of us. And I want you to wear this ring, it tells the world that as of today we are engaged."

Fred places the diamond ring on my finger and kisses my hand. I am more emotional than I thought I would be and my eyes become suddenly very warm. The situation is saved by the elegant waiter who brings us a magnificent baked Alaska.

We bundled up into our heavy coats and leave the restaurant. Outside, the cool air takes away from our faces the warmth from the fireplace inside and, hand in hand, we walk towards the lake. The sidewalk and the jetty are almost empty; there is a cold breeze blowing but it doesn't make me shiver because Fred is with me and my heart is very warm. We talk of the wedding, the guests, the reception and many other things; Fred says we can choose to live in his present home, minus his parents, or in a new home that he and I can select in town, the decision is mine. We both think of next Spring for the big day. Everything looks and feels perfect, we have talked about everything except religion. This is most serious and I decide to head back to Fred's car where it is warm and comfortable. I rest my head on his shoulder and think of Lord Buddha, the pagoda, the spirits who often visit me from beyond, the soothing comfort of deep meditation, the oneness with the pagoda's surroundings, the feeling of belonging. How I love all this. I must now ask the only important question that must be asked tonight, now.

"What about religion, Fred?"

"You need not worry about it, sweetheart, everything will be taken care of. My parents will help you and guide you every step of the way and my cousin the rabbi will be delighted to teach you everything about Judaism. In no time at all you will be ready for your immersion into our religion and you will become one of us. You will be my perfect Jewish wife and we will be happy for ever."

I cannot believe the words just spoken, my head is near explosion point, my body shakes and I have only enough speech power to say,

"Quite a discourse, my dear. Please take me home now."

I am thinking 'control, I must control myself at all costs'.

Before Fred stops the car at my gate, I discreetly remove the engagement ring from my finger and, just as he opens the door for me, I place it in his hand. He is in shock and wants to speak, but I cut him short.

"Take it back, Fred, there will be no wedding. I will never, ever, leave Buddhism. Good night."

Silently thanking Ramon for having cleared our driveway, I run into the house without slipping or falling, and slam the door shut. Around me all is quiet, I can hear the furious pounding of my heart. Inside my head all is insane. How dares he, oh, how dares he insult my intelligence so; how self-centered and possessive of him; another Fred all together, a total stranger. I am angry, humiliated, sickened and feeling like a complete idiot.

Even my comfortable and peaceful bedroom cannot bring me peace. Sleep is too disturbed to be restful. Fred's words still hit my brains, they return by waves each time I wake up to push away one nightmare or another. The merry-go-round is constant and brings on the most dreaded of migraines. If migraine is lethal, I will surely die tonight.

NINE

When morning asks for permission to enter my bedroom, I let it in and we keep company for a little while. It looks bright and light as it plays with a few tiny rays of sun that have pushed their way in between the curtain panels. A new day beckons and I must brave it straight in the eye. I must go back to the 'me' of before, I must not allow what took place yesterday to destroy my sanity or my inner peace. I will not be devastated and I will not cry for the rest of my life. It is easy to think these thoughts when you're lying in bed and the day is still just a baby. How will it be in two, three hours? Next week? Next month? Can I stay in bed for ever?

The answer comes from the kitchen where Maria is —already?- preparing breakfast. It is not like me not to be in the dining room before she arrives. But then today is not like every day, at least for me. Never mind, I will join Aunt Sumi for coffee and, if she asks, I will tell her what happened last night, coolly and truthfully, without volcanoes spitting lava. What happened last night was, I am sure, an obstacle thrown in my path by destiny telling me it was the wrong way to walk. I must confess that my pride was more hurt than my feelings. I could not, and still cannot understand why Fred did what he did. He is not a mean, cold person, but why did he take me and my religion for granted? In so doing he destroyed the love that was budding between us, and perhaps even our friendship of so many years. The questions I have today are a world apart from the questions I had yesterday. I hope Aunt Sumi will help me and make the migraine disappear.

The aroma of coffee hits me where it works most wonders: my nose. And when the smell of pancakes joins in, the dining room becomes a paradise where I hope to get rid of my still complaining migraine.

"Well, well, my favorite niece is already up and ready for the day; how did you sleep, Raffee?"

"Not too well, but with this very tempting breakfast I think I can kill my horrible headache. How did you sleep, Auntie?"

"Soundly as always after I have had a long and peaceful meditation. You can try to get rid of your migraine with a cold towel on your neck and forehead, it works for me every time. What caused your headache?"

I decide to take a detour around the main subject for now.

"It started during the night, maybe it was a leftover from that awful snowstorm that hit us. Earlier this morning the outside thermometer showed a temperature of two below, and it's only the end of November. Do you think we'll have a white Christmas?"

"I am not sure, I've noticed that when it is extremely cold, there is no snow, everything looks frozen solid, and then when the temperature goes up a little, the snow arrives with a vengeance. Cold temperature and snow are two things I loathe. The third thing is a migraine. What caused yours, Raffee?"

There is no cowering this time, I plunge head first into the sea –no, the ocean- of what took place last night; my not understanding, my questions, the total surprise at Fred's selfishness, the hurt and humiliation; what do I do now? Where do I go? Do I see him again?

Maria peeps in, sees the look on our faces, turns around and goes back to the kitchen without uttering a word. Bless your consideration, Maria.

"So, you see, Auntie, this is the culprit that caused me to have this horrible migraine. I cannot for the life of me understand why Fred acted that way. Within mere minutes he killed a wonderful friendship of so many years."

"I am totally stunned, words escape my lips to describe how I feel. Talk about taking for granted! He took everything for granted, you, your feelings, your religion; how can the kind Fred that we know do such a thing?"

"Perhaps we didn't know the true Fred? All these years we've been close friends, there has never been anything of this magnitude. All of a sudden, because love is involved, everything tumbles down into oblivion: friendship, respect, love, a future together. Everything. Auntie, I confess I am lost, I have lost my way, I don't know any more what to do or not do, what to think or not, where to go. I am numb, except for the migraine that refuses to go away."

"We need quiet and much peace. You know where we can find both. I'll do the driving, we are taking one dozen incense sticks with us and soon we will forget about time and earth, hurt and bitter disappointment. Let's go."

Aunt Sumika, model of serenity, has once again poured honey on my 'wound of the heart' just as she did when my parents died and she and Uncle Chris took me in and gave me their love and their home. I am blessed and profoundly grateful. Why did I for one moment think that I could also be happy somewhere else, with someone else? How ungrateful of me. And how dumb. This is a lesson I won't forget, it is opening my eyes, jogging my brains, and warning my heart against man's lies. My Aunt, gentle, generous, quiet, so kind and selfless, I owe her so much. Suddenly I see before my eyes my secret mission, clear, precise and very strong. I shall avenge you, Auntie, remove the cloud of sadness from your beautiful eyes, and bring you the satisfaction to know that she who hurt you can never hurt you again. And when Uncle comes home, he too will see in your eyes the light of life returned.

We both jump when somebody sneezes behind us; I turn slightly to see a man with brown hair and blue eyes sitting on the floor of the pagoda deep in concentration. It is extremely rare to see other Caucasians worshipping in a Buddhist temple; I hope this man is sincere and doesn't come here out of curiosity as many do. Aunt and I call such people 'clowns'; they are shallow, empty beings who do not know what they are missing because they do not know Lord Buddha. Actually they don't know much at all, some of them call the Virgin Mary 'the mother of God'. They forget that Mary was created by God, not the other way around; that God is the universal creator, He created you, me, Einstein, Buddha, Mohammed. He is the Father and nobody created Him. Therefore no woman can be called 'the mother of God' because no woman created Him. The wrong belief has been passed on and on to gullible people for millennia. Today they still say in their prayers 'Saint Mary, mother of God, blablabla and blablabla'. When my mother was alive, she used to say the same prayers without thinking, without asking questions.

"You don't ask. You believe," she told me each time I had questions. So I stopped asking them.

Aunt Sumi turns to me and I nod. We are ready to leave the pagoda and, after bowing respectfully to Lord Buddha, we walk to the side door and exit. I am a fetus leaving the womb, there is a mean world outside, am I strong enough to brave it? Was I better protected in the waters of meditation?

"Lunch is my treat, Raffee. Tell me what you feel like eating."

"Auntie, you are an angel. How about the Golden Lotus, they have ample supervised parking, your car will be well protected. I am not very hungry but perhaps reading the menu will inspire me."

I admire the inside of this beautiful restaurant; everything is sparkling and the waitresses are always polite and friendly. The food is divine and I have become very hungry all of a sudden.

The meal was succulent, we are leaving now and, as we reach the parking lot, we see a gray BMW pulling in next to Aunt's car and a man getting out in a hurry, almost colliding with my aunt.

"I am awfully sorry, Ma'am, please forgive me, I am very hungry and this is my favorite restaurant," he says.

"It's all right, no harm. Go eat before you starve," Aunt replies. The man smiles and suddenly stares at us, as if recognizing us from somewhere.

"It was you at the temple, two rows ahead of me. I must apologize again for startling you with my sneezing. I am Francis Ratzavunnag of the Thai Consulate." He bows, we shake hands and Aunt makes the introductions.

"I am Mrs. Luens and this is my niece Raphaëlle Luens. We too like this restaurant very much."

"Perhaps I will have the pleasure of running into you again," and looking at me he adds "soon". Aunt does not miss a thing while I feel my cheeks starting to burn.

"We also go to the temple often during the week but not on week-ends. Have a good day, and enjoy your lunch," Aunt says, and we take leave.

"Raffee, you didn't say a word, you were very far away. Are you all right?"

"Yes, Auntie, I am all right. You can't really say much in a parking lot, just hello and goodbye; besides, I didn't forgive him for sneezing so loudly in a place of worship, he should know better unless, like so many, he goes there just out of curiosity, you know that kind of people, the clowns, those who…"

"Hold it, Raffee, what's got into you? We don't know him from Adam or Eve and already you are hacking him to pieces… What is this? Does it have anything to do with what happened last night? I am not angry, honey, just curious and a bit worried."

"Please, Auntie, don't worry. You know me, I'll get over this hurdle and be like new again soon, I promise. It's only temporary insanity; find something to occupy me and I'll forget the whole nonsense."

On our way home we see department stores with some windows already beautifully decorated for Christmas; other windows show children, small Christmas trees and hundreds of toys around. Capitalism does attract many religions.

"There will be many Christmas parties in town as usual and there will be people dressed in extravagantly expensive clothes which they will discard the next day. What a world and what a waste," Aunt says.

"Yes, but if you don't waste, you are not "in". Have you noticed how men dress up nicely for the occasion and women dress down to near bare breasts and legs, and shoulders? What a degradation! Yet, I am willing to bet that women's party clothes cost much more than men's suits. Yes, what a shallow world and what a deep waste. The world has gone very far away from the birth in a manger of that little boy eons ago; the world has forgotten the treasure of simplicity and sincerity."

"And we live in this world, we witness all this nonsense, it makes us angry, maybe judgemental, but, sweet Raffee, we have something much more precious than what these people have. We know simplicity and we have sincerity, we are blessed. Is your employer going to give you time off during the holidays?"

"I don't know and I won't mention it. These are not our holidays, Auntie. We don't observe, we only give presents to our friends who do. I will buy a box of chocolates for Francesca of the employment agency. I can't believe it's almost the end of the year, I do wish Uncle Chris would end his retreat and come home. I miss him."

"He'll come home, honey. We only have to wait till he is ready."

Ramon must have come while we were out because the driveway has been cleared one more time. What a wonderful helper he is. It will make it easy for me when I go to work tomorrow morning. I will probably work like a possessed in an attempt to kill and dispose of all the bruised feelings that are still pounding in my head. Aunt Sumi often says that time is the Master Healer and she is almost never wrong. Time will probably heal my wound if it did not hers. Her wound is so deep that decades have not relieved one bit of it. I am putting all my hopes in my mission. Perhaps once the perpetrator has been removed, Aunt will finally take a deep breath in and exhale out for good the bitterness and sorrow she has carried in her heart for so long. Is it possible to love another human being that much? She must have loved Neil to a degree that I cannot fathom. It must have been an infinite love beyond human comprehension. And it was a human who put an end to it and a knife into my aunt's heart. That human has to pay and I have to make my aunt happy again.

After dinner we settle in the living room with a cup of warm honey each, it is time to unwind and enjoy the comfort of our home. Though unfriendly feelings still haunt me, I want to push them away and have a light and interesting chat with Aunt Sumika. As if on cue, Aunt asks,

"Are you sure you want to go to work tomorrow, Raffee? There may still be much snow on the roads outside the city and I am a little worried."

"The lady said to come tomorrow, so I will. Don't worry, I'll be careful driving. The woods near her house are very beautiful in winter, they look like a gigantic painting on pure white background with blue sky and sometimes there are one or two dots of red; that's when cardinals fly in and out of their nests; I like when they come and beg for seeds in my boss's backyard."

"These beggars we like a lot. What about those we see on the city's streets and sidewalks who have become so bold as to touch you when they want money or cigarettes, or drugs? I often wonder what brought them down to this condition."

"Sometimes the police round them up and take them away. But, Auntie, these beggars are not the worst ones, they don't ask much, just enough to satisfy their hunger and then they go home, wherever that is. The bad ones are the big charities, big hospitals, who demand money via the television, radio, postal services, marathons, and other events. They force their way into our homes at any time of day or night and their begging messages are repeated over and over with insistence and without respect for people's privacy. They do all this but the police never take them away, do they? It is the poor man in rags who is removed from sight because he asks for a buck or two, not the high and mighty charities, hospitals or others who want hundreds, even thousands of dollars. We have all heard of how much money some of these people make yearly; it is absolutely shocking and shameful. How true the saying 'the more you have, the more you want'."

"Phew, honey, what a discourse! You must have felt these feelings for a long time and today they are coming out en masse. You know what? I feel the same way, I find it sickening that the 'high and mighty' keep asking for millions to fill the ever hungry bank accounts of their executives. This is how I see it: a day has twenty-four hours for both the executive and the man in rags. They both work. The executive goes to work in a luxurious office downtown. The pauper braves the elements to go to his office: one square metre of sidewalk at the corner of A and B streets where he will stand and beg until evening regardless of rain, snow, frigid temperatures or scalding sun. The executive makes over a million dollars per year; the pauper may take home twenty dollars per day if he is lucky. And the police have the nerve to round up and take away these paupers. It is an easy job to hurt the poor. Could it be that society prefers to help the rich and kick the poor? Do we really live in this society, this nation of beggars?"

"Yes, Auntie, we live among these birds of prey, we see them in their luxury cars downtown; some drive, others are driven and on their faces we read the same message 'I am rich, you are nothing', 'I can do as I please, even kill cyclist messengers, you can't', et cetera, et cetera…"

"Cyclist messengers… you mean the one killed by our attorney-general?"

"The very one. The attorney-general went scot-free because the courts dropped all charges, do you remember? Lesson to learn: in Canada when you have money and connections, you can kill and never see the inside of a jail. Isn't this a beautiful country?"

"I'm afraid it is the same in many countries. The poor everywhere are treated like garbage, the rich are worshipped, and the powerful have the license to kill cyclist messengers."

"I wish I had the license to kill people who make other people very sad and bitter."

"You mean Fred?"

"Not really. Fred disappointed me, he didn't make me very sad or bitter. I mean other people, there must be thousands of them around us."

"Have you just appointed yourself savior of the downtrodden?"

"Not savior, Auntie, avenger."

"Then you must proceed with caution because often vengeance has two very sharp blades."

"I will be extremely careful. Shall we say goodnight? I am falling asleep."

"Happy dreams then, little Raffee."

TEN

Today is a day to be remembered, it is the confirmation of Andrew as a full-fledged doctor; the crowning of many years of studies and hard work – Andrew calls it the *gulag* -. He will not forget the endless night calls, the two-bite lunches taken at supersonic speed, the stolen naps in linen rooms, the exhaustion. Today he can push all this aside, take a deep breath, then fly with his own wings. Doctor Andrew Kozell is ready to start his own practice, life will be *his* life, not the General Hospital's, not part of the lives of his buddies the other interns. Patients will be his own patients, not someone else's. He will not forget the first time he delivered a baby in the emergency room because the Ob-Gyn was attending to the premature arrival of problem triplets two rooms away. But he will try, hard as it may be, to forget the mass of torn flesh and thick blood he placed on the operating table that turned out to be a three-year-old boy who expired within seconds. It was Andrew's first loss and for weeks he could not erase the scene from his mind; it followed him day and night, often taking his attention away from a patient under consultation until the attending nurse nudged him gently back to the work at hand. Yes, he will try to forget the devastating sorrow on the face of the boy's mother. He was her only child and she could not have any more children. Her world shattered then and there and it left Andrew speechless, feeling useless and desperately alone. He felt so inadequate and incompetent.

It is said that the first blow from life is always the hardest to take. It is also the first lesson we learn. Smart people will remember the lesson and put it to good use. Others will shove it away and never learn. There are good doctors and bad doctors everywhere. They all take the same Hippocratic oath and their actions thereafter will separate the good from the bad. The former will soar to success, the latter will be shunned. Andrew is among the very best, he will soar rapidly. We are all very happy for him, he has worked so hard and sacrificed so much.

His parents arrived two days ago from Oregon to celebrate their son's success. We will all be together at Stephie's home this evening for dinner. Mrs. Rowlands has invited everybody; there will be good conversation –there always is when Mr. Rowlands is around- and gifts for Andrew. The Rowlands' home is huge, the driveway can accommodate four cars, there are two living rooms and two dining rooms, chandeliers in each. I am sure we will use the master dining room this evening, there are just too many of us; and since it is too cold outside, nobody will want to go to the immense patio near the pool for after-dinner drinks. I asked Stephie's mother the other day if she would like me to bring something for the evening. She said to bring joy and a good appetite. I took the liberty of spreading the word among our group of friends. There will be joy and good appetite and, I am sure, intelligent and interesting dialogue. If Walter spits fire, we will extinguish it gently.

Dinner was a resounding success, everybody was high-spirited, talking and laughing at the same time. When dessert and champagne arrived, we were spellbound and silenced, it was as if the king and queen of the evening had entered the room and demanded respect. Once their majesties had settled on our plates and in our flutes, silence disappeared in an instant and the wonderful cacophony returned. Somebody asked, "Where's Fred? Anybody know where Fred is?" Aunt Sumi's eyes and mine met for a fraction of a second but we said not a word.

"He is in Dubai on business for his father," Stephie said.

"Is he buying more real estate for his dad's company?" Rhys asked.

"I don't know, but he'll be away for a while."

"Maybe he'll come back with a beautiful Muslim fiancée," Andrew said. I took it as my cue and jumped in.

"Not in a millions years, Andrew. Judaism does not get along well with Islam, nor does it with Buddhism."

"Oops, my mistake, I didn't think of that."

From the corner of my eye I saw Aunt nod in my direction. We smiled and said nothing, we understood each other, we are in the same camp, and my heart is not broken, just slightly rumpled.

When Mrs. Rowlands invited us to the master living room for after-dinner drinks, some of us took their half empty flutes with them, the champagne was just too divine to leave behind, they were going to sip it to the last bubble. Stephie asked if we wanted music, we opted for conversation instead.

"Ah, good! We have tons to catch up on since that walk on the snow eons ago; who did what? When? Let's talk," Alexa said.

The floodgates were opened, we all jumped in. There were stories to tell and stories to listen to. Questions here, exclamations there, and warm drinks everywhere. The living room really deserved its name. Turning to Arielle, Mr. Rowlands asked, "Did you see on the news the poor dog that had to be euthanized because a drunk driver had injured him so badly there was no hope of saving him? I know you have two dogs and you love animals."

"Yes, Sir, I saw the televised report and my heart broke to pieces for that dog. I hope the drunkard will be severely punished and his license taken away.

When I walk my dogs, I stay on the inside of the sidewalk, well away from the traffic, there are so many reckless drivers out there. I hope the dog did not suffer too much before he was put down."

"At least there was euthanasia for him and he went peacefully. We can't say the same for humans who suffer hell and beg to be let go. They are refused euthanasia because somebody, somewhere, played God and made it a law that humans must suffer until their last breath. Pity and compassion for animals only, not for us humans," Josh said.

"In Switzerland and the Netherlands there is compassion and there is euthanasia. For people who are very sick and for whom there is no hope, the medical authorities, in agreement with the patient's family, assist with euthanasia. It is done with great compassion and dignity. And it makes great sense. But not in North America, not in Canada, oh no, Sir. Doctors let us suffer until we croak," Aunt Sumika added vehemently, having joined the debate started by Mr. Rowlands —who else?

"Remember when my nephew, little Marcus, was so ill and in excruciating pain for so long? When the three doctors we consulted told my sister that 'they were sorry, they've done all they could, that Marcus will be kept pain free and comfortable', etc..etc..? Not one of them offered to end the boy's suffering for good, not one. At least the dog on the news received compassion, was put out of its misery and died peacefully and quickly. Seems to me Veterinarians have more courage than Physicians. And that's a shame, really," Walter said and sighed. Little Marcus was only five when he died. Walter had become virulent against the medical powers that be. When Walter talks about one of his strong opinions, the surroundings look and sound like a volcano in eruption; he brings fire and lava to the conversation and soon there is not one person who remains silent, everybody wants to join in, has something to say. It is happening now. We all have a story to tell, an opinion to share, questions to ask.

Kevin mentions mercy killing and how a mother was sent to prison because she put an end to her hopelessly ill daughter. Her action was called 'murder' by some and 'mercy' by others. The debate was never cleared because nobody dared give it the light of day, it was considered taboo and no one wanted to talk about it openly or for long. The curtain of cowardice fell on the population of Windoaks.

"I don't know for sure what I would do if I were ever faced with such a situation," I say.

"You would side with the suffering person you love, the one begging the doctors to stop the pain for good, to let life go out of a hopelessly deteriorating body. Because you love, you have the strength to let go, Raffee, you are more courageous than the doctors who refuse your loved one euthanasia," Rhys answers.

"It is not that easy, my friends. You have your opinions and I respect them, but you are painting a rather simplistic image of the situation. You think that because somebody is in excruciating pain and medicine has no hope for them, they should be euthanized, one, two, three, and they are gone? Why don't you go back to the source and find your answer?" Doctor Andrew Kozell steps in with poise and peace.

"The source… the source… what are you talking about? Where is the source, or don't you know what to say any more, Andrew?" virulent Walter tries to provoke our new doctor.

"Gosh! Let's not fight over this, let's play scrabble, I dare you. Just one question, Andrew, where is the source? I want to find answers," Josh says.

"The commandment 'Thou shall not kill'. Read all ten of them and forget not one of them," is Andrew's answer.

"Very commendable and very high up. But we are humans, we live down here; sometimes we suffer something resembling the hell we see in books; that's when we want out, that's the only time we want out, but we are refused the last compassion, we are told 'to hang in there, to be brave, etc.' even when there is not a shred of hope left for our recovery," Walter insists.

"True, it is extremely difficult to accept and very hard to understand, but it is the law in North America. Maybe with time it will change as it did in some other countries, but for now we must obey the law."

"You mean we must watch our loved ones suffer hell and do nothing about it?"

"Medicine has a great number of pain relieving products to keep patients comfortable at all times. We do not relish the sight and sound of a human being in excruciating pain, we do everything we can to alleviate the suffering."

"But you refuse to 'alleviate' it for good, that's sadistic," Walter spits out.

"You are free to feel the way you do, Walter, I am only telling you where medicine stands on the matter of euthanasia. I didn't make the law, I obey it," Andrew says.

Alexa, whose father is a doctor, steps in now with a different thought.

"When the pain is too much and there is no more hope, why doesn't the patient simply take his own life? Why does he want the doctor to do it? You mentioned courage where doctors are concerned, did you not?"

One minute of deep silence sets in and suddenly everybody is talking at the same time. Gosh Josh stands up and asks for order, "One at a time, please."

"Maybe, just maybe, the patient doesn't have the courage to end his life and wants someone else to help," Kevin says.

"Does the law also apply to the patient?" Arielle asks.

"What if the patient is too sick and too weak to end his own life? He would need help, wouldn't he?" Stephie joins the debate.

"There is something called assisted suicide. It's up to the patient and his family to go that way or not. And now, let's talk about life and living. Let's raise our glasses to Andrew's success today, tomorrow, and for years to come," Mr. Rowlands says.

"Hear! Hear! To Andrew" we all speak in unison as we raise our glasses.

"Thank you all, this is indeed a day to remember, you have been wonderful. In one week I'll be back at work, in my own office, not at the hospital. From now on I won't depend on the hospital but on the patients who come to see me. I hope they will be many."

"We'll send you as many as we can, that's a promise," Josh and Rhys say together.

"Bound to happen when a pharmacy and a medical lab are in connivance," Mrs. Rowlands adds to the merriment of all.

"Where will your office be, Andrew?" I ask.

"Two blocks away from the medical lab, across from "Sweetsie" the coffee shop. And about twenty minutes drive from the apartment I am renting a little out of town."

"No more dorm for you, hurrah!" Arielle says.

The clock in the vestibule rings one single chime. I didn't realize it was that late. Almost in unison we all prepare to take leave and thank the Rowlands warmly for a wonderful evening.

"It was very nice meeting you, Mr. and Mrs. Kozell," I say to Andrew's parents.

"We feel the same way meeting you and Andy's other friends. You have an interesting name, where does 'Raffee' come from?" Mr. Kozell asks with a mischievous smile.

"Oh, it's short for Raphaëlle; friends and family call me Raffee. Are you staying long in Windoaks?"

"Another two days to help Andy settle in his new abode, and we'll head back to our little farm in Oregon," Mrs. Kozell answers.

"While here, if you need anything, please don't hesitate to call me, I'll be delighted to help. Andrew has my phone number."

"She is an angel with a name like that, I've noticed your halo all evening. Andy is lucky, yes he is," Mr. Kozell says and causes my cheeks to burn a bit. We say good night and Aunt Sumi waves goodbye as we pull out of the driveway behind Josh's car.

During the night more snow fell and, once again, our driveway is covered with a white blanket that shines under the morning sun. When the snow is all new and no one has yet walked on it, I call it 'virgin snow' and I delight in looking at it. Our pine trees are bending under the weight of the same blanket and I see a vibrant red cardinal darting in and out in search of food. The temperature is not too cruel and, once the driveway is plowed, I will go downtown to buy a box of chocolates for Francesca and more incense cones for the altar in my bedroom. Aunt Sumi burns incense sticks in her room; I prefer the cones because they burn straight down to the base and the ashes stay right there whereas the ashes from sticks may disperse around and fall outside the bowl that contains the sticks. But cones or sticks, the objective and the result are the same: to respect and communicate with Lord Buddha who rewards us with inner peace and serenity. I also look for the strength and courage needed to succeed in my mission. This mission stays alive around me day and night, it is not pushing, not screaming, not demanding; it is just here with me like a second skin covering me entirely, body and mind, and I know it won't go away until it is accomplished. I call it mission, but perhaps it is also an obsession, so strong and stubborn is its presence.

Mr. Kozell called me an angel… that was sweet of him. When I told Aunt Sumi, she smiled and said, "Well, of course you are an angel, Raffee." To which I added, "An angel of revenge maybe." She shook her head and declared that I was full of mysteries. It was my turn to smile, mysteriously, just before we wished each other good night and happy dreams. It was very late and my sleep was not once disturbed by dreams or nightmares.

Maria arrives and I hear her talking to the pots and pans in the kitchen. Soon the divine aroma of coffee reaches my room and catapults me out of bed. The first sip of mocha in the morning is, in my opinion, the best of the day. It wakes me and my brains up, helps me to focus on the day ahead, why it often decides what I'll do and how I'll do it for the entire day. It is my memory jogger, the dissipater of night's foggy cobwebs, the bearer of a new day's promises.

"Well, if it isn't my angel Raffee ready for breakfast," Aunt Sumi says as she walks into the dining room wearing a lovely sky blue Thai outfit.

"And top of the mornin' to you too, favorite Aunt. How did you sleep?"

"After that wonderful evening with the wonderful food and drinks, I slept like a log. And you?"

"Another log. The Rowlands definitely know how to give a party, everything was perfect. And once again Mr. Rowlands masterfully steered us all into a fantastic conversation and a hot exchange of opinions."

"And he had the magic ability of changing the subject when it became too hot. What an intelligent man."

"He did the same thing last time we were there for Stephie's birthday; quite a leader he is. What do you think of Andrew's parents?"

"Nice people, quiet and friendly, very observant, they didn't miss a thing. I admire them for the sacrifices they made for Andrew's success. They must be very proud today."

"And relieved too because now Andrew will fly with his own wings, he has arrived. Mrs. Kozell told me that it was the death of his baby sister at age two that steered him towards medicine. He was eight at the time and has never changed his mind. What strength and determination."

"And yet the Andrew that we know, the everyday Andrew is so gentle and helpful; he doesn't strike me as someone hard and stubborn."

"He may be a very sensitive person if the death of his sister touched him deeply enough that he kept his childhood decision until it bore fruit in his adult life. I'll give him an A1 for determination. What are your plans today, Auntie?"

"I will see to the birds that have made their homes in our pine trees; seed to fill the feeders and lint from the laundry room to put out for their nests. Are you going somewhere?"

"Just out to buy chocolates for the lady at the employment agency, the one who said I was overqualified for the housecleaner position, ha, ha!"

"She was absolutely right. I still don't understand what got into you when you applied for it."

"It was temporary insanity but I am having fun with it. You won't tell Uncle, ever, will you?"

"Not if you don't want me to. That employer of yours doesn't know what a gem you are; I hope she treats you well."

"Oh she is all right, doesn't bother me at all, and speaks good English. I don't mind cleaning the mansion. Well, I'd better get ready for the candy store if I want to be back in time for lunch. See you later, Auntie."

The employment agency has not changed much except for a few Christmas decorations made in China. There is a dark green plastic tree trimmed with colorful plastic lights and glittering tinsel hanging on the branches; background music plays 'Silent Night' and on the still wobbly table I see small candles shaped like roses placed in small saucers. Somebody made an effort to decorate the place for the holidays.

The receptionist calls my name and I walk into Francesca's office. It has not changed, neither has she. We shake hands and she invites me to sit with her in a tiny area she calls 'my office coffee room' composed of a tiny coffee table and two chairs that are fighting for space.

"How have you been, Raphaëlle?"

"Very well I must say, considering the bad storms we've had and the amount of snow this early in the season. Roads are not always plowed early in the morning and driving can be a nightmare."

"I think of you driving out to the mansion, it is very hazardous, how are you coping?"

"So far, so good. I've come today to give you a little something for Christmas. I hope you have a sweet tooth." And I place the box of Golden Buds on the coffee table.

"Raphaëlle, you shouldn't have! It is very kind of you, thank you. Yes I have a sweet tooth and it will sing me many songs later. How is it going at Mrs. Jahe's?"

"It is going well, the lady is all right, and I am punctual on my work days. She hasn't said a mean word to me, so I suppose she is satisfied with my work."

"Oh Raphaëlle, she is more than satisfied. We've spoken on the phone a couple of times. She likes the way you hum tunes while you do the chores, she says you are a happy youngster. And then she made a confession: she has become quite fond of you. If we have ever wondered about job security, we can now rest assured that your job is totally secure. Congratulations."

"Thank you, Francesca, this is an absolute surprise, I've never thought of such a possibility, but 'like' is better than 'dislike', right? Now I must run home. Have a very merry Christmas."

"The same to you, enjoy the holidays. Goodbye for now, Raphaëlle."

The cold air outside brings reality back to me; I am still disturbed by what Francesca said, embarrassed and feeling uneasy. Mrs. Jahe is fond of me... good heavens, please let it not be so. My mission must not totter, I must not falter. Aunt Sumika's happiness depends on it.

I need to walk a block or two in the snow before I can return to my car and drive home.

ELEVEN

THE ROAD to St. Thomas is buried under tons of snow, there are icy spots to avoid here and there, the whole scenery is white, the ditches on either side of the road are invisible and, to make one's sense of direction worse, all the trees are uniformly and heavily covered with snow. I feel wrapped in cotton; whichever way I look, I see white and the silence is so deep it gives me the shivers. Will I arrive alive or half dead at the mansion? Will I be late? I've never been late before. Maybe I should have stayed home and called the lady, but I didn't expect to see so much snow on the road.

Last nigh Aunt Sumika wasn't sure it would be safe to drive such a long distance, but I reassured her and promised to be extra careful. If only I could see the tall pine trees and their different shapes and looks, I would be able to estimate my position and the distance to the mansion. As it is, I keep driving blindly on a white carpet, not knowing when I'll see the first house that will definitely tell me where I am. There's a ghost on the horizon, it's a car! It drives slowly past me going the other way. Phew! I am not alone, not lost, not crazy, somebody else is driving on this road today. I am so relieved I want to sing or at least whistle a tune. I know now that I will arrive alive at my destination. It was a temporary loss of control on my part, but all is fine now. Here comes the first house; then I see the convenience store and I know I am not far from the mansion.

My boots sink way down into the deep snow as I ring the bell on the front door. Mrs. Jahe opens very quickly.

"Right, please come in, Raphaëlle. How brave of you to drive today, thank you for coming."

"Good morning, Madame. The road is a murder (oops! bad choice of word) but I did see another car go by. I'm sure by noon the road will be more passable."

"It'd better be, I have a doctor's appointment at eleven. Would you like a cup of tea before you start?"

"No, thank you. I'll start right away if you don't mind."

In the living room among the exquisite objets d'art, I see Christmas decorations tastefully arranged, a small live pine tree streaming with silver tinsel and, on the coffee table, half a dozen small red holders with red candles looking magnificent and seemingly impatient to be lit.

The lady did not react when she saw my lime green smock earlier. She never comments on the outrageous colors of my coveralls whereas Aunt Sumi always tells me I am eccentric, which makes me laugh heartily. Yesterday late afternoon I noticed clouds in her eyes and instantly a hundred questions assaulted me. Is it her health? Can I help? Is it something beyond this world? Can I help? Is it Neil? What on this earth can I do? In the evening Aunt was more silent than usual and the clouds grew darker. How was I going to enter the world in which she has retired? Does she want me there? Yet I knew that she was sad, very sad, but I didn't know what made her sad. If I knew why, I could try to help push the clouds away. Does she want the clouds to go, or are they there to hide a much deeper sadness? Is Aunt's life going to be a constant seesaw between joy –rare as it is- and sadness? Was she away in the beyond with her beloved Neil? If so, I had no right to interfere and disturb their dialogue. Divine love belongs in the beyond; I have no business stepping in between the two of them. So, very quietly and discreetly, I retired to my bedroom where I sat in front of the altar and talked to Lord Buddha for a long while. As usual, I was the beggar asking for inner peace, courage, and direction to succeed in my mission. I felt –and the feeling was powerful- that accomplishing this mission would definitely bring happiness back to Aunt Sumika.

And here I am in the home of the woman who is the cause of so much sorrow and unhappiness in my Aunt's life. I shudder to control my hatred, I smile to her to hide my death wish, and I proceed with cleaning her house while keeping the scalding lava and the venom well inside my mind. There is a time for everything, I tell myself. Her time will come. It is ten o'clock, the ballet of mops and dusters begins, then the vacuum cleaner joins in and I go to the bedroom upstairs where the photographs are. I never tire looking at the one of Neil so handsome and so kind. And I never stop asking, "Why? Why did you let her kill you?"

"Right, Raphaëlle, I am off to my appointment now; your money is on the kitchen table. Have a nice week-end," Mrs. Jahe says

"Thank you, Ma'am." And I think suddenly to myself "Why don't you have a fatal car accident on your way? The road is very accommodating today with snow and ice aplenty. Go meet your Maker and beg for mercy."

I continue the cleaning until quarter to twelve. The telephone rings, I don't dare pick it up, we have never discussed this before. If she has questions, she'll ask me next week. I place every tool back where it belongs and, famished, I leave to go home to a warm lunch. Will I see the unwelcome clouds in Aunt's eyes again? When I left this morning, she was still in her bedroom and I didn't see her.

The road looks more civilized now and the driving is less scary. A few evergreens have gotten rid of some of their snow and they now look bicolored, dark green and pure white. The scenery is still beautiful thanks to a blue sky and a blazing sun. In the summer when the same sun visits us, everybody heads to the lake and the beach, our summers are so short, there is not a minute to waste. When we were little, my brother Peter and I would scream at Nanny to take us there, "Now!" Peter said and I added, "Right now!" We never had enough of the lake, we were 'water kids' as Mother would say. And then one year, a road accident abroad took my parents away. I became an orphan. No word can describe the feeling of utter loss and despair that I felt. Peter had died a few years before, now it was my parents. I was left alone in a world that was still very big and forbidding to my young teenage eyes. My reaction alternated between sorrow and anger, one day of tears followed by one of rage because of the injustice done me; then back to tears because I knew I would never see them again, never confide in Dad again. Days became sheer agony. I was lost and didn't know what to do, where to go. The lights in my life were extinguished.

When Uncle Chris and Aunt Sumika offered to take me into their home, my heart exploded with relief and gratitude. They gave me love and treated me as their own child. Uncle said I was the daughter they never had, and Aunt added, "You are the princess in your new home." They did everything for me, gave me all that I needed, showed great patience when teenage rebellion took me by the hand and tried to run things the wrong way. They have never hit me and never yelled at me, though there were times when both treatments were needed; like the time when Fred and I played hooky because we didn't like the history teacher; or when I called the science teacher a witch to her face and she sent me to the principal's office. After class that day, Rhys told me I went too far; I just shrugged my shoulders.

"Stop doing that, Raffee, you don't want to stain your report card," he said.

Years passed, teenage was shoved away, adulthood replaced it. Today we are all working and living adult lives. Childhood friends remain good friends. Uncle Chris is away on a religious retreat at a Buddhist temple in Thailand, Aunt Sumika has gray hair around her forehead and I no longer play hooky, not even with my ridiculous housecleaning job. With the passing of time there is the passing of childhood into adulthood, and the many silly things we did as children now make us smile. As an adult I recently made a serious mistake, I trusted Fred enough to accept our engagement only to be terribly disappointed when he wanted to take my religion away from me. I will survive, I will turn the page of that book and look ahead, not back. There are many more chapters in the book of life, it will take me a lifetime to discover them and learn from them.

At home Aunt Sumi has placed a lovely cloth on the table for lunch; this is unusual as we often have our noon meal on trays. Could this be a sign that her 'crisis' has passed? I don't want to pry, but I sure want to help if need be. What wouldn't I do for her.

"How was work today, Raffee? And the driving?" she asks as she comes in from the kitchen with a basket of small golden loaves that smell like warm delight from the best bakery in town. My nose is in seventh heaven.

"Work was routine, driving was not. On the way to work I thought I was lost and tightly locked in a box of white cotton and I got scared. The snow was very deep and almost got into my knee-high boots. On the way back it was a little easier but not completely safe."

"Let's have lunch, you must be very hungry after such an expedition."

"I am famished, Auntie, I could eat a horse."

"Oh don't say that. You know in France they eat horse meat."

"Oh don't say that yourself, Auntie, it is awful. How could they eat horses, it is so primitive of them. One of these days the horses will get their revenge and I will clap my hands."

"So speaks my angel of revenge! Have you heard from the Kozells?"

"No, I haven't. They have our phone number and I've told them to call me if they needed help. About the horses, I am serious, Aunt, sooner or later animals will turn against us for all the misery and injustice we inflict on them day in, day out through the years. From the tiniest to the biggest beast, they will punish us and they will be right. We abuse them and mistreat them because they do not have the power of speech. Do you know why they cannot speak? Because the Creator knew that if they had speech, they would be the ones governing Homo Sapiens, their intelligence is that much superior to ours. And so, pitying us, the Creator withheld speech from animals and told Man to occupy the earth and have the animals in subjection. He did not give us carte blanche to abuse and mistreat them. I am very strongly in favor of all animals."

"So am I. When I see somebody hitting a dog, I want to run to him and hit him too."

"Yes, hit him where it hurts the most. It is so coward to hurt an animal, any animal. Rest assured, Aunt, there will be an animal revolt and then..." The telephone rings and interrupts me. How rude. Maria picks it up in the kitchen as I want to stay with Aunt and the horses.

"For you, Raffee." There is no dodging now, I pick up the phone in the living room.

"Hello, Raphaëlle, this is Eva Kozell, Andy's mother. I hope this is not a bad time, is your kind offer still on? I need to buy some linen for Andy and I don't know the city at all. Could you spare a couple hours?"

Suddenly the horses have galloped away; I look at Aunt with raised eyebrows as in "can't help it".

"Hello Mrs. Kozell, it'll be my pleasure to take you out shopping, I can pick you up at two thirty if it's all right with you?"

"Wonderful, you're an angel as my husband said. Two thirty is quite all right, thank you so much."

Andrew will have new bed linen and new kitchen towels. Aunt and I are giving him dishes, glasses and some cutlery. In two days he will start his new practice. Mrs. Rowlands found him a receptionist named Marilla. I hope she doesn't look or act like Francesca's receptionist, it would scare away Andrew's first patients. Aunt and I won't be his management and won't intrude, but we'll step in to help at the first SOS sign. I am very fond of Andrew and he has always been Aunt Sumika's protégé. Now that he doesn't have to work twenty-eight hour shifts, our group will find ways to entertain him often. With Gosh Josh on board, he may very well have to recuperate from too much fun instead of too much work.

Mr. and Mrs. Kozell will soon leave to go back to their farm in Oregon. Last night we had dinner together at our place. It was a nice and friendly affair, very comfortable. Aunt has the knack of putting people at ease, especially our guests.

"You have a lovely home, Mrs. Luens," Mrs. Kozell said.

"Oh, please call me Sumika," Aunt replied.

"You have a lovely home, Sumika." We all laughed at her impishness.

"She does that all the time, and with a straight face too," her husband said.

"When you work on a farm and you get up at four in the morning every day of the week, you need to find many imps on your path throughout the day or else you go insane."

"What happens to farmers when they go insane?" I asked.

"They abandon the farm, sell the livestock, let the house go to the weeds and then they cry. You see, they couldn't find imps on their property and they didn't laugh every day; their brains went out first, then all the rest tumbled down. We know a few farmers who ended up in homes for the mentally depressed."

"Farming is certainly not for the weak-hearted, it is hard labor and it never stops. If we didn't have the two sons of our good friend Henry to help out, we wouldn't have been able to come at all. It is winter and we don't expect any birth, but any kind of emergency could still occur; Jeff and Paul are young, strong and knowledgeable, we trust them totally," Mr. Kozell said.

"We are, the three of us, in hard-labor occupations, I mean farming and medicine; we are expected to give and give with no limits, we don't have much free time at all. It is harder for Mom and Dad, they have to work every day of the entire year whereas I can probably have a short vacation now and then and I am compelled to observe statutory holidays. There is no such a thing for farmers," Andrew said.

"You must love your professions since you chose them," Aunt Sumi joined in.

"Yes we do," three voices came in unison and Aunt and I smiled warmly.

"Do you see farmers abusing and mistreating their animals?" I asked, ignoring Aunt's frown in my direction. I am sure she was afraid I would once again embark on a crusade against cruelty to animals.

"Farmers do not abuse their animals because they depend on the animals for their livelihood. Ask Eva about our cow Daisy, you'll like the story," Mr. Kozell said. I was anxious to hear it and instantly turned to Mrs. Kozell with questions jumping out of my eyes. I was becoming a sponge, thirsty for new things to hear and to learn.

"Daisy is a six-year-old brown cow with big and beautiful eyes and long eyelashes. She knows her name very well and if you pronounce it in a conversation with somebody, she will run to you because she heard her name. I tell her she is a cow, not a dog; she answers with a light Moo, rubs her nose against my arm and goes away to rejoin the rest of the herd. She is always the first in line to be milked and she stays motionless during the entire milking. You know why? Because when she behaves and doesn't throw her tail in my face, when the milking is over, I pat her on the head, give her a treat and tell her she is the best. Again her little Moo and off she goes."

"That is so funny and so cute, I think I am falling in love with Daisy," I said.

Mr. Kozell gave me a warm smile as his wife continued,

"In the summer when the weather is nice, sometimes I dare take a few moments to rest sitting on the grass. Guess who joins me? Daisy comes and gently nudges my elbow. I ask her what she wants, she says Moo and, to tease her, I invite her to take a nap with me. The silly thing lies down on the grass next to me and peacefully chews her cud. How can I not pat her then? She behaves more like a dog than a cow and I must confess she is my pet. Yours too, isn't she, Robert?"

"Yes, she is for sure, she has a way of knowing when we want her, when she would be welcome, it's like a sixth sense if such a thing exists in animals.

Some people say cows are dumb. Well, these people are totally wrong, Daisy could teach them a lesson or two."

"It must be a very big job to keep a herd and tend a vegetable garden, and there are only the two of you," Aunt Sumi said.

"It's not too bad in the winter because everybody is indoors and everything is done indoors. Mind you, there is more cleaning up to do, but we manage between the two of us. It's later in the spring and summer that we sometimes call Paul or Jeff to the rescue although our herd is small, just one bull and five cows. There is so much to do during the rest of the year, sometimes getting up at four in the morning is not enough. But we are not complaining because, as they say, if you like your job, you like your life."

Before they left, we promised to stay in touch and Aunt whispered to Mrs. Kozell that she would always be ready to help Andrew if he ever called. Mr. Kozell asked if he could give me a hug; Mrs. Kozell said yes but not a bear one because Raphaëlle is also the name of an angel in the Bible and you don't bear hug an angel. The lady sure can talk. What a happy household theirs is and what a pity they live so far away.

Christmas is now three days away. It will be a white, very white one, the snow has not let up, we can hardly see the green of our pine trees and, I am sure, when Ramon comes to clear the driveway, he will want to shake the snow off the branches so the trees can breathe. Aunt Sumika will give him a fat envelope with fat money in it for his Christmas, he is such a good and reliable worker. I find it very endearing when he comes timidly to ask for my opinion on one topic or another, showing me that he trusts me. Each time it happens, I am always happy to help clarify an unclear situation or explain some rules or customs unfamiliar to him. It is amusing that when we talk in the garden, he calls me Raffee, but when he comes to consult with me, he uses my full name Raphaëlle, which makes it sound more formal. When I mentioned this to Aunt, she said that Ramon takes seriously what I tell him and he shows respect by using my full name. What a dear soul he is, knowing the formal and informal of things.

When Maria comes tomorrow, we will give her the gifts we bought for the boys and Aunt will give her a fat envelope with a fat amount of money to thank her for her service through this year. She has been with us for many years and we are very fond of her. I think she guessed that something happened between Fred and me, but she was considerate enough to not mention it. I like this quality in a woman, it is rare. Other women go ladida dida non stop when they get hold of something as serious as the breaking of an engagement. Just think! An engagement, and they broke it! Tongues work overtime for days but in the end they get no overtime pay because the subject is soon discarded, the principals themselves not giving a hoot about it.

Earlier this morning Francesca called to wish me happy holidays. Her office will be closed for three days; she asked if I would be attending midnight mass, I told her no, I don't go to church because I am not a Catholic but I wish her a merry Christmas all the same. I didn't want to embark on an explanation of Buddhism, nor did I want to shock the religious beliefs of an Italian Catholic. I happily let them go to midnight mass and, while they sleep the next day, I happily go to the pagoda.

Rhys made an incredible effort this year, he has invited our group for dessert the evening of Boxing Day and threatened punishment if we brought anything to the party. Walter had a brilliant idea, we went along with it and, the night before Boxing Day, we deposited our contributions, nicely wrapped, at Rhys' front door. In the cardboard box there were one cookie, one can of beer, one box of pretzels, one apple from each of us and a greeting card with seven indecipherable signatures and a P.S. "See you soon".

Needless to say, the dessert party was a sweet success, Rhys outdid himself and served drinks like a pro.

"Hey man, did you work in a bar before you entered the medical lab?" Kevin asked.

"He must have because in the lab he has to handle bottles and vials and what not," Alexa added.

"Yeah and in the lab you won't find Drambuie or Grand Marnier; I don't want to tell you the 'what-not' that you see in the lab, it would spoil your appetite. Tonight we have a taste bud festival, let's enjoy it," Rhys said.

The cakes were sinfully good, the music was very muted, the friendship very warm. We reminisced together and talked about our school days, the various universities we attended, our travels, experiences –good and bad- We told anecdotes, some hilarious, others terrifying. Somebody mentioned Fred, but I remained silent. Andrew liked his new pad and the fact that there was a convenience store near by.

"Convenience stores are a bachelor's best friends," Walter said.

"Very true and bless them. Gosh, I always shop there myself for last minute stuff," Josh added.

"And we always have last minute stuff to buy," Andrew concluded.

It was one in the morning when we left amid warm Thankyous and Goodnights.

TWELVE

CHINATOWN is always too busy on week-ends, but I decided early this morning to go shopping anyway because Aunt Sumi heard about a large shipment of longans being delivered at the Asian market and since we both love the fruit, I thought I'd go buy some before lunchtime. Crowds of shoppers are milling around and moving like huge waves, entering and leaving the various stores; children and dogs get in people's way and make a nuisance of themselves. A woman with three children is bargaining loudly with a store owner, it sounds more like an argument than a transaction; passers-by stop and look for a moment, then walk away. It's everyday business, you look knowledgeable if you bargain, you never accept the asking price. Vendors call you, show you their wares, tell you they have the best merchandise; they invite you to come in and see, very beautiful, very reasonable price, you will like very much, etc. A shopping trip soon becomes a full-scale expedition testing one's patience and self-control. It also tends to last much longer than you had planned. If you don't know for sure what you are looking for, you will fall prey to the all-absorbing atmosphere of the market and will go home with a disparate assortment of objects you will not use in a hundred years. Our friend Arielle once bought two dog dishes she found "absolutely adorable" and went home with them happy as a lark. Only she had no dogs and no cats.

Today I know exactly what I want to buy, there will be no wasting time chatting with vendors. I walk to the fruits and vegetables display, ask for longans, buy a large bag of four pounds and, after paying the toothless grandma who is tending the table, I literally fly to the parking lot and my car. A look at my watch tells me I have time to stop at the pagoda for a conversation with Lord Buddha. I have missed the pagoda. Along the streets and on sidewalks remnants of winter can be seen; the snow that was pure white is now brown and slushy and doesn't look pretty or ready to welcome spring, a mere fortnight away according to the calendar. When quiet rumors of spring take over the town, they also take over our mind and heart, but less quietly. We jump for joy, sing from morning till night, plan a million things to do or to buy; we discover that the trees and plants in our garden look more beautiful today than they did a mere two weeks ago. The shy snowdrops timidly show their heads crowned with their first two leaves, how frail they look. Underneath the thin blanket of snow life is at the starting block, ready to pounce forward. After the many deaths that winter brought us, we, too, are ready to pounce forward to welcome a life renewed. Though the renewal is thousands of years old, it is still new to us and we welcome it year after year as if it were the first. This may very well be our unperceived way of thanking the Universal Creator, we, his otherwise ungrateful creatures.

Inside the pagoda all is quiet and slow, earthly life is taking a break. My incense sticks are lit and placed in a container on the table. I go to my regular spot and, without wasting a minute, close my mind to the outside world to better concentrate on my dialogue with Lord Buddha. Soon I am bathed in peace and serenity, it is as if somebody had come and taken away a great weight from my being, leaving me feeling as light as air; even my breathing has slowed down. If I have often wondered why I could not reach this perfection outside, I know now the reason. It is the presence of Buddha and the peace and love that radiates from him. His peace covers us all, whether we be one person or one hundred; we all feel that the gift is given especially to each one of us directly from him. We receive it humbly and we thank him humbly. Inevitably we are the beggars, we always have something to ask or implore for. But we also come to thank him with gratefulness and humility as we reap the rewards of silent lessons learned in both. He is the teacher and the giver. And I am honored to be his obedient servant. He is kind and gentle, he does not force us to come on Sundays under threat of ending up in some hell. He does not demand money or donations from us, and he does not terrorize us with the fires of purgatory. Yet he is more present and more respected than many priests or pastors or rabbis. He is simply Lord Buddha. Bowing to him now, I leave by the side door, closer to my car parked outside.

As I was about to open the car door, I hear, "Miss Luens, Miss Luens, please wait!" Who on earth calls me Miss Luens? I turn around and see a man running towards me from the pagoda's main entrance.

"Please forgive me for bothering you… I am Francis Ratzavunnag… we met in a parking lot not long ago…" he says breathlessly.

"Slow down, Mister, or you will stop breathing for good. Did you really have to run so fast? I have longans, would you like some to quench your thirst and control your heartbeat?" I look at him and see that his heartbeat is already under control, he smiles; suddenly I recognize him, the man who dared sneeze inside the pagoda weeks – or months – ago.

"It's very nice to see you again, Miss Luens. I was praying in the pagoda, we must have been in there at the same time and didn't see each other." And with a very impish smile, he adds, "I didn't sneeze this time."

"It's a plus for you then. And my name is Raphaëlle. It's almost lunch time and my Aunt is expecting me, I should head home. Have some more longans, and see you around, it's been nice seeing you again."

"Please don't run away, I have an idea. Would you have lunch with me? I have a mobile phone, you could call your Aunt and apologize... that is if you'll have lunch with me, of course." Seeing my hesitation, he adds, "Please, Raphaëlle?"

Oh wow! Has he been to a charm school for men, I wonder? He knows what to say and when to say it. All right, I'll have lunch with him.

"It's very kind of you, I accept the invitation; where do we go?"

"How about the Golden Lotus?"

"That's your favorite place, isn't it?"

"You remembered! Do you like the place?"

"You did not remember! That's one minus for you."

"Please punish me for forgetting, I'll do everything under the sun to be forgiven."

"Careful what you ask for, Mister."

"My name is Francis, you are most welcome to use it."

"All right, Francis, let's go. You take the lead, I'll follow. First, help me call my Aunt, I have never used a mobile phone before."

Sunday. Lunch time. The Golden Lotus. The supervised parking lot has turned into a maze of glass and metal forms with hundreds of vehicles nearly touching door to door. I look around and want to leave immediately. Francis stops and comes to my car, "Don't worry, I'll show my special card and the supervisor will help us in two minutes. Follow my car closely, Raphaëlle." For once I'll do what I am told. He was right, his car is now driven away by one attendant who returns and takes my car too. Phew! What a mini ordeal it's been.

"This monkey business has made me very hungry," I say.

"Let's hurry inside where your wish will be my command." Charm school again, Mister?

His mysterious card is working overtime, the waitress miraculously finds us a table near a window and takes us there, smiling and bowing. After we placed our orders, Francis asks for two glasses of wine. I look at him with a question.

"You drink and drive?"

"Only one glass and not a drop more. With food on top, my driving won't be affected. How about you? If you need a chauffeur later, I'll be happy to be him and drive you home. Remember, your wish is my command."

"Put that way, how could I say no, thank you."

The food is always delicious at the Golden Lotus, more so when you are famished. I enjoy baby cuttlefish in curry pâtés while Francis fights with crab legs placed lengthwise on a long platter. I must give him credit, the white wine gets along splendidly with our seafood.

After dessert, the best part of any meal, we move to the Coffee Room and order mocha. Francis drinks his black, I add everything in mine. The waitress also brings a dish with mint candies and places it on our table with a smile and a bow. It is time to unwind and chat.

"How is your Aunt, Raphaëlle?" he asks.

"She is well, thank you. She is alone for lunch today because Maria, our maid, doesn't come on week-ends. I'll make it up to her later, she is so wonderful to me."

"You love your Aunt very much, don't you?"

"Yes, she is my world. Without her I'd be a total orphan. With her and Uncle Chris I am only half an orphan. They are all I have and I love them dearly."

"And nobody can hurt them ever, or else..."

"Absolutely, or else I kill." For a fraction of a second Mrs. Jahe's face appears before my eyes. I quickly chase it away, "Not now, your time will come," my mind whispers.

"Strong and passionate, aren't you. I am sorry for the loss of your parents; were you very little when that happened?"

"Not little, pre-teen. If you don't mind, can we talk about something else? Like who cooks for you, do you live alone, do you like living in Canada, etc?"

"Sorry, I won't talk about it again; I will only listen if and when you wish to talk. I love this country, it is huge and very friendly; I cook for myself, although "cook" is rather pretentious. A bachelor's cuisine is rarely cordon bleu, but I survive my own cooking and am in perfect health."

"What do you do when you are not working? Do you get bored?"

"Bored, me? Never, I don't have the time. Work keeps me away from my apartment twelve hours a day. When I am not prisoner in my office, I often go and converse with the monks at the pagoda. I learn so much from them. Or I listen to classical music in my little place; I write home to my father and friends. That reminds me I have to buy ricin for my grandmother, she makes ricin oil out of the plant."

"And where do you find the plant?"

"In Oriental pharmacies, there is one two stores away. When ricin is in its natural state, it is the most powerful of poisons, it comes from the castor plant and has to be handled with the greatest care. I have to send the ricin home to Thailand where my grandmother will turn it into a mild and harmless purgative for children. But enough with pharmaceutical talk, tell me about you, your interests, what you like to do in your spare time."

"I was born and raised here. My mother was a Catholic and my father a Buddhist. I was raised between two religions but never really had my own until my Aunt and Uncle took me in when I became an orphan. My Aunt, who is Buddhist, taught me Buddhism and I soon decided it would be my religion. It is now. Aunt travels to Nirvana, I have not yet reached that dimension but I am working hard on it. I like to get busy around our garden as soon as the weather allows it, soon I hope. I am interested in what pains and angers our society. When our friends come and we talk about this, sparks fly and lava flows around. And last but not least, I like an intelligent interlocutor with whom an interesting dialogue can be had. Very invigorating for the brains. Am I hurting your ears yet?"

"Oh, Raphaëlle, it's wonderful and refreshing to hear you talk; my ears are not hurt, they thank you. I almost didn't dare breathe, let alone interrupt you. Society's aches and pains are also on my mind but, up until now, I've had no one interesting or interested enough with whom to discuss them. It seems everybody is too busy to stop, talk and make sense; people run around like lost souls, they have not one moment to think; they exist but do not live is my opinion."

"An opinion I share with you and my Aunt. We have interesting conversations at home sometimes. And also when my friends get together for one occasion or another, there is always some hot subject to discuss; it is intelligent, and intellectual too."

"How come your Aunt is a Buddhist? Your Uncle too? Don't answer if you feel I am prying."

"Not at all. My Aunt embraced Buddhism years ago, before I was born. She was at the time a teacher in Bangkok and she has lived there for decades. My Uncle was already a Buddhist when he met my Aunt. They both lived in Thailand for many years."

"We have one important thing in common, we are Buddhists. I am half Thai and half Irish and I've lived all my life in Thailand until two years ago when I was offered my present position with the Thai Consulate. This is only my second winter in this beautiful country. In Thailand there is no snow and no ice; what we have is heat and humidity."

"And leeches and gorgeous orchids, so says my Aunt."

"True. Leeches are used in medicine and orchids are offered to Lord Buddha. These flowers, so ridiculously expensive here, are grown everywhere in Thailand, from the grandest palaces to the humblest straw huts in the countryside. Have you been to Thailand?"

"No, I haven't. I hear everything about it from my Aunt and Uncle. I am sorry to interrupt our chat, but I think it's time for me to go home. Lunch was superb, thank you Francis."

"Shall we meet again to discuss our society's booboos? I'd like that very much."

"Yes, let's. How do we get in touch? Chance encounter at the pagoda?" He smiles and shakes his head.

"No, here I'll give you my phone number, call me any time. If I am in a meeting, make sure to leave a message with my secretary . If you wish, you can give me your phone number too and tell me when it is best to call as I don't want to disturb; it's up to you."

We exchange phone numbers and walk to the parking lot. The supervisor takes us to our cars and hands over our keys.

"Goodbye for now. Thank you, Francis, for a very pleasant afternoon."

"The pleasure is all mine. See you soon, Raphaëlle. Give my respect to your Aunt."

The drive home is intentionally slow, I need to process everything I heard and saw this morning, to tidy up things in my head, it keeps headaches away. Francis is nice, very polite and friendly. His conversation is interesting and intelligent. What was that with the special card? Who is he? What position does he hold at the Consulate? He couldn't be a Thai prince… princes don't need to work, least of all overseas. If he is Thai and Irish, then he is Eurasian. What else do I need to know? Lots. Maybe if and when we meet again, we'll talk more and reveal more. For now I am content with the knowledge that he is Buddhist, one of us, one faith. And in my book that's a huge plus.

Our driveway is free of snow, the asphalt is showing. What a difference after so many months of whiteness. The lawn has a strange look of green, brown and white, it is in the process of cleaning up the remnants of winter. The pine trees have shaken all the snow off their branches and now show the majestic dark green that makes Aunt and me so proud.

"Welcome home, sweet Raffee," Aunt Sumika greets me.

"Sorry I didn't have lunch with you, Auntie, but I did buy a large bag of longans. We are going to have a longan orgy this evening, are you game?"

"When there are longans, all is permitted. Sit down and tell me about your morning –if you wish."

"After a stop at the pagoda, I ran into somebody we met not long ago."

"Who was it?"

"Mr. Rats Away."

"Ha! Who? Who do you mean?"

"Mr. Rats Away, the sneezer at the pagoda… do you remember?"

Aunt bursts into loud laughing and shakes her head as she laughs; I swear I haven't seen her laugh so much in years. I look at her, surprised, not believing. All I can do is wait till she stops.

"Oh, Raffee, you are impossible and impossibly funny. His name is Francis Ratzavunnag, very much a Thai name. I hope he never finds out what you called him just now."

"It's not so bad if he can really keep rats away from people..."

"Oh no, stop it or I'll get a headache from laughing too much. Let's relax for a minute, then if you want, you'll tell me more."

"Have some longans, Auntie, no rats have been near them, I promise. Look in the bag, there are a few missing because I gave them to Francis to help him regain his normal breathing."

"Was he out of breath? What happened?"

"He saw me ready to leave the pagoda and decided to run a marathon to stop me. He called me "Miss Luens!" He was breathless, so I offered him the only thing I had in the car: longans. While he was chewing them, his breathing returned to normal. We talked and he invited me for lunch. He helped me call you on his mobile phone, you know I've never touched that gadget before and didn't know how to use it. We went to his favorite place, the Golden Lotus. We talked some more. You know, he has a priority card and uses it to obtain...well, priority, such as parking privilege, best table in the restaurant and the Coffee Room."

"The card is very important for sure, but what is much more important is how he used it. Arrogant? Loud? Demanding?"

"Not at all, Auntie, he used his card only twice and very discreetly. I am sure not many people, if any, noticed. I didn't dare ask him about it, but I was rather impressed. Who get such card, Aunt?"

"Only people in high places. Francis must hold an important position at the Consulate."

"He is Buddhist, his father is Thai and his mother Irish. This is only his second winter here. Like me, he is interested in society's maladies; he likes classical music and he also told me something I've never thought about before: Auntie, he goes to the pagoda and chats with the monks. Is this possible? We almost never see a monk when we are there, where are they? And do they really have time to talk with visitors?"

"He is Buddhist, he is one of us, same religious family, same faith; it is wonderful to know such a person outside our close family. Yes, the monks give time to those who seek private conversations with them; monks speak to men, nuns to women. A number of monks live in the back of the pagoda. Nuns have separate lodgings and they, too, give time to those who need to see them in private. You see, our Buddhism is discreet and humble, not loud and ostentatious like its westernized version. Looks like Francis practices true Buddhism, his father has raised him well. Will you see him again?"

"If he calls, yes I will. It is interesting to talk and listen to him. And he likes longans too."

"I don't know many people who don't like them; that's why it was a good idea when you decided to run to Chinatown on a Sunday to buy them before the crowds empty the stores. Between the two of us they won't last long either, they are so easy to eat and the taste is like heaven. Too bad they don't grow here and have to be imported."

"I bet they grow everywhere in Asia. Francis also said that leeches were used in medicine and orchids offered to Lord Buddha. Who on earth wants to handle leeches? And in medicine? Do they make pills or tablets out of them and have people swallow them? The thought is so repulsive."

"You think that is repulsive? Wait till I tell you how leeches are used, you may have nightmares tonight. They are used as special cupping glasses to suck out patients' blood. The patient lies on his stomach, the leeches are placed on his back and start their job right away. When they become full and dark red with the patient's blood, they are removed, leaving tiny marks on the skin. The nurse cleans and disinfects the marks and the patient can go home until the next visit. When I lived in Thailand I used to call leeches 'creatures from hell'."

"Absolutely nightmarish. I don't ever want to see a leech. Where do they live so I won't go there?"

"They are invisible until they find your leg or arm and stick themselves there to start sucking your blood. Once blood gets into them, they become larger and can be seen with the naked eye, and the sight inspires terror and nausea. They swarm by the thousands in stagnant waters and in rivers. They were everywhere in Thailand, especially when monsoon rains stay stagnant in one place for an hour or so. You don't want to step in any of those puddles, believe me. I used to wear rubber boots to walk on the grass in the garden and around our house after a downpour. Uncle Chris didn't like them either. One of his agents once came back to the office with an enormous leech black with blood and wiggling on his foot. The beast had been stuck there for a while and the man begged for help to remove it. Know what your Uncle did? He took a lit cigarette from one of the employees and literally barbecued the leech; it fell off the foot, the agent sighed with relief, the employee threw his cigarette away and simply lit another."

"Well, a leech is certainly not an animal I wish to protect. They can stay for ever in their puddles, I'll never disturb them. Orchids are offered to Lord Buddha?"

"Yes, the most beautiful orchids are raised in Thailand, that's a well known fact. When you visit the magnificent Wat Arun (or Temple of Dawn), you cannot believe your eyes how beautiful and exquisitely arranged orchids are near the central altar. It is a picture that remains in your memory for a long, long time. I know, I remember it as if I were there last week. Uncle Chris wanted to raise orchids on our huge property, but the work involved was more than he bargained for. So we settled for gardenias and had great success with them. They are still my favorite flower. The gardenia is called 'Dream Flower' because it is said that one sniff of their incredible fragrance will take you miles away into dreamland where you can dream the most beautiful dreams without being interrupted."

"How fascinating and dream-inspiring. Thank you, Auntie. Maybe Francis will, miraculously, buy me a gardenia if we meet again. How about dinner now followed by longans galore?"

"I am game, thank you, sweetie, for buying them today."

THIRTEEN

YESTERDAY during my work at the mansion, I kept thinking of what Francis said about ricin and I decided I would find out more about the plant. But how to find out more without inviting questions and, perhaps, even suspicions? Surely an Asian pharmacist will raise his eyebrows when a Caucasian woman – young on top of that – enters his store and asks about ricin. Will he believe me if I tell him it is to make ricin oil purgative? Or will he sell anything the customer wants in order to feed his cash register? As I found no answers to my questions, I decided it would be too embarrassing to go to an Asian drugstore alone and much wiser to go with Francis whenever the occasion arose. Which means waiting for the occasion to come up. Time involved when I am so anxious to accomplish my mission. When Mrs. Jahe said that the man who raped and killed a high school girl last week should be sentenced to death, I felt the hair on my head raise, my heart began a marathon of its own and I found it extremely difficult to control myself. But control I did and I told her she was right, that anybody who kills somebody should die. With one exception: self-defense. She had the audacity to agree with me. Has she forgotten? It was no self-defense when she decided to kill Neil slowly, it was malice at its worst and premeditation at its best. She succeeded, didn't she?

When Neil died, Aunt Sumi was still living in Thailand, patiently waiting for the end of the pledge they took many years before. At the end of the pledge they were to meet again and be united for ever; the end of their pledge would have been the peak, the culmination of years of waiting. Did Mrs. Jahe somehow find out about this pledge and hated it? Why did she kill Neil? There are questions I want so much to ask my Aunt, but I am too afraid of stabbing her again and again where it hurts her the most: her heart. I fear the mere mention of Neil would throw her back into the hell of despair. From the moment she learned of his death, the light of life left her and has not returned. Although our home is the picture of happiness, I know deep within myself that Aunt is missing Neil, her heart has never stopped bleeding and she does not understand why the cruel blow was delivered. I also have the strong feeling that once the killer has disappeared from the face of this earth, my Aunt will begin to heal and life will again reside in her eyes. I want this very much to happen before my Uncle returns. Because we don't know when this will be,

I must be ready to act without delay. All these thoughts and questions kept me company yesterday.

When I came home for lunch, Aunt Sumi was not in. Maria heard me calling and came quickly to the dining room.

"Your Aunt got a phone call and left in a hurry."

"Did she say who called?"

"Not to me, but I heard her say 'I'll be right over, Walter'."

"So it was Walter. I am calling him right now. Thank you Maria."

While my call was put on hold, I ate whatever I found on the table, I was famished.

"Hello, hello, Raphaëlle?" the phone said.

"Walter?"

"No, it's me the old secretary; there was an emergency at the women's shelter, Walter is there now. Would you like to leave a message? He'll return to the office as soon as the crisis is over."

"No, I am going to the shelter to help, thank you."

After a sad goodbye to an untouched lunch, I put wings on my car and flew to the shelter, some distance from home. At the gate, I saw Aunt's car and parked mine next to it. The shelter is located far away from the downtown core to better protect its occupants from drunk and violent husbands or partners.

The women who come here are always in desperate condition, horribly beaten by their men. They arrive with children in tow, dirty, smelly, rude and undisciplined. They swear and curse and do not seem to mind their embarrassing odor. When the women are too badly hurt and cannot stand up or speak, the attendants take them to the infirmary and direct the children to the main reception room where they can have food and drink and where the guard on duty tells them the same thing over and over, "And behave yourselves or else." George is sixty years old, a huge man with gray hair, bulging biceps and a stentorian voice that can be heard two corridors away in the attached garage turned kitchen. He used to be a security guard for an insurance company downtown. His job at the shelter is not too different from his former job, only, as he says, "Now I guard the little ones."

Today's emergency concerns a middle-aged woman who was brought in by kind neighbours in an incredible state. Her face has an uncertain shape, it has been smashed and dry blood covers half of it from the forehead to the chin. All she could say was, "Husband did, husband hurt." Walter was called immediately by Helen, the old secretary. The police were alerted and are out looking for the husband. Aunt Sumi left home before I arrived and neither of us had had any lunch at all. She is looking after the babies in the nursery while the attending nurse runs to the emergency room of the infirmary. I will take over George's duties when he goes out to have his lunch. If any of his "little ones" misbehave, I will use the strident whistle I have in my purse, the sound of which is guaranteed to lift their bottoms off their "little" chairs; and when their eyes meet mine, the message will be clear, "Watch it, kiddo, I am not as patient as George."

"Hello Raffee, thank you for coming, we are so badly under-staffed, it's a miracle that this place is functioning at all. Your Aunt was the first to arrive, I called you but you weren't home. How did you know where to find your Aunt and me?" Walter greets me.

"My friend Sherlock Holmes helped! It doesn't matter, I'm here to help, make me help please, as soon as George comes back. I can be here till tonight if necessary."

"You are one in a million, Raffee, thank you a million times. Come see me after George is back. I am waiting for the inspector from General Hospital, we don't know yet whether the woman can be kept here or has to be transferred to the hospital. Apart from this, I would love to do the same face job on the husband's mug if I could find him."

"The police and the law will never let you. They are here to protect scums, all scums. Since we are not scums, we don't have their protection. Right?"

"Right. More on this later, I promise a group discussion. Here comes the inspector, let me resume my marathon." And Walter runs off again.

In the reception room one little boy has climbed on his chair and pretends to sing in a microphone. One blow of my whistle and he is sitting down looking like an angel. I wish I were allowed to smack his bottom, but we live in a society that frowns upon disciplining children and calls it child abuse. If these children are not disciplined now, they will grow up smashing people's faces. The vicious circle goes on and on and taxpayers will pay on and on for facilities such as this one, and for absurdly high police wages. A little girl is crying all alone in one corner of the room, I see her shoulders move slowly up and down. She wears a dress of an uncertain color and her hair is all tangled up. She sniffs and, to my horror, blows her nose into the hem of her dress. I grab a pink candy from the jar on the desk and walk to her.

"Why are you crying, little one? What's your name?"

"Rose and I want my mommy." She says this in one breath making it sound like "RoseandIwantmymommy".

"Rose is a nice name, it means pink and, look, I have a pink candy just for you; take it and enjoy, then we'll chat, all right?"

She nods and her hair moves all together like a bunch of stiff reeds. When did she last have a bath and a shampoo? She doesn't smell of Barbie cologne either. Wretched humanity. And to think that our friend Walter works in this environment; our virulent Walter with the strong opinions helps the human wrecks that are deposited here. He sees the lowest of the low-life specimens around him almost every day. Is this why he is so strong when we discuss human vulnerability? And why he is always ready to fight virulently for the defenseless? He holds a high position in the community and chairs important meetings, yet when the shelter needs extra help, he never says no.

"Was the candy good, Rose?" I ask. She smiles, that's an improvement.

"Where is your mother?" She points to the corridor on the left and I grit my teeth and close my eyes. That's where drunk women are taken to have strong coffee, a wash up and a rest before they are let out to go home. Rose will be here till late afternoon. She was given lunch at eleven o'clock with the other children, the candy is an extra dessert.

I hear whistling, George is back from lunch. I hand over his desk and duty.

"There is a little girl named Rose, she misses her mom, please make her laugh, it will dry the tears. Thanks, George."

Now the question is Where do I find Walter? There are many rooms, doors and corridors. Is he still with the inspector? I knock and open a door hoping to find him. I see Aunt Sumika with a crying baby in her arms; she whispers 'hush' to me and I stay motionless for a while until she places the little bundle back in its crib. The other eight bundles are sound asleep, they look like angels with folded wings. We move to the farthest corner of the room to chat without waking the little ones, and we whisper.

"Walter called for you but you were still at work, so I volunteered. My God, they desperately need extra help here, why doesn't the City do something about it? I am fuming at these conditions; the nurses are overworked, the so-called cleaning staff consists of one woman in her sixties, the secretary is Helen, age seventy; George is the only guard in this building, he can't be on each floor at the same time, etc. This situation is unacceptable, it is bound to explode sooner or later, and I believe it'll be sooner," Aunt says.

"I agree with everything you just said but, Auntie, there is not much we can do, except help out when they send an SOS. Did you see the woman who was brought in today? I wouldn't mind going to jail if I could find the husband and smash his drunken face myself. Walter feels the same way. Were you able to grab anything to eat since you had no lunch at home?"

"Nurse Patricia brought me two large cookies and a huge mug of tea, I thanked her from the bottom of my heart, believe me. And you, did you eat?"

"No. But there are candies in a jar on George's desk; I helped myself to a handful and now I am terribly thirsty. Can I take a drink out of that plastic bottle?"

"Absolutely. The cleaning lady brought it in for me. Everybody does everybody else's work here, the place looks like a busy anthill. What do you do next, Raffee?"

"I have to find Walter, he told me so while I supervised the reception room with all the children. I must go find him now, see you later, Auntie. We'll go home together later."

Walter is in the last room at the very end of the corridor. As I enter, he opens his arms and gives me an extraordinary hug that almost chokes me.

"Whoa! Wanna kill me? Thanks for the hug. Did the inspector order the injured woman to the hospital, or is she still here?"

"She is in the hospital as we speak; a great weight has been lifted off our shoulders. She will probably need plastic surgery to repair her face, but that's between her and the hospital. I have decided to go to City Hall to present and discuss our case, this situation cannot go on, lives will be lost and children will suffer. Thank you so much, Raffee, you have no idea how much your help and your Aunt's is appreciated. On a day like this, to have two pairs of extra hands to help is like a gift sent from heaven. We owe you a big one."

"You don't owe us anything; we would do it again at the first call for help, remember that. It's almost six p.m., are you going home or back to your office?"

"Office until perhaps ten tonight, but don't tell our group, please."

"If you need anything or anyone with regard to your trip to City Hall, you know where to find us, we are still 'one for all and all for one' like in Grade Eight. Don't get exhausted, Walter, you'll need all your energy to face the rabid dogs of City Hall. Take care, bye for now."

Aunt and I arrive home at quarter to seven. Maria has already left for the day. We find a note on a nicely set dining table; there is duck à l'orange in the oven, we need only heat it up for twenty minutes; vegetables are in the microwave, and dessert is in the fridge. We are famished and, while dinner is heating, we quickly freshen up, change clothes and drop together on the sofa in the living room, totally out of life. When one ounce of energy returns to me, I take out a bottle of rosé wine, fill two glasses and rejoin Aunt.

"We definitely need and deserve this today. Santé, Auntie." And we clink our glasses.

"This will go perfectly well with the duck," Aunt says.

"And if we feel like it, we can finish the bottle too as there'll be no driving tonight. What a day!" I sigh.

"And if the wine and the duck have revived us enough, we can sit on the sofa later and talk for hours about today," Aunt suggests.

"I am game, and I don't mean the duck. There is much to say about the shelter. Let's eat and enjoy. Maria is really a wonderful person, look at the table she has set for us."

Duck and Rosé are working wonders on two very hungry souls; chocolate cream pie is the crowning, and finally the curtain falls on our feast. They say you have to move after a big meal, so we move to the sofa in the living room ten steps away from the dining table, lights are dimmed and for a few minutes we welcome a friendly and comfortable silence. An excuse to allow our stomachs to say their thanksgiving. I go to the kitchen and prepare two hot drinks of tea with three drops of dark rum in each. Aunt likes very dark tea with two sugar cubes. After the first sip, tongues are usually eager to chatter.

"The shelter is almost the twin sister of a mad house, how do they function in there? They need at least four more workers on a full-time basis if they want to help all the women and children who come every day," Aunt says.

"I agree completely. Look at today; on top of all the chores the staff are expected to do, there comes an emergency, a serious one. It sent the two nurses scurrying around, one to receive the injured woman and the other to prepare a room and a bed for her. In the meantime there is nobody attending the babies on your floor or the teenage girls on the second floor; and the poor cleaning lady is told to forget her mop and get lunch ready for everybody. This is no way to run a business. So they call for help. Walter, the executive at the main office, has a heart and cannot say no; he calls you and you cannot say no. What a circus I saw when I arrived. You know, I didn't get a chance to eat anything before I went to the shelter, this means that my last meal was breakfast this morning. Thank heavens for George's candies, they were most welcomed."

"There were nine babies in the room and I told Walter I'd look after them as long as I was needed. I didn't have lunch at home either, just two cookies and tea at the shelter. There was much hullabaloo when they brought the injured woman in. Why didn't she go straight to the hospital instead of showing up at the shelter in her condition, I'll never understand," Aunt Sumi sighs.

"And how about the drunk women! A drunk man is an ugly sight, but a drunk woman is hell on earth. And there are too many at the shelter. They are poor, have no money for food or clothes...but they can buy alcohol? Cigarettes? And they have dozens of children? Have they never heard of contraception?"

"What is worse is that the shelter *does* give these women contraceptive pills free of charge. What do they do with them? They sell them to who ever wants to buy them. Then they go home and make more children. Laughing at society is a hobby they enjoy. You can't imagine how angry this makes me, my blood boils and I confess that at times when I look at these women, I say to myself, 'You are filthy parasites, you don't deserve my help'. But I have never said No yet. Strange, isn't it?"

"Not strange, Auntie. Your blood may boil, but your heart knows better, it shows you the way. In the reception room where I took over George's duties, there was a little girl named Rose, she was crying all alone in one corner, the other children just ignored her. When I asked her name and gave her a candy, she said to me in one word 'RoseandIwantmymommy'. I swear the kiddie had had no bath or shampoo for weeks and she smelled really bad. I felt sorry, even sad, but what could I do? And when she pointed to where they took her mother, I shuddered. It was the room for drunk women. Why do these women let themselves fall so low? Don't they like themselves? Don't they see that there is something better for them out there than what they have? Don't they want it? Auntie, is this rotten life a choice they made?"

"You'd be surprised at what these women do. It is totally incomprehensible to me and I will for ever wonder why they do it. A battered woman almost always chooses to return to live with her husband or partner, the wife beater. I am willing to bet that the injured woman who was brought in today will do the same once she is discharged from the hospital. I could scream, it makes me so mad."

"If they do that, it is definitely their choice. If they choose it, it is because they like it and want more of the same treatment; so they return to the table for seconds, thirds, and more. They must be masochists. And masochism is a mental defect, a taste for suffering. When I think that there are hundreds of them out there, all coming to the shelter to have their wounds licked, I grit my teeth in anger. They do this so often, it kills in us all feelings of compassion and pity. They sound like a broken record, 'I'm hurt, my husband did this, please help me.' Why don't we send them away after the third visit? I should mention this to Walter, maybe he can do something."

"If this were feasible, I think the shelter would have done it a long time ago. The place is called Shelter, it is compelled to take in anybody who needs help and care, and refuge. We cannot put a number or a limit on people's suffering. When we are called 'shelter', we do just that, we shelter the needy and the suffering who show up at our door, regardless of how many times they come. They need shelter, we shelter them; they need food, we feed them. They don't pay a penny. You and I and everybody of sound mind and body pay for these parasites who refuse to take care of themselves. You see, Raffee, I am getting angry again."

"Don't worry, Auntie, you are a normal human being and anger is a very normal feeling when we see that we are being taken advantage of by these low-life specimens. I am no angel and I, too, get enraged sometimes. The more so when I know perfectly well that for these women the shelter and the local health authorities have many better things to offer at no cost, things that are almost always rejected. It seems the women don't want a better and healthier life, or food and clothing for them and their families. They are so used to poverty and to being abused and beaten, they take it as being an integral part of their lives. It is extremely difficult to change such bad habits. I think of the children and it is something I can't swallow. Poor little Rose, poor all the others who have done nothing wrong but are bearing the brunt of their mothers' actions Where are these children headed?"

"Some of them will, miraculously, turn out well; others will follow in the footsteps of their parents and eventually end up at shelters' doors. It is a pity to see a human mind go to waste because it has had no food for its brain to grow on. What a strange world we live in."

"When I talked with Walter earlier, he had had enough with the conditions at the shelter and had decided to take on City Hall for more and adequate funding to run the place; more staff to look after the poor wrecks who knock on their door every day of the year. When we left the shelter, Walter went back to his office, there to stay until around ten p.m. He asked me not to tell our group; I guess he doesn't want to show how hard he works. And yet, the shelter is not his job, he is an executive at the main office downtown. Can you believe this is "our" Walter? If he brings his strength of character and virulent opinion to City Hall, maybe, just maybe, he'll get what he wants. What do you think, Auntie?"

"City Hall is a mad place with mad dogs running around. Some of the dogs are rabid, others are plain mad. Walter will need steel muscles and a voice louder than the dogs' bark. He will have to put his foot down and perhaps play dirty."

"Play dirty, Auntie? How?"

"If with a loud voice and bulging muscles he sees nothing coming, all he has to do is throw one name on the table and I can assure you, the atmosphere will change like a live chameleon."

"Oh, I see. Name dropping? I wonder if Walter will use such tactic. He is usually so sure of himself, he wants to win the war by himself, with his own artillery."

"This time he will do it not for himself, but for all the pitiful creatures he sees at the shelter. If he needs our help, he knows where to find us, we'll always be ready to support his efforts."

"Amen. And now I would like to present a motion: Let's go to bed, it is one in the morning. Seconded and carried?"

"Unanimously. Happy dreams, Raffee."

FOURTEEN

THE NEXT DAY when we told Maria where we were and what we did yesterday, she immediately from the kindness of her heart offered to give away to the shelter clothes that her boys no longer wear or want. Aunt and I looked at each other and the same spark touched us: we will start collecting clothes for the shelter; it was a brilliant idea Maria had, we thanked her warmly.

"It's nothing really. In my country and in the village where we lived, there is much poverty and hunger, so help each other was very naturally. If you want, I bring a bag or two and leave in the garage and when you go to shelter you take them with you. If it's all right with you?" she said.

"That's very kind of you, Maria, and it's all right to leave the bags in the garage. We will add our own bags and ask our friends to join in. What a superb idea you had. Thanks a million," Aunt replied.

"A million maybe I no have, but clothes I have many and I will feel happy to help. What sad life the shelter women have."

"A million is a figure of speech here, it means much, very much. Yes, the women who arrive at the shelter are always in horrible condition, abused and beaten. The staff look after them, feed them and treat their wounds. Then they can leave and go home."

"But why they go home? The husband abuse and beat them so bad, they not afraid? Or, excuse me, maybe they like?" Aunt and I looked at each other again. Maria had thoughts that are close to mine, I think I said about the same thing to Auntie last night.

'We don't know, Maria. It is possible that these women have nowhere else to go, no relatives, no friends. And when they have children with them, nobody wants to take them in. They have no choice, so they go back to the man who beats them. They are like the dog who returns to its master regardless of how many more times it's going to be beaten and kicked."

"But surely the government he can help?"

"The government is governed by greed —you know what greed means?" Maria nodded and Aunt continued, "People who work for the government have one thing in mind: money, money by all means, any means. Their pockets have to be filled and heavy with our money. From time to time one of them will play monkey on TV, gesticulate, and say beautiful things that are music to our ears. We agree and applaud. We think 'here is a good man'.

When the program is over, he goes home and returns to what he was before: money famished."

"Why they want so much money? I think they are very well paid already because I see their cars and some drivers, no, er...chauffeurs. When they buy one litre of milk, they pay same as I pay, why they think they need more money? Is there gold in their carton of milk, maybe?"

"There is much worse than that, Maria. For example, when the government wants to install a new door to an office at City Hall, it costs five thousand dollars or more. When we do the same in our house, it costs one hundred and eighty dollars, the job is very well done and the door is of high quality. They pay several millions of dollars for snow removal in one season just for our city , not the suburbs."

"Ah, Dios mio! It gives me headache. Where they get the money? If I know where, I go there too."

"They get it directly from our pockets, all of our pockets, it's called taxes. It is their God, and every year they invent new taxes. We bow our heads down and we pay, pay and pay."

"Why nobody starts a war against the taxes? If we are together, all of us, we fight together and we can win; no more taxes. I think it is now like this: we pay more money and we get less service. Look at the garbage removal, only one per week and they still complain. What they want? No removal but money still comes in their pockets? The government he must be loco (crazy). And last year the garbage removal was on strike for many months; the city became one huge mound of rubbish and smelled so horrible, people got sick. I thought this only happened in Mexico's poorest areas... not here in super modern Canada. Something wrong here?"

"Yes, Maria, something is very wrong. Workers go on strike and cripple the entire city. These workers can be mailmen, street cleaners, airline pilots, teachers, nurses, and many more. Why? Because their unions dictate it, and they worship their unions. As long as there are unions, there will be strikes. That's what you called 'super modern Canada."

"Excuse me, you say 'war ship'... what is war ship?"

"No, it's 'worship', it means they adore their unions."

"All loco, all not free, all prisoners of unions. Unions same as Mafia?"

"No, it's not the same thing." At this point I decided to join in with my contribution.

"Although, Auntie, we can say that they are very close friends. If you look carefully, you will find many affinities between them; you will find strings and string pullers. There is not one unionized worker who would dare disobey his union's orders. We still call our country a democracy, government by the people, etc. You and I know who these people are. They have many strings in their hands and have a great time pulling them at will. They dictate and workers bow. Ambulance drivers on strike? Sick and injured people will die, so what? The workers' union prevails and nobody outside the union can come in to replace the striking workers and, perhaps, save lives. No. Dead bodies must be shown and seen to better strengthen the unions' position and demands."

"You say dead people, Raffee?" Maria wasn't sure she heard right.

"Yes, Maria. Some people will die during a workers' strike. The sad thing is, even if you, Aunt or I want to step in and help, we are not allowed to do so, we would be called scabs. Striking workers would rather let innocent people die than break strike orders. Mind you, not all workers are heartless, some feel very bad about the whole situation, but they are tied up, they have no choice. This is called democracy and Canada wants to teach it to certain other countries, at the cost of our soldiers' lives."

"Sorry, I don't understand how to teach democracia with soldiers' lives," dear Maria asks.

"When our soldiers are sent to far away countries, their mission is to promote peace and bring democracy to all. They get killed by the dozen, the mission lasts many years and nobody ever sees democracy. They die for nothing and at home they are called heroes. You are lucky that Mexico doesn't send her sons and daughters abroad to be killed."

"No, they are killed at home by the drug cartel people, and more than a dozen per day. In my country there are two diseases: poverty and illegal drugs, and no doctors to treat them. So we come here to Canada, my dear husband liked very much here and the boys and me too now." She turned to Aunt and asked, "Can I bring tea for you and Raffee?"

"Yes please, thank you Maria, you're a dear."

"You say 'deer'... it's Bambi in the movies, right?"

"No, it's 'dear' or cara in your language."

"Same sound. Tea comes in five minutes."

Aunt and I couldn't help smiling at Maria's question.

"She has good ears, Auntie. English language has so many "sound-alike" words with totally different meanings."

"They are called homophones. I am sure her three boys know all about them by now. Why, one of them even writes Haiku, which one?"

"It's Raul who also likes to fly kites, remember?"

Maria brought us tea and cookies and returned to the kitchen to start preparing dinner. We are very fond of her and our conversation has endeared her to us even more. Here is a solid woman with a solid head on her shoulders and a heart of gold. So what if her English is not perfect? You don't need to be brilliant in languages to show your true personality and feelings, that's a job done by your brain and your heart; in Maria's case it is a job very well done. Her three boys are excellent students and – is this possible in our century? – models of sons and young men. I remember once when Roberto, the eldest, brought home a 'C' in science. Maria had a quiet talk with him while the other two boys were doing homework in their room. I sat next to Maria and remained as silent as a mummy.

"What happened here? Did you 'go' hooky because teacher is a woman? I want to hear truth only," she said.

"Sometimes I find science boring and I let my mind wander out the window; when tests come, I don't remember much. I prefer maths, you know I am good in maths."

"We are not talking about maths. Today it is science. I am not happy when you bring me a 'C'. You have good brains and good willpower, God gave you brains when you were born and life taught you willpower. God wants you to use them both all the days of your life, especially when something bores you. It is when the going gets tough that you need to use more of your brains and willpower, not so much when the going is smooth and easy. Science bores you? Then the going gets tough and you must immediately use your willpower to listen to your teacher, learn well, and bring home at least a 'B+'. I work hard and I ask my sons to work hard too. The moon I don't want and don't ask for it. Just better grades. So, what will you decide? Learn well, or next time bring home an 'F' and make all of us sad?"

"I am sorry, Mom. I will concentrate more and stop looking out the window when Mrs. Long is teaching. I want to bring you an 'A', I really do. But if I don't reach it, will you accept a 'B'?"

"Are you bargaining with me? A 'B' will be fine IF it has a + stuck to it. You are worth much more than that, Berto. So, be good, work harder, and make us happy. All right?"

"All right, will do, thanks Mom." She smiled, shook her head, and they sealed their agreement with hugs and kisses. Roberto has willpower and from that day on, never brought home another 'C'. I don't know if there were many '+' stuck to his 'Bs', but Maria had not complained about him and science since.

How many teenage boys listen to and obey their mothers nowadays? The number is frightfully small, you would need a magnifier to see it. Teenagers, boys and girls, tend to suffer from short memory syndrome. They have forgotten who pushed them out of the womb and sacrificed a lifetime to care for them from day one. The woman who nursed them, fed them, cleaned their dirty bottoms and changed their soiled diapers. She had to be mother, doctor, friend, confidante, teacher, police, healer of heartsickness. If there ever was a profession requiring all these qualifications and more, motherhood it is. We are given one true mother, the woman who gives us birth, the one who has nurtured us inside her for many months. She is our real mother. To her we owe everything until our last breath because without her we would never have been able to take our first. She is the second life giver, the first being the Universal Creator.

As soon as children reach their teens, they think they are gods and own the world. Mother? What mother? Don't you see I am an adult now and don't need a mother or a father? I can ride a motorbike and drive a car; I can play hooky with my buddies, drink beer or do drugs, and nobody will know. I don't need a mother, I don't need parents, I know everything, I know my rights.

Where do you go when your buddy John The Brute smashes half of your face? To whom do you run? Remember, you don't need your parents, you said so yourself in your know-it-all statement. What do you do now? We all know what you do. Like a dog with its tail between its legs, you run home to Mama. She'll take care of god's booboo and god will feel no shame receiving the care. Suddenly god has become a little child again, desperately needing his mommy.

What if mommy was not there? You would run to your father who would smash the other half of your face to teach you a lesson before taking you to the hospital. And you realized that you could play god only with your mother, not your father. Will the lesson be learned? Not a chance, teenagers are blindly recidivists. They will take years, if not longer, to learn the first of life's lessons. "But I have rights, I know my rights," they say. Yes, you have rights but they come with duties attached. Have you ever heard the word 'duty'? Or does it not exist in teenage kingdom? Have you forgotten the golden rule of your father when he told you, "In my home I am king and I have all the rights. My only duty is to raise you to become an honest man. As long as you live under my roof and eat my food, you have only one thing: duties. You can exercise your rights after you have left my home and can fend for yourself on your own. It's a savage world out there, sonny." Your father was not being mean to you, he only wanted to show you the right way to walk to become a respected adult. He may sound strict, even harsh; it comes not from malice but rather from love because you are his son and he loves you. Smashed face or not.

Maria's boys lost their father and are raised by their mother. She is doing an excellent job and all three are a huge success both in school and out. Alejandro, the middle boy, is the thoughtful type, always ready to help around the house. Sometimes his mother has to tell him to go outside and play and "take" the sun. It seems he wants to replace his father more than do his brothers. When a question comes up and they don't find an answer, they unanimously decide to consult with Raffee. Their call is always well received and I am always happy to help. Aunt Sumi is very fond of them. I am too.

"Are you ready for dinner, Raffee?" she asks.

"Yes, Auntie. What did Maria fix for us?"

"Something very nice, I can tell by the aroma coming from the kitchen."

As soon as dinner is served, Maria takes her leave and we say goodbye, see you tomorrow. Her day is not over, she has another home to care for: her own, with three other mouths to feed.

"Auntie, would it be a good idea to call Walter and ask him about clothing donations? I don't know if it is the shelter's job to provide clothes. Maybe he will know where we should take the bags," I ask.

"Yes, that would be good. At least we wouldn't embarrass the shelter by just showing up with bags of donations. Yes, call Walter and we'll take it from there. I am still amazed at the conversation we had with Maria. The woman can really think, she speaks with logic and sincerity; what she feels she tells without innuendos or double meaning. It is very refreshing."

"Quite unlike our politicians, wouldn't you say?"

"Oh dear, don't mention them while we are eating, they are a rather nauseating crowd. For the life of me I don't understand why they behave the way they do. After all they are human beings like all of us, they have a family, children, pets, friends, etc. Do they behave the same way at home, outside their official quarters?"

"And why do they say such nonsense the moment they hold a microphone or face a camera? For crying out loud, these people are educated, they don't come crawling out of sewers to climb into ministerial chairs. They are expected to do a good job for us, their employers. Instead they talk nonsense and make promises they never keep. They are called public servants... who do they serve?"

"Their pockets, they serve their pockets first and foremost, and the more they have, the more they want. City Hall should be called Octopus Boulevard, there are just too many tentacles reaching out to grab our money. Did you notice how often they invent a tax and slam it down on us? Tax here, tax there, we all have to pay. One of these days they will tax us for the air we breathe. Where are we headed?"

"I don't know where, Auntie, and I am too insignificant to start anything, but if somebody starts a counter-tax movement, I'll be the first to join. It is high time the population made itself heard. Why do we never say anything? Never complain or threaten? Are they the all-powerful ones? Are they holding a sword over our heads like in countries run by dictators? If so, why do we call ourselves a democracy? We should have the freedom to refuse to pay all those exorbitant and unfair taxes. Many small businesses have had to declare bankruptcy and a number of store owners have committed suicide."

"The government has blood on its hands and doesn't care one bit. All it wants is money, more money. The more money they take, the more misery we see around us. Entire families are evicted from their homes because they can no longer pay rent. Children stand and beg on crowded sidewalks when there are no policemen in sight. All of us are sick and tired of this situation, we look up to the heavens, we sigh and we do nothing."

"I am sure somebody will do something, this state of affairs cannot go on for ever. It is like the animal world where animals are abused and beaten; one day there will be an animal revolution. It will be the same with overly taxed people, they will revolt. I know I am right, Auntie, just wait and see."

"I know you are right in your thinking, but I wonder if there will be one of us out there brave enough to start a much needed revolution."

"Remember the French Bastille Day? Ah, those were courageous people! They thrashed a system they hated, and it stayed thrashed for good. Crowned heads never returned to full power, monarchy was abolished and people took into their hands the future of their country. Why can't we, the people, do the same?"

"Why indeed. All I know is that when it's time for elections, we the people will show them the abusers how we feel and what we want."

"Yeah, and the newly elected people will soon drag us down into a new tax pit. Auntie, we can't trust any of them. I suggest we stop voting, pure and simple."

"And I suggest we turn in ballots with this mention 'No more taxes'. Serve them right."

"Good idea. Maybe we can have a discussion with our group of friends and spread the word. I am sure Gosh Josh will jump on the wagon right away."

"And he will say, 'Gosh! What a good idea,' too. We laugh at dear Josh's trademark interjection.

After we have cleared the dining table, Aunt and I don a warm sweater each and dare to sit on the patio. Spring is still a newborn, not yet very warm, but the evening is so peaceful and gentle, we cannot resist the call to keep it company outside. Soon the first stars are winking at us, I try to count them but quickly lose count, there are just too many of them. A shooting star zips by and disappears in the depth of heavens.

"Did you make a wish, Auntie? When we see a shooting star we are supposed to make a wish quickly before it vanishes. When I was little, I was always too slow and could never say my wish. And when the star went away without my wish, I would cry. Dad always said, "It'll be for next time, there are millions of shooting stars up there, honey'."

"You know that you can talk to the stars, all the stars. Among them there is one very special, it is the star of a beloved departed person. Because there are so many stars up there and they all look alike, all you have to do is look into the night sky and think of your beloved, tell the stars your feelings, your thoughts, your longings, and your message will be delivered to the one you love; it never fails."

"What if you don't have a beloved one up there?"

"Then you are lucky because he is still alive somewhere on earth. If you still talk to the stars, they will hear you and, with time, they will send one who will become your beloved. Patience is the golden word here."

"Oh, Auntie, I am not impatient to find my beloved, believe me. I like my life as it is now and I don't feel like changing at all. Are you talking to someone special up there?" She remains silent, I'll respect her silence and won't push. This very silence is answer enough to my question. What comes next belongs to her. I can only wait and hope with flutters in the area of my heart and eyes that are beginning to burn.

"Yes, sweetheart, there is someone special up there looking down at me and talking to me. Someone I will love till the end of time."

"It is Neil, isn't it? You told me a little about him some time ago. It is so unfair that he died and left you suffering so much. What ever became of the person who killed him?"

"Oh she is very much alive. It is always the same, you see, the good ones are taken too soon and the perpetrators go on living as if nothing happened. Life is very strange and very cruel, you don't always understand the blows it hits you with. Life is dog's vomit."

"Please, Auntie, let go, don't allow sadness and bitterness to get the better of you. One of these days Neil's killer will disappear from the face of this earth. And with her your sorrow and despair; you will again embrace life and not insult it. It is the law of life, you kill an innocent being, you will pay sooner or later. Neil was an innocent being, his killer will die, there is nothing we can do about it, is there?"

"Is it my angel of revenge speaking?"

"Maybe yes, maybe no. Let's say good night and happy dreams for now, Auntie. I love you and I make it my duty to bring joy back into your life."

FIFTEEN

IF STARS do talk to us, I want to prepare a list of subjects to discuss. And if they really help us, perhaps I can ask them to show me the path I must follow to bring joy back into Aunt Sumika's life. The sooner, the better, as we don't know when Uncle will return. Mrs. Jahe must vanish from this earth and I must make it happen. How and when? I am still locked in a box of dark clouds hermetically closed with not even a hole to let in a speck of light from outside to direct my steps. All I have at this time is feeling, knowledge, and determination. I deeply feel the injustice done my Aunt; I know that she will erase all sorrow when the cause of the sorrow is erased; and I am determined to make my Aunt happy again. Why, I am even ambitious, I want to do it before my Uncle comes back from his religious retreat abroad. So help me, Spirits.

Watching Aunt watch the night sky yesterday hurt my heart so much, the pain felt almost physical. She was so intent in her dialogue with him in the beyond, I kept my breathing in check as I didn't want to intrude on her private conversation or distract her with even a single sigh, silent as it would have been. The moment belonged to her, I was then an outsider. Can a human being love this much? Suffer this much? Why was she the chosen victim? Why is the killer allowed to live a normal life? If I am to bring joy back to Aunt, it is my duty to erase the cause of her sorrow; there is no other way. I am willing to try anything. With the exception of a fishing line because it requires too much strength to decapitate a person, and the sight would be too gory. I much prefer a quieter way (I almost said 'a gentler' way). Something as silent as a python swallowing its prey without hurry.

As long as Aunt knows that the killer is alive, she will not forget the cruel blow; she won't be able to let go of her sadness, her despair. The injustice is hurting her every day of her life, the loss is more than she can take. And though it's been years since Neil died, her pain is the same today as it was then: unbearable. When she looks at the stars and remains motionless, almost not breathing, I know she is hurting and communicating with him; the moment is sacred and her soul has left earth. Sitting next to her, I become non-existent, I am as meaningless as a speck of dust. How I wish to know what they are saying to each other. I look at the stars too, but they won't tell me a thing, except 'Stay out of it and let them unite their love in peace, you don't understand.' No, I don't understand, that's why I am asking you to help me. If I understood, perhaps I could better help her bear her sorrow. You who have millions of years of wisdom, why don't you tell me and explain to me? 'Because what they are saying to each other is private, it belongs to them alone. You have no right to step in, we have no right to speak out. What you can do is remain silent and talk to your soul.'

So, instead of asking more questions and begging for help from the stars, I take my soul by the hand, we sit on the chair next to Aunt Sumi and start a silent dialogue.

"Tell me, Soul, why doesn't she eradicate that painful past? It has been so long, so many years."

"When you love deeply, you hurt deeply."

"Do you mean to say that my Aunt doesn't love my Uncle deeply?"

"It's not what I mean. Your Aunt and Uncle love each other very much, their love is sincere and beautiful."

"How can she love Uncle so much and at the same time worship Neil?"

"One is alive, the other is dead. The spirit of the dead is stronger and, when it is the spirit of your beloved, it comes back to visit with you the moment you call it. In the spirit world there is no time or hour, or days. We, spirits, look after the humans assigned to us, we come when called, we help when help is needed, and we answer questions when we are allowed to answer them."

"Does my Uncle know all this?"

"Yes, and more. Your Uncle is a very deep thinking man; very often he doesn't need to see to know what is going on, his soul already knows and communicates with him. He loves your Aunt deeply."

"Then why did he decide to take such a long retreat away from her?"

"He didn't decide, Lord Buddha called him. Before your Uncle met your Aunt, he was prepared to become a Buddhist monk and live a monk's life in poverty and peace."

"How did he know he was called?"

"His spirit conveyed the message to him. He is very much in tune with his soul and the world beyond; when he reaches Nirvana, it is the highest and most beautiful of all, a dimension rarely attained by others. Your Uncle is protected by Lord Buddha himself, a distinction not granted to all."

"When he comes back, will life be as it was before?"

"Life will be as sweet as before because during his absence, your Aunt and Uncle have remained in touch through their souls, they have not been separated; nothing has changed."

"Will I be permitted to call you again when I need to talk silently?"

"Yes, any time, day or night. I am your soul."

"Thank you, Soul. Oh, another thing: Will you help me to dispose of Neil's killer?"

"Yes, when the time comes. You will have to be extremely careful."

"Thank you a million times. I will be very careful." It is wonderful to have such an understanding and helpful soul, I am very grateful.

When Aunt Sumi returned to earth after her visit with Neil and after my own visit with my soul, there was an unusual feeling of deep peace surrounding us. There was no need for words or conversation. We remained silent for a long while until an owl flew past us and hooted gently in the chilly night.

"I love owls, I find them beautiful and fascinating. There is an air of mystery about them. Do you like them, Auntie?" I asked.

"Yes, I do. I admire their big, round eyes, and I love to see the mother owl feed her voracious young."

"Baby birds are always ravenous, they all want to be fed at the same time."

"It's quite a job for the parents to hunt for food and fly back to the nest to feed their young."

"But they all do it well and the babies grow up fast. I would love to be able to converse with the stars as you just did. What should I do?" I was trying to invite her to open up and talk to me of things dear to her and unknown to me.

"First you need to have a beloved one who has left earth and now resides in the firmament among the stars and the spirits of beyond. The link between you and the night sky is the love that unites you still to the departed one. Without such love, there is no link. And without such link, there would be no communication. Between Neil and me the link has existed for many years and will exist until I join him, nothing can break it."

"Do you mean that I can never communicate with the stars as you do?"

"Not the same way I do, but you can converse with your soul and, if you look up in the night sky, your soul will talk to you and even share your words with the other spirits who live up there. You are never alone, for the moment you consult the stars, you have an attentive audience. All it takes is sincerity; your words and your thoughts must come directly from your heart. If something that comes from you is tainted with the tiniest speck of falsehood, the entire firmament will remain mute and you will have no dialogue at all."

"If the link between Neil and you is that strong, does it mean that you love only him? What about Uncle Chris? Don't you love him?"

"Your Uncle and I are very much in love, else why would we marry and stayed married for such a long time? I have loved Neil before I met your Uncle. What Neil and I had was something beyond earth, something called the perfect love, it can happen only once in a lifetime. When Neil died, he took my heart and soul with him because I belong to him and he was my owner. I wanted to die too so I could be with him. Your Uncle saved me, he loves me and I will never leave him."

"Is what you feel for Uncle more gratitude then love per se?"

"Absolutely not. Both my gratitude and love for your Uncle are deep and sincere."

"Then why do you so often leave earth and take off to be with Neil where we cannot reach you?"

"You sound a bit belligerent, honey, but I'll answer you all the same. It is because the spirit of the dead is stronger than the spirit of the living. When it calls, I am there. I will never say No to Neil."

"Why did Uncle go on such a long retreat away from us? Did you quarrel? Are you going to separate?"

"Certainly not! Never. You don't need to worry about it because it won't happen. Take a deep breath of relief, I hear uncertainty in your voice. Your Uncle was called away on a long religious retreat. In the temple where he lives, he prays and meditates every day; he also goes with the other monks to villages near and far where people will give food in return for blessings from Lord Buddha. To give is to receive. He does this every single day, he wears the saffron colored robe of the monks, he is one of them, one hundred per cent one of them. Your Uncle is a good and fervent Buddhist."

"Does he know of your link to Neil's star?"

"He does, he has seen me many times lost in contemplation of the night sky. He has always respected my travels in the beyond. Your Uncle understands a great many things."

"And he is not jealous?"

"Not at all. Sometimes he tells me impishly, 'But I have you here on earth with me, you are alive in my arms and in my heart.' Yes, Raffee, on earth I belong to your Uncle. In the beyond I belong to Neil. Your Uncle is never the cause of my sorrow. If I am so often sad, it is because of the profound injustice done Neil. I cannot accept that he died and left me here. I cannot accept that his killer has never been punished. All these things are boiling in my head and I don't know if they will ever disappear. It's been so long."

"Oh, but they will, Auntie, they will. I only wish I could help you when you feel so bad. What wouldn't I do to make every day a joyful day for you. As a start, I want Neil's killer to die, then I want Uncle to hurry home, and finally I want to celebrate all this with a huge party. In that order, please."

"Raffee, you are a sweetheart. It is getting late and too chilly out here, let's get back inside."

We both shook off the cold that had covered us like an icy blanket and hurried in to the living room. Though I wanted to explore further into Aunt's invisible world, I knew the subject was exhausted. For now.

"Would you like something to drink, Auntie? Something warm and soothing?"

"Both warm and soothing, please. Surprise me."

I brought two mugs of hot tea with a heavy dose of rum, we warmed our hands around the mugs first and then enjoyed the beverage with eyes closed, in delight.

"Thank you, Auntie, for lifting a little of the curtain that was blocking my view of the world beyond earth. I realize how ignorant I am and I hope you will teach me more soon. The stars, I see them, I feel them, but can never touch them. What a pity. I a man falls in love with me, I will order him to bring me a star."

"May as well ask for the moon, Raffee! Stars belong in the sky, they live there and give us light both on our earth and in our souls; they will always be up there if we won't down here. Some day we will be called away, we will leave earth, our souls will soar upwards, the spirits will welcome us and assign us a star, our very own star. That day will be joyful and peaceful."

"You mean the day we die, don't you? Isn't it rather a sad day? A day of everything ending?"

"Most people see it that way; they think death is final, the closing of a book, the ending of everything we know. They make themselves sad and they cry many tears. If only they would dry their eyes and look just a little beyond earth's horizon, allow their inner self to think and feel differently. Little by little they will understand that death is not an end but a beginning; the earthly path has been walked, now there is another path to walk and there our departed begin their new cycle, one that will not end. It is a beginning that will last for ever. I think our departed loved ones are very lucky indeed."

"But we miss them, we think of them all the time, life without them is unbearable. If life on the other side is so peaceful, why don't we put an end to our miserable life on earth?"

"Because suicide will take you straight to the other eternity: hell. And because a true Buddhist respects Buddha's law and will not kill himself; he lives his everyday life on earth until life itself leaves him. When our earthly cycle ends, another begins for us in the beyond. That's where Neil is and that's where I will go when my name is called."

"You are not afraid to die, then? Everybody is afraid of dying, I mean everybody, Auntie."

"You should not, because death does not hurt you, death just takes your heartbeats away and severs the link between you and earth, thus liberating you from what you just called "miserable life". I know, many people are petrified of dying, that's because they have never heard of the other cycle that has been pre-designed for them, where there is only peace and serenity. A good man who has lived an honest life on earth will be rewarded and welcomed by the spirits in the life beyond and he will for ever be happy."

"But, Auntie, once a human has reached his other cycle somewhere out there, can he not return to earth to see his loved ones and to help?"

"No, he cannot. Once he has crossed the bridge and touched the rainbow on the other side, he belongs on the other side and can never touch earth again. He waits there for his loved ones, and we wait here until it's time for us to cross that same bridge and join him. That's why I say that you should not be afraid to die, because death will walk you gently towards the rainbow and you will then know eternal joy and happiness. We can look forward to death while living our everyday lives, but we cannot force death to come."

"What about humans who kill humans, do they reach the rainbow too?"

"That decision will be made only by the highest of all spirits who live in the beyond. There is justice, compassion, and what we call mitigating circumstances. All will be judged before they set foot on that bridge, and no evil will be allowed in the spirit world. We, Buddhists, trust Highest Spirit and deeply respect him."

"Is he higher than Lord Buddha?"

"Yes, he is. He gives orders to his servant Buddha and to all the other spirits. In Thailand we often hear Buddhist monks sing prayers to Highest Spirit during their walks through villages; I could never catch the words but even today remember well the melody."

"Auntie, why do the monks beg for food when they go from village to village?"

"They don't beg, Raffee, they offer; not food, but blessings from Lord Buddha. The person who bows to the monks and gives food is in fact asking, begging, for blessings. To give is to receive for, what is a bowl of rice compared to spiritual favors?"

"Have you lived in a pagoda among the monks when you were in Thailand?"

"In a pagoda, yes. Among the monks, no. I stayed with the nuns for many months, teetering between life and death. Your Uncle saved me and took me home. We are both deeply grateful to these nuns."

"What happened? Were you in an accident?"

"No. It was severe depression upon learning of Neil's death. I simply didn't want to live any more. But the nuns, and especially your Uncle, wanted me to live and did everything to keep me alive."

"So, Uncle knows everything about Neil?"

"Yes, and he has helped me every step of the way back to good health. It was not long after that when we married. The wedding took place at the same pagoda before two monks who blessed our vows and sent us 'into the world to live happily ever after'. We are happy today as we were then."

"And Neil, wherever he is, is happy for you, or jealous?"

"He is happy that I am happy. Jealousy does not exist in the world beyond; remember, no evil? As much as I love your Uncle, my heart still belongs to Neil and some day he will give it back to me, when we are finally reunited. I live one day at a time, never knowing when my name will be called, but as long as I am on this earth I will truly love your Uncle and make him happy. When love is mixed with gratitude, double happiness is given to the loved one."

"I never thought it was possible to truly love two persons at the same time."

"Don't forget that one is dead, the other alive. In this case it is possible. Love encompasses all boundaries, frontiers, space and time; it knows no obstacles or barriers. True love will always live between the loved ones, whether they are together or separated by the great beyond. Some day, Raffee, you will find true love, I know it for a fact."

"And I know with some regrets that it will not be Fred."

"Not to worry, there is a wide ocean with millions of fish in it, you will find your special one and the rest of your life will begin with him. Until such a time, you can talk to your soul and to the stars in the sky, they will give you their light and make your steps more secure along your earthly path. They have been a great help to me for many years, and I still consult them now and then. It is good that you, your Uncle and I know about this other world; we travel there to obtain our supply of peace and serenity. And it is a pity that people in general choose to ignore this world."

"Probably because they don't see it and so they don't believe. This is such a see-and-believe universe, so much wisdom is wasted because it is unknown to people who choose to be blind. I am so happy that you have accepted to teach me Buddhism, it's been the light of my life ever since. There is so much depth in it, I am learning more each day."

"Your Uncle will be delighted to see you thus transformed when he returns. What did your soul tell you tonight before the stars took over? Answer only if you wish, I don't want to pry."

"Oh it was a very simple conversation from a novice to the residents of the huge celestial palace. I have never before talked to them, so for this first time I was more all ears than all lips. I am sure with time it will become rich with lessons learned, and I can't wait. Speaking of lessons learned, do you think the badly abused woman at the shelter returned to her abusive husband or, hopefully, found another place to live?"

"I sincerely hope she found something else, but I am very afraid she went back to that horrible man. It is a tragedy when a person falls so low and has nowhere to go; a human being who has become a human wreck. To think that in this day and age society still allows it."

"It is not so much society, Auntie, it is our politicians, the powers that be. They choose to close their eyes and bury their heads in the sand. As long as they can gorge themselves on our hard-earned money, they don't see anything else; not the poverty, not the misery, not the hunger. They are another breed of leeches. I am sure this calamity does not exist in pagodas or among the monks. Am I right?"

"Yes sweetheart, you are absolutely right. Monks have no money, no palaces and no greed. They own nothing and demand nothing. Prayers, meditation and helping others are the essence of their life. And what a rich life it is! How many times and how many people have sought to learn from their wisdom; even royalty have consulted them and received guidance. The Buddhist monk is humble, quiet, wise and totally disinterested in money or riches. He is far removed from the political intrigues that plague our daily life. At a pagoda, life knows no calamity."

"Let's send our politicians to a pagoda for six months with no contact with the outside world. Perhaps they will learn one or two valuable lessons."

"I truly doubt it, Raffee. They will learn nothing, their minds are too polluted and their hearts too rotten to allow them to see the slightest sign of goodness and honesty among their human brothers. I am afraid the majority of our politicians are for ever lost. Those who are not yet may need several years at a pagoda to realize how wrong their former life was and start making amends. But we are talking nonsense, there will always be among men abusers of the system and of society. Only within Buddhism do we find the true meaning of peace, love, and understanding."

"Have you been a Buddhist for a long time, Auntie?"

"Yes, very long, long before you were born."

"How long have you known Nirvana?"

"Aha! This has been on your mind all these months, hasn't it? Nirvana is not something we can have because we want to have. It is a special blessing granted by Lord Buddha himself to his most deserving and appreciated servants. To reach Nirvana is to travel out of Earth towards the perfection of Buddha in his own world above and far away from our pathetic world. Nirvana is a place of limitless peace and happiness where we, mortal humans, are allowed to taste eternity if for but a moment. It is that very moment that we seek to hold through prayers and meditation, and service to Lord Buddha."

"It sounds so beautiful and rather difficult to achieve. But I will keep praying and meditating because, first and foremost, I want to be a good servant to Lord Buddha."

"And you will be rewarded ten fold."

"Thank you, Aunt Sumi. I love you very, very much."

SIXTEEN

ALL THE LESSONS received last night from Aunt Sumika will keep me thinking and pondering for weeks. It was an enriching evening under the stars, sitting close to Aunt. She was the giver and I the taker, a very grateful taker. For the longest time ever I have wanted to hear more about her past and about Buddhism. She is a good teacher and yesterday sitting with her on the patio, I became a sponge, drinking in and absorbing every word she uttered and every answer she gave to my neophyte questions. Today I admire her knowledge, wisdom, and patience. Of course I want to hear and to learn more; if it took her all those years to acquire the knowledge that she has today, I can expect to be a student for many more years.

To know that she and my uncle are still in love after more than twenty years of marriage is something illuminating for one who has recently thought she was in love only to discover that it was not love at all. This matter of love is still nebulous to me, I have doubts and more questions about it. Aunt said there was a huge ocean full of fish and that I would find my special one. I hope he is a good swimmer and can take the lead because I am a total novice in this domain. I only know what I want and don't want. If the fish is intelligent enough, we'll have a chance to succeed. If not, he'll be kicked back in his ocean without further ado.

Nirvana. Aunt knew instantly that I've had this on my mind for a long time. Her answers and explanations literally transported me into another world. I realize now how deeply religious she and Uncle are, how close to the world beyond they live. And how difficult it will be for me to achieve their level of religiousness. To be granted Nirvana by Lord Buddha himself is in my opinion the highest reward of all. I am determined to learn, to pray and to meditate as much as I can in the hope of, some day, reaching Nirvana and sharing with Aunt and Uncle this extraterrestrial dimension.

Her love for Neil. It is unfathomable because it is so deep and undying. Neil's death has killed her earthly soul and heart, and ability to think; though she is alive and breathing and lives the normal life of a human being, her thoughts and every heartbeat belong to the other world where her beloved lives. She looks forward to death but will not force death to come. She loves my Uncle and worships Neil at the same time; dual personality? In my humble and limited knowledge of matters of the heart, I confess that I have difficulty comprehending this. I will have many more questions about it as time moves on, but for now I will order myself to accept the fact quietly and to concentrate on finding a way to dispose of Neil's killer; I feel determined and ready to act. All the more so because I now have a partner and a helper in this mission: my Soul.

Stars in the night sky. How beautiful they are; they look so tiny in that immensity, but I know now the power they have. Why, they talk to you, listen to you, give you advice and, if you so ask, they will direct your steps so you can avoid the many traps placed on your path. The link between you and the stars, delicate as it looks because of the distance between you and them, is actually very strong and long lasting. As long as you live, the link will be there, reachable and ready to bring you help and guidance. All you need do is call the stars and establish contact, then pour out your sincere thoughts and questions; they will listen to you and answer you. Somehow they will know how to calm an anguished heart or a worried mind. Trust them, they will never disappoint you, their mission is to take good care of you. There are millions of them up there and you have your very own star among them. I think I am falling in love with all the stars in the firmament, so I solemnly promise to always keep in touch with them.

All these thoughts and recollections occupy my mind as I hasten towards the mansion for another cleaning day before the week-end. Every time I look at Mrs. Jahe, I shudder because it is always the same thought that comes to mind: she killed Neil, she must die. Followed by 'I must find a way'. When I am away from the mansion, the thought bothers me less. But when I see the gates, my head begins to pound, I wonder what the day will bring, what she will say, and most of all I ask myself 'how can she feel so free and so happy?'. Then my feeling of inadequacy intensifies, I am close to giving up everything, and my eyes fill up. But then Aunt's face appears, I see in it kindness and love and generosity. I also see sorrow and despair. This vision soon causes my defeatism to melt away, I feel strong again and more determined. It has to be done.

"Good morning, Raphaëlle, how do you like this gentle spring day?" the lady says when I arrive.

"Good morning, Madame. Spring is a time for rebirth, I like it."

"A family of blue jays has moved in at the back of the house, soon there will be chirping."

"And a lot of noise, they are such loud birds." She laughs, I don't.

As I walk to the large closet to retrieve the tools of my trade, she opens one of the living-room windows to let the sun and the breeze in, and I think 'This breeze will scatter the dust all over the room… what's the point of dusting the furniture?' But I dismiss the thought and start my work as usual by cleaning the small guest washroom on the main floor. She will entertain this week-end and on Monday I'll do the work all over again. One of these days when I've had enough with this menial job and this killer, I will let go of both, one to eternity and the other to whoever is willing to clean a ghost's house.

When I go upstairs to clean the bedrooms and main washroom, I cannot help entering first the room with the brown curtains and the photographs. I feel as if Neil is calling me and the call is insistent enough for me to choose this room to clean first. Silently I tell him about Aunt Sumi, how she feels, how she misses him, how much she loves him. I tell him about the stars in the night sky and how I know now that Aunt talks to his very own star. Though he remains the silent prisoner of a framed photograph, I have the strong feeling that he hears every word I am saying and he is happy that I am saying them to him. My heart aches to see him here and to know that at home someone misses him so very much. I ask him if he wants me to do away with his killer, but my question remains unanswered, proof that I am not yet able to communicate with the spirit of a stranger. All in due time, I tell myself.

"Hello Raphaëlle up there, I am going out, your money is on the kitchen table," Mrs. Jahe calls from the base of the staircase.

"Thank you, Madame," I reply and, before she is tempted to say anything else, I turn the vacuum cleaner on high; this way I can't hear her and she can't hear me. She can go where she pleases and it will please me very much if she has a fatal car crash on the way. A little voice in my head says, "Don't be a coward, don't rely on a third party, do the job yourself, you'll have much more satisfaction'. Ouch! Get the message, Raffee?

After the cleaning is done upstairs, I gather my tools at the top of the stairs to bring them down two at a time. My foot catches on the tear in the carpet and I almost tumble down head first, swearing like a trooper and very angry indeed. Why on this godforsaken earth has she not had it repaired? Is she waiting for an accident to happen? It almost did. She must have the tear repaired, or else... She has a beautiful home with beautiful things everywhere, but she is not a very tidy person. There are half empty glasses of fruit juice lying around on tables and countertops, her metallic coffee pot is full of finger marks, and the tear in the carpet has not been repaired. She is inviting accidents. One of these days she will spill a cup of coffee on the gorgeous light colored carpet in the living-room; I can just picture her face at that moment, but I certainly won't clean the stain when I come. Taking a deep breath, I let my anger fly away slowly.

All the tools are back in the closet and I am ready to leave this beautiful mansion with its prisoner in a framed photograph upstairs. How lonely it must be for him. How long has he been there? And how long must he wait to be liberated? I don't know you, Neil, but I feel very close to you through Aunt Sumi's love for you. Some day we will all be happy together in a better world. I see clouds gathering in the sky; the window in the living-room is still open, I hesitate half a second and decide to close it. Dark clouds herald rain and I am sure the lady doesn't want rain on her beautiful carpet and table, I am doing her a favor here, me the angel of revenge! Too bad I can't share this joke with Aunt Sumi.

The road back to Windoaks is clear of traffic for a long stretch, but past the convenience store I see a crowd and police cars blocking the way. Time to slow down and stop. A yellow tape runs on poles from corner to corner, the intersection is totally closed to traffic; I am not even allowed to try the one small side street that would allow me to rejoin the highway two or three miles from here. I must get home quickly or Aunt will worry sick and think the worst. I don't have a mobile phone and I don't like them. Explain to the policemen? Forget it, they are too busy attending to the body lying in the middle of the road; I see them pumping the heart of the injured person whose face I can't see. In a flash my mind shows me Mrs. Jahe's face but I push it away and the flash vanishes. There are three other cars stopped and drivers have stepped out of them. I am beginning to get angry and very hungry at the same time. All I have in my car is a bottle of water, not even a fruit or a cookie. How long is this chaos going to last? Now the policemen are placing a yellow blanket covering the injured person from head to toe, and the heart pumping has stopped; I know what this means: the injured body is now a corpse, it could not be saved. What a tragedy. I mention this to the woman standing next to me and ask her what happened.

"So the poor man died, eh? How sad. He was hit head-on by the gray car parked along the sidewalk opposite us. His motorcycle flew up but not as high as the man himself who was catapulted towards the lamp on that pole there and then smashed down in the middle of the intersection and did not move. Somebody called for help, I don't have a mobile phone or I'd have called myself, and within minutes the police and an ambulance arrived. Immediately the police asked for witnesses and since I was here first and saw everything, they asked me to stay; the same with the two men standing on your right. We have to remain until all has been cleared. I was on my way back to work but now I'll probably be detained here until late."

I walk towards the gray car and see that the driver is a woman with hair the color of snow. She has opened the door on the driver's side and looks so stunned and shocked, I fear she'll have a heart attack. Older drivers are sometimes – not always – a real threat on the roads, and this may not always be caused by diminished reflexes as it is by the effect of various medications taken. I am afraid this woman will never be allowed to drive again, she has lost her independence for good, her life will change completely. Is she going to be prosecuted for vehicular homicide? Can she live with herself knowing that through her recklessness she has taken the life of an innocent human being? To be faced with this situation at her age must be sheer nightmare, I feel for her. I also feel for the man lying here, dead; a father, a brother, a son, a boyfriend? I know not, but it is certainly a terrible loss. One minute his heart was beating and the next it stopped for ever. Life, our life that we take for granted, clings to such a tiny and weak thread, we could say that it clings to air because in an instant the thread can break and create chaos in one's family. We are such non-entities in this universe although we continually claim our superiority over this or that, here or there, willfully ignoring that we could become corpses within a second or two. Did the Creator make us this way or did we acquire this stupid trait?

I walk back to the woman and we chat a little more until the ambulance takes away the victim and the policemen remove the yellow tapes.

"I guess I can go home now," I say to her.

"But I must stay with the other witnesses. Nice talking to you."

"Nice talking to you too." And I drive slowly away, careful not to pass too close to where the body was lying, it still bothers me.

At home Aunt Sumi had lunch all by herself, wondering and worrying about me. Although I am literally starving, I tell her immediately what happened that detained me so.

"The poor man! Little did he know when he left his home that he would never see it again. If he has a wife and children, my heart goes out to them. How frail we humans are when faced with destiny, there is not one thing we can do once fate has spoken. And yet we never stop boasting and bragging as if we were immortal and nothing could touch us. I hope the dead man is now on the other side of the bridge and has his own star in the sky," Aunt says.

"But what about the woman who caused the accident? What will happen to her now?" I ask.

"She will appear in court and probably lose her licence. I don't think she can invoke any mitigating circumstances, the fact is too clear and simple: she was not paying attention, hit the motorcyclist and killed him."

"Can she say that it was not intentional, it was an accident?"

"When you cause an accident, any accident, tiny or huge, you pay; no ifs or buts about it."

"Can't she be excused on account of her age and white hair?"

"Do you mean to say that older people have the privilege of being excused for taking the life of another human, accident or not?"

"I guess not, that was a silly question. I wouldn't want to be in that woman's shoes right now, she must be scared out of her wits."

"It's a wonder she didn't have a heart attack!"

"Oh but when I looked at her, she had all the signs of one coming up, I didn't stay around though. Sorry you worried about me and had lunch all by yourself. I'll make it up to you and treat you to dinner in town tonight. What do you say, Auntie?"

"It sounds really nice. What food do you have in mind?"

"A big change. We'll dress up and go to a very chic French restaurant on Main Boulevard. We've been in that area only once or twice before, let's do it again."

"Big spender are you, Raffee? What's the occasion?"

"We don't need a special occasion to enjoy fine foods and superior service, and it's spring, everything is reborn, we must join in the celebration of its return."

"So, we'll be two Madames this evening?"

"No, you will be Madame, I will be Mademoiselle."

"Right you are, I forgot my French, shame on me; it is such a beautiful language."

"I am not sure it is beautiful when one of their terms of endearment is 'chou' meaning cabbage. How would you feel if Uncle Chris called you 'my little cabbage'?" Aunt laughs and adds,

"It wouldn't be an endearment at all since he would demote me to a vegetable status. He may as well call me 'my dear aubergine, or darling tomato' for that matter. On the other hand, they have an adorable term for window shopping which they call 'lèche-vitrine' or window licking! How do you like that?"

"Very cute indeed; we'll go window licking downtown one of these days you and I and have a very good time doing it."

Since it is Friday and we won't have dinner at home, we give the rest of the day off to Maria who can certainly use the extra time to do her grocery shopping before going home to feed her boys. Aunt and I relax on the patio and chat about everything and nothing.

"Auntie, I am still disturbed by what I saw at noon, I keep seeing the body covered with the yellow blanket, it's a vision that doesn't seem to want to go away. What is this?"

"It's because you are very sensitive and the event has troubled your sensitivity; you have never before seen a fatal car accident, it is understandable that it bothers you so. But you'll be all right, it'll go away."

Main Boulevard at night looks magical with its many luxurious store windows beautifully decorated and sparkling with bright lights. It is a long boulevard of enchantment where in the evening you don't see many people walking outside; they are all inside the numerous five-star restaurants having the most delicious and finest foods money can buy. Each restaurant competes with the next. They all have a uniformed doorman to usher you in and another uniformed attendant to drive and park your car in the covered parking area. You are treated like VIPs and your hand never reaches in your wallet for a tip because these restaurants consider themselves above tips. It would be improper and frowned upon to give a tip to any of the restaurant's staff. Tips are included in their exorbitant bills. That's why Aunt Sumi called me 'big spender' earlier when I suggested we had dinner here.

We choose a restaurant with a lovely name "Le Bijou" and I give the car key to the uniformed parking attendant. The doorman, dressed in a red uniform with gold buttons and epaulettes, folds in two to greet us and, standing up, shows us the way in with a grand gesture of his right arm and another bow, not as deep as the first one.

An elegant waiter wearing white gloves directs us to our table. We take time to admire the room, the chandeliers, the décor; then, and only then do we reach for the menus to study what is offered tonight. A very muted and soft music is playing, conversation around us is also muted. I am looking at the dresses worn by the other women and nod inconspicuously in appreciation. We are surrounded by good taste and elegance, it'll be a lovely evening. Aunt Sumi deserves to be treated to the best of the best, she has done so much for me. I know she loves fine foods, and when she dresses for a special occasion, she always attracts the admiring look of many men. Uncle Chris is a very lucky man indeed.

"How is your lobster gratin, Auntie?"

"It is out of this world. You may say a lobster is a lobster is a lobster... Not so here, this is heaven on earth, I could kiss the Chef."

"Oh, you wouldn't, Auntie! I'd tell Uncle and you'd have an argument and he'd win for sure. The wine is superb, I must congratulate the head waiter who suggested it."

"How do you like your Pacific salmon?" Aunt asks.

"I love it and the special sauce it is swimming in, I could kiss the Chef too!" We both burst out laughing; the wine is helping too. Yes, the evening will be very enjoyable and the night is still so young, there will be more laughing coming later.

"Top of the evening to you, gorgeous ladies!" a gentleman says as he approaches our table. Who is he to take such liberty? I squint my eyes to see better and breathing stops in my chest: it's Mr. Rats er... it's Francis! How handsome and very elegant he looks, my heart misses a beat, it's never done this before.

"Auntie, it's Francis," I say as he is now standing right in front of us.

"Hello Mr. Ratzavunnag, it is nice to see you again."

"I feel the same way at seeing you and your niece again. Please don't let me disturb your dinner, the food here is too divine. If you will allow me, when you are ready for dessert, please join me and we'll enjoy it together?"

"What a good idea! We'll let you know somehow then."

"Just signal to the waiter, he will direct you to my table; my guests are leaving very soon, I shall sip a coffee in the meantime. Enjoy your dinner." He bows and leaves. I am still speechless and my mind is traveling I know not where.

"Raffee, wake up, what's got into you? You recognized him, didn't you, honey? Was it his extreme elegance that knocked you out?"

"Whoa! Auntie, I don't know what hit me, I almost didn't recognize him, he is so handsome and elegant, we've never seen him dressed so chic. He has guests, he says? Do we want to share his guests?"

"No, he said his guests were leaving. There will be only the three of us. Let's finish our cheese before we signal to the waiter."

"I will call him now to bring me the bill before we join Francis. Unless you want more cheese, Auntie?"

"No, this is just perfect and the Brie is from heaven. Can I share the bill with you, sweetheart?"

"No, Auntie, this is my treat. You worried about me today and you had lunch all alone. I hope I am forgiven."

"It was not your fault, you don't need to apologize. At least I had food while you were famished waiting for the police to open the roads. Thank you for this wonderful dinner."

"Let's go join Francis for dessert, shall we?"

"More food? Can we eat more after what we have just enjoyed?"

"With conversation appetite will quickly return and we'll eat a mountain of dessert, I know it for a fact. Besides, there will be after-dinner drinks and we both love them."

We signal and the waiter kindly takes us to Francis' table.

SEVENTEEN

AT FRANCIS' TABLE we see a red rose in front of two still empty coffee cups. I look at him and thank him with a smile while Aunt Sumi buries her nose in her rose.

"What a kind thing to do, Mr. Ratzavunnag," she says.

"It's my pleasure, Mrs. Luens. Flowers have feelings and appreciate being admired. These are roses, but if I could, I would gladly replace them with gardenias."

"Gardenia is my favorite flower, we had many in our Bangkok garden. They don't grow well in this climate here, it's a pity."

"But if you have a greenhouse, they'll do quite well, even here."

I watch as Francis and Aunt Sumi talk about gardenias and travel towards the same destination: a meeting of their Thai souls. It is wonderful to witness the birth of a friendship. These two have much in common, they will become good friends, to my greatest joy.

A white-gloved waiter brings dessert, three different ones; we don't waste time and put our forks and spoons to work right away. After seafood and French cheese, I find my crème brûlée a delight almost of the gods. Aunt is having a Savoie drowning in raspberry cream, and Francis is enjoying an oversized chocolate éclair. Three sweet teeth at the same table, there is no talking in our corner for the moment. Francis recovers first and starts a friendly dialogue.

"This is a very nice place to dine, the food and the service surpass everyone's expectations. I am happy to run into you today. Raphaëlle, tell me – if you wish – what you've been up to since last we met; have you uncovered new booboos in our society?"

"No, not yet, but I was a few feet away from a dead body today."

"Good heavens! What happened?" I tell him all about the fatal car crash. Aunt Sumi tries to stop me, but Francis looks so interested, it wouldn't be fair to stop.

"How awful and tragic to die so violently. How are you doing now with the after-effect? Are you going to be all right? Sometimes it is difficult to push away the vision."

"I know, I still have it in front of my eyes. You know, it's the first time I've ever been so near a dead person who was alive a mere two minutes before. It is hard to understand how quickly life can end."

"Life ends on earth but immediately begins in the beyond. It is our belief as Buddhists. Please try to think of the new life and let go of the previous one because it has ended." I see Aunt nod very appreciatively.

"Thank you, Francis, it is good thinking and I will keep the thought close to me for comfort. You said earlier that you had guests with you… I hope they didn't leave on our account."

"No, not at all, they had to get ready for their return to Thailand on a late night flight. It is an extremely long trip, they'll be exhausted on arrival." And turning to Aunt, he adds, "You have lived in my country, Mrs. Luens, so Raphaëlle told me. Have you mastered the language?"

"Not mastered, but I understand much of the everyday language, although having been away all these years, I am afraid I've lost most of it. It's the written language that I was never able to conquer, it is so difficult! What other languages do you speak, Mr. Ratzavunnag?"

"Please use my first name, Francis, it's shorter and easier to pronounce, and much less formal. I speak two and a half languages. Two and a half… Seeing Aunt and me stare at him wide-eyed, he explains, "Thai and English first, then some Mandarin."

"Where did you learn Mandarin? In an orchard?" I ask and realize how absurd the second question is. He laughs, but Aunt shakes her head, obviously not approving.

"Raffee is educated but can be quite silly sometimes, don't mind her, Francis," she says.

"Yes, don't mind me, Francis. Your turn, what have you been up to these past few weeks?"

"I've had many talks with the monks at the pagoda, conversations with them are always interesting and uplifting, and every time I've talked with them, I tell myself 'I've learned something today'. What a well of knowledge and wisdom they are. On the business front… but do you really want to hear?"

"If you want to tell, we want to hear."

"For the past week, my guests at dinner tonight have worked with me to try to find the parents, or rather the mother, of two mixed-blood Thai children presently living in a Thai orphanage. The information we have is that the mother is a Canadian who has lived in Northern Thailand for many years and has abandoned her two little girls when she left the country, leaving no forwarding address. Canada is a huge country, our search will take months if not years. We don't even know if the mother still lives here, or if she is even alive. But at the request of the orphanage, we have accepted the mission."

"What about the father?"

"He died of kidney failure waiting for a kidney transplant. The little girls were only five and six years old. After the cremation ceremony, they went with their mother to a small pagoda run by nuns in the country side. They stayed there for several months and one morning the mother vanished, leaving her daughters in the care of the nuns. Not long after, the girls were placed in the orphanage where they are now."

"The poor things," says Aunt Sumi.

"And coward mother," I add.

"It is a sad story for sure. And we don't even know if the mother will accept her children if and when, and ever, we find her. At this early stage of the search it's all shoot in the dark and see where it lands us."

"We don't have many connections in this city, but we have many friends. If you ever need help and it is in our power to help, we will be very happy indeed to assist; just let us know," Aunt offers and I agree wholeheartedly.

"You are very kind, I much appreciate your offer. The monks at the pagoda will also help us, they have discreet ways of finding the truth and, in this case hopefully, the whereabouts of the mother."

"Do you know the names of the girls?" I ask.

"I can only give their first names due to the confidentiality of the case. The older one is Maneeya and the other is Marulee, they are now eleven and ten years old."

"Is the orphanage well run and safe? Are the children in good health? It can get very cold in Northern Thailand. Forgive me for asking these questions, but I have seen too many unhealthy institutions when I lived there a long time ago," Aunt speaks.

"Please don't apologize; it is true, many years ago we did not have the modern medicine and facilities that we have now. Today orphanages and hospitals in Thailand come under the Ministry of Health and Welfare, everything and every place is strictly controlled regularly by experienced and dedicated social workers. These orphans are in good hands."

"That's one good news we are happy to hear. Tell me, if the mother is found but rejects the children, what will happen?" Aunt asks.

"Under the law she must take custody of her daughters or she goes to jail for abandonment of minors, unless she is found mentally unfit by a specialist; in which case the little girls will be handed to Childhood's Help who will find them a foster home."

"I don't trust foster homes," I say.

"As a whole they are all right and children do grow up happy. From time to time there have been problems but these homes are now closely monitored by Childhood's Help and we have not heard of any wrong doing for a while now."

"All the better for these poor children," Aunt Sumi says.

"But, Francis, how are you going to do this search job on top of all your other responsibilities at the Consulate? Aren't you taking too big a bite?" I ask, concerned.

"You are sweet, Raphaëlle; I have helpers in other departments of the Consulate who will do the job and report to me weekly, more often if necessary. I have no idea how long it will take or if we'll be successful, but we have to start as soon as possible for the little girls' sake."

The waiter returns, refills our cups and asks if we would like some more dessert, a drink, anything else. We look at each other, wondering.

"How would you like after-dinner drinks?" Francis offers. What a good idea!

"Oh yes, excellent! May I have a Crème de menthe, please?" I volunteer.

"For me a Curaçao, please." That's Aunt's favorite.

"And for me a Bénédictine." The waiter bows and leaves.

"These drinks will warm our hearts for sure, they are close to divine; especially after a delicious dinner and dessert and most of all in such elegant company as ours," I say, raising a yet invisible glass. Aunt and Francis laugh with glee and sparks in their eyes. This little interlude seems to have lightened up our serious dialogue.

"Mrs. Luens, does Raphaëlle always hit the jackpot when a jackpot is needed? She shows a superior sense of balance between heaviness and lightness of conversation. Good timing too."

"You haven't heard her speak when all our friends are together and a debate takes place about one topic or another. I doubt if any sense of balance shows up then!"

"It's not always true, Auntie. Not when Walter spits fire."

"You have a Spitfire friend?" Francis asks. It's my turn to laugh at Walter being called a Spitfire. I picture him flying in the sky and actually spitting fire at imagined enemy warplanes. Dear Walter with gold in his heart and lava in his words. Aunt Sumi comes to my rescue.

"Our friend Walter is the executive director of the local women's shelter, he has strong opinions and a strong personality. What he says makes good sense, at times he may sound excessively strict, but today's society is in desperate need of strictness. Look at the leniency and weakness of our government and of too many people around us. We are surrounded by degradation and disgrace. What's your opinion, Francis?"

"I agree with you totally and I think a little strictness won't hurt the people of this great nation. If nobody acts now, the situation will degenerate into sheer chaos where anybody can do any harm they want without ever being punished. Total anarchy. That would be a sad day."

"On the other hand, there are good people who get together and fight this new monster. At least they try. Unfortunately as is always the case, evil enjoys majority and victory, and the good people are not noticed, not listened to, discarded into a far corner of the very society they want to help. The circle is vicious, how do we get out of it?" I ask.

"By demanding stricter penalties for law-breakers, thieves, criminals; something like this: you steal a bicycle, you go to jail for one week; you hurt an animal, it's two weeks; you deliberately kill a person, you go lie down for the lethal injection. All this has to take place now or we will all suffer terrible losses," says Francis.

"Unfortunately, Francis, nobody cares anymore. What's worse, murderers will not be put to death and they know it well. That's why many people come to this country to settle their scores by killing their adversaries, knowing full well that their own lives will be saved, even protected by our laws. How do you like that? Our country protects murderers! Wouldn't you say it is an open invitation to kill?" Aunt Sumi is getting angry and caustic, watch out, world! I have to simmer it down a bit.

"Auntie, our country does not welcome murderers. These people come under false pretenses with false papers and once admitted in, they start their quest for revenge; they easily obtain firearms and kill for the most stupid reasons, 'he insulted my mother', 'he *say* I look like a pig', 'he *call* my girlfriend whore', etc. And so they kill. If they were known killers, they would not have been accepted by immigration."

"Don't be so sure about that, honey. Looking the other way is so easy, it even brings lots of money. Immigration workers are not known to be law-abiding and honest, the temptation is just too great in their profession. If we don't hear much about it, it's because their punishment – if caught – is a slap on the wrist and, 'Don't do it again, bad boy or bad girl'. That's strict penalty in their book."

"That's how unfortunately they sometimes let in terrorists, the worst of the worst of mankind's diseases. It happens in my country too," Francis says.

"Then it is a global disease proliferating at great speed and I don't see a remedy, do you, Francis?" Aunt asks.

"I don't either. Or rather I do but dare not mention it." With our eyes we both question him.

"My solution is too explosive and not entirely successful, there would be some who, like the phoenix, would rise again to resume their place in the axis of evil and form new cells."

"So it would be an ongoing fight with no end in sight?" I ask.

"There is an end, we only don't know when or how it will come about. Rest assured, there will be an end to terrorism. It is a disease. Man has conquered and erased diseases before, remember poliomyelitis for example; it no longer exists, it's gone for good. So will terrorism."

"That's an optimistic point of view but, with help from Curaçao, I'll take it as the gospel according to Saint Francis of Thailand," Aunt says with an uncanny smile. He laughs out loud and I join him, but not so loud.

"Mrs. Luens, you make us laugh with such a serious face, I almost took you seriously for a moment there."

"It's the surprise effect, it does the trick and it's not often that my Aunt toys with people's attention in that manner. She really got us, didn't she?"

"And it's very good because laughter makes miracles both physically and mentally. That's why they say it's the best medicine. Have you noticed how after a good, long laugh your body feels relaxed and your mind lighter? No wonder professional comics are paid so much money," says Francis.

"This morning at the scene of the accident, I could have used the service of a professional comic. Everything was against me, I was famished, had no food in my car, the police didn't allow me to drive on home, I didn't know anybody around, couldn't call Aunt on any phone, and then the injured man died there in front of me. An accumulation of negatives, for sure."

"And look at you now, Raphaëlle. You look like a princess, stunning and very elegant. Both your Aunt and you are attracting much attention from the gentlemen around us, don't think I haven't noticed. It makes me feel like a million to be in your company and they are not!"

"Hear! Hear! You sure can talk, Francis. Thank you for the compliment, we are delighted to be here with you and have your full attention to ourselves, not to mention your elegance and good taste," I speak for Aunt and myself.

"Motion seconded and carried," Aunt Sumi says.

The waiter returns and we ask for hot tea to wash away the alcohol and sugar of our liquors, it will make for safe driving later. Speaking of driving...

"Did you hear about the drunk driver who caused a five-car collision on Highway 49? Three people were taken to the nearest hospital and one of them is in critical condition. It happened four days ago early morning," Francis says.

"Was it the one where a child was seriously injured?" asks Aunt.

"The very same. The boy was with his mother and their car was hit in the back by one of the five cars involved. What a pile up it was."

"I bet the drunk driver was not hurt," I say with rising anger.

"And I believe he is the same reckless driver who has been arrested six times before on the same charge: drunkenness. I don't understand why he is still allowed on our roads," says Francis. By now my anger is dark red with sparks jumping in my eyes.

"I'll tell you why, my friend. Because this is Canada, we don't have stiff penalties here. Six times arrested and he continues to give hell to other drivers and to the authorities. He is probably driving without a licence because his was taken away. What is the point of withholding a licence? The driver very soon resumes driving under the influence as usual. This time again he will be arrested, taken to the police station, scolded, fined, and released after a few hours sobering up in a cell. For him it is routine, the same today, tomorrow, next week, what does he care?"

"Until he kills somebody," Aunt declares, frowning.

"Then, what? He'll be offered free lodging and free food for a couple of months. If this happens in the winter, it's a windfall for him, our jails are heated and have the latest comfort, a comfort which many law abiding citizens cannot afford in their own homes. This drunk driver will have everything he needs in his cell."

"Except for what he wants most: freedom and alcohol. He will face a ceiling and four walls for many weeks, and he will drink tap water till he vomits it because the taste is so alien to him," Francis adds.

"Still he is the lucky one. Think of the injured people he sent to hospital, will they make it or will they succumb? Does he care? Absolutely not. All he wants is his bottle of whisky or whatever else he gets drunk with. He is so saturated with alcohol, it has turned his brain into a mop that will never dry and he will never be able to think or feel again. He is no longer human, he has become a big hole where alcohol is poured in twenty-four seven. He doesn't live, he exists. What do we do with such a creature?"

"One thing is certain, we don't want him in our midst or even near by. The Courts must declare him a dangerous offender and lock him up for good. It's the only way to keep him from driving again and perhaps killing somebody next time," Francis answers.

"Problem is, he will be released, will drive again and this time will kill an innocent person to make up for time behind bars and to enjoy the full taste of his new freedom. The vicious circle continues. It makes you wonder what the powers that be have under their skulls in lieu of brain; maybe human waste on the wrong way out settling in comfortably for a long stay. It looks that way anyway, don't be shocked by the comparison," I say as both Aunt and Francis frown.

"You know, Raphaëlle, you'll never qualify for the job of government's

speaker, you would scare the crowds away!" Francis tells me with a very faint
smile.

"That's because the crowds are not used to frank and straight talk, they
have been fed for too long with liars' and hypocrites' discourses, beautiful
words, marvelous promises. Of course they'll run for cover if I ever step on a
podium and reach for a microphone, wouldn't you?"

"Oh, Raffee, you're impossible. Where did you learn to speak your mind
without the slightest embarrassment?" Auntie asks.

"Francis, do you think I am impossible?"

"Your Aunt said it in a very affectionate way and, if I may say so, with a
touch of pride?"

"You are very observant, young man, and you see the invisible. Very
sensitive, indeed. Buddhist training?"

"Yes, Mrs. Luens. My father is a devout Buddhist and has trained me
well. We observe before we speak. When he was offered the post of speaker
for the Thai government a long time ago, he declined; he didn't want to tell
lies and he didn't want anything to do with corruption," Francis says, and
turning to me, he adds, "So you see, Raphaëlle, this problem is rampant in
many countries, not just here. The name of the disease that consumes our
authorities the moment they take office is called corruption, an extremely
contagious condition. Nobody has yet found the cure."

"That's why our present mayoral candidate is so hated by all the other
candidates: he wants to fight corruption! Brave Don Quixote," Aunt says.

"Auntie, this time his adversaries are not windmills but a horde of
screaming and swearing jealous people; they will lose, I am sure. Then after
the final votes are in, let's see some sparks at City Hall! Something like the
First of July, eh?" Now they both laugh out loud. Goodie! I made them laugh
on an "unlaughable" subject.

"Have you been following the mayoral race?" Francis asks me.

"Not very closely but enough to see who does this or says that. It is such a
nonsensical race, sometimes I am embarrassed to see only greed and hypocrisy
in some of the candidates, young and old. To think that most of them believe
people will vote for them is beyond comprehension. If there are this many
nincompoops in our government, where are we headed?"

"Let's hope our one good candidate wins. And may I suggest we head
home now, honey?" Aunt Sumi says.

"Francis, thank you a zillion for an enchanting evening, you're the best,"
I tell him.

"It was more enchanting for me because I had the company of two
gorgeous ladies, not just one. I hope to see you again soon."

"You will, soon, I promise," I say.

"Next time, you will come for dinner at our place," Aunt adds.

"I'll be delighted for sure."

The evening ends on a joyful note as Aunt Sumi and I head home.

EIGHTEEN

WITH SPRING come the rains and when it rains, Chinatown is a jumble of water, umbrellas and dripping gutters. Drivers enjoy drenching pedestrians and pedestrians enjoy swearing at drivers with fists thrust at them and angry words shouted in a language I don't understand. It may be Cantonese or Mandarin, or Vietnamese. It may also be any of several other Oriental languages, this area of the city being the business heart of the Asian community. A woman carrying a child on her hip and an umbrella in her hand pushes people out of her way as she hurries to catch the bus at the next stop, about a hundred feet away. A man pushing a cart is literally drenched from head to toe by a passing truck; he is not a happy camper and explodes in a litany of insults, gesticulating like a puppet. A driver coming behind him impatiently sounds his horn and gets a torrent of insults; as he passes the cart man, he takes a mean pleasure in splashing him all over. Insults versus drenching, four wheels versus two, the rain continues unabated, business carries on, transactions are completed, the beehive is in constant motion. Wet or dry, shopkeepers will never be caught grumbling because of the rain. Or the snow in winter. The keen sense of business shown by members of this community never stops to amaze me. Could it be the secret of their success and wealth? When they first arrived in our country from faraway places, they had almost nothing to their names, except perhaps the strongest will to make it no matter what. They worked hard, made unlimited sacrifices, ate rice and one vegetable at a time; grandmothers made clothes for the entire family; everybody walked miles each day, they did not spend money on transportation because 'you have legs, you walk'; they did not turn down any task demanded of them because 'you have hands, you work'. It is not unusual to see a child of eight or ten minding the store while the parents are busy elsewhere; and don't you try to cheat this little person, he is not easily deceived or frightened and within seconds you would be faced with an angry and menacing adult who would show you the door in a very direct way. There are always adults working in the back of the store, it is team work and business thrives. When the child is relieved of his duties, he goes to the kitchen and does his school work on the table where the family have their meals. Oriental families eat together in a close-knit group; this makes for a strong bonding rarely seen in Caucasian homes.

The father is the indisputable head of the household, on his shoulders rests the welfare of his family. His day begins at four in the morning and seldom ends before eleven at night. The children respect him deeply and would do any chore he assigns to them, even if it encroaches upon their allowed play time. The mother is a priceless helper to her husband, she looks after all his needs and their children's needs, she cleans and cooks and manages the store when the children are in school. Each member of the family is part of a well oiled and functioning machine; together they prosper and succeed. They are very honest people, if they owe you money, they will pay back to the last penny; it is face saving, an extremely important element of Oriental life.

From the coffee shop where I am sitting and waiting for my friend Arielle, I watch Asian life go by, everybody looks preoccupied, busy, and in a hurry. Do they ever take time off? Do they work like this all their life? If so, how long is their life? I will ask Arielle if her mother's family back in Vietnam live and work this way. I know she writes to her many cousins who still live there, it would be interesting to know more about her background. Here she comes now, beautiful as ever, attracting attention from all, males and females. I greet her and we hug.

"Hello Arielle, wonderful to see you, how is everything?"

"Super nice to see you, Raffee, how are you?"

"My horizon is clear. Yours?"

"Clouds. But before we deal with them, let's have some delicious cakes and more coffee. My treat." We order and sit back to wait for the cakes.

"It's brave of you to go out in this weather, but then I know you're a good swimmer," she says.

"Well, the garden needs all this water to give us lovely flowers later. I didn't need to swim much, my car is parked just around the corner. Where is yours?"

"It's part of the clouds, we'll get to that later. Here comes the pick-me-up stuff, let's enjoy!" And I think to myself 'She needs a pick-me-up, something is wrong'.

A bus stops by and lets out a motley crowd of busy workers scurrying left and right, ignoring the heavy rain.

"Would you look at them! How they hurry to their shops. Every one of them has a business and a place to go, and not even a downpour can stop them. What an industrious people they are," Arielle says.

"Yes, I've noticed it too, these men and women seem to live for only one thing: work. If we did the same, we'd be called over-zealous and get no kudos for it. What a different world theirs is. Are you ready to share some of your clouds with me?"

"Yes, thank you. When you've had enough with them, just let me know and I'll stop. My cousin Simone is in the hospital's emergency department. My Mom is with her now."

"Good heavens! What happened? Is she going to be all right?"

"This is a horror story, please control your anger if it shows up. Simone went to see a new doctor at one of the city's walk-in clinics to establish contact and say that she now has her own family doctor. She is not sick, has no health problems whatsoever. But the doctor decided to prescribe a medication for something or another; Simone had no idea what it was for but trusted the doctor and had the prescription filled. She was to take one tablet per month, it was going to keep her bones in good health if she planned on keeping her daily jogging and hiking around the lake. She thought one tablet a month sounded very light and gentle, she would start right away. Remember, she was not sick or ill with anything. So she took one tablet. Soon she began to feel pain from the waist down and complained about it. Very quickly the pain intensified and became unbearable, Simone could no longer stand up or walk, she screamed and her body began to shake uncontrollably. Mom wanted to help her walk a few steps to her bedroom; she stood up and went crashing to the floor straight down, her legs were like cooked spaghetti, they no longer supported her."

"Where were you? Did you help?"

"I was in her bedroom pulling the cover off to let her in. She never made it. Mom cried out, I ran over. Simone was on the floor, not moving, only moaning in pain, she sounded like a wounded animal close to death. The sound was not of this world and I got scared. Mom pointed to the phone, I picked it up and called Emergency. About ten or fifteen minutes later the ambulance arrived, the attendants placed Simone on a stretcher and asked questions. She only moaned, semi-conscious. Mom explained the situation and answered several more questions, then we left in Mom's car and followed the ambulance to the hospital. Simone had lost consciousness and sunk into a coma. I was frantic and Mom was crying. This was two days ago. When I left the hospital just before coming here, she was still comatose."

"Was it because of the medication?"

"We don't know for certain because we are not professionals, but I'll bet a million it is."

"If it is, what are you going to do?"

"First thing, first. We must pray and hope for her recovery. I will take turns with Mom to be near her every day until she opens her eyes again. This has taken a big toll on Mom's energy, I must look after her too and make sure she eats and rests properly."

"Ari, let's go home now, my home. We will talk more with my Aunt, she is full of good ideas and will be happy to help, and I want to stay close to you. Shall we?"

"You're the best, Raffee, thank you."

At home Aunt Sumi leads us to the covered patio where we sit comfortably on the settee with more coffee and small butter cookies from Brittany where the best butter in the world is produced. Arielle tells the story, Aunt listens intently and I become more and more convinced that the doctor has made a terrible mistake. I am also thinking of Andrew, our dear Doctor Kozell; perhaps he can help us find our way in this near total darkness. I cannot believe that a doctor, someone we trust intrinsically, someone who has had years of training and experience, could do something like this and not double check his prescription records. If he had checked, he would have seen the mistake and taken the necessary steps to nip the harm in the bud, and none of this would have happened. Instead, an innocent person is in a coma and a family stricken with fear and deep anxiety. Will Simone make it? Will she die? They say to err is human. We say humans don't have to suffer and die at the hands of the very people whose sacred duty it is to keep us alive and well. If mistake there be, shouldn't there also be retribution?

"My mother is worried sick, she doesn't want to leave the hospital, I had to insist that she go home to eat and rest. We decided to take turns. In about two hours I'll have to take over her duty. Before I came to meet you at the coffee shop I had cooked a meal for her, she only has to heat it up in the microwave oven; then later, she can take a long rest while I stay with Simone," Arielle says.

"Did the doctors at the hospital tell you anything?" Aunt Sumi asks.

"No, they have no time, we are not VIPs. Only the nurses talk to us now and then for a second or two; the hospital staff go through their daily routine, and don't you dare interrupt them, they are knowledgeable and we are not, so, don't bother them."

"This is unacceptable, totally inhuman, how dare they?" Aunt says angrily.

"Oh, they dare, Mrs. Luens. This once highly regarded profession has degenerated into a disgraceful run-of-the-mill job. Dedicated nurses are hard to come by compared to ten years ago when I underwent an appendectomy. How quickly things have changed. And not for the better, I must add." At this point I want to put in my contribution.

"It's worse than that, Ari. Nurses go on strike now! Yes, they stop work when their Union says the word, how do you like that! Do you know how highly they are paid? It is insane, I tell you. The more they have, the more they want."

"That's the bad side of humans, it is called greed."

"It is also a disease that has contaminated almost all workers, especially those who already make a bundle."

"I hope when you are with Simone later you will see an improvement in her condition. Try to find out if it was the medication prescribed by the doctor that is the cause of all this. We may have good grounds for a legal suit. Our friends will help us, I know we can count on them," Aunt says.

"Especially Walter. Do you remember him, Ari?" I ask.

"Yes, I do. He is at the Women's Shelter, isn't he?"

"Not at the shelter. He is the executive director at the main office downtown. He would be a strong ally."

"You two are talking legal suit and ally... what do you intend to do? I am a bit nervous, lawyers are a breed I simply loathe, what are your intentions?"

"Relax, Arielle. We won't do anything until we have proof that the doctor prescribed the wrong medication and until we have your approval," Aunt tells her.

"And then sparks and lava will fly and flow," I add.

"Hold your horses, Raffee, or you will scare Arielle. All in due course, honey. The most important thing right now is for Simone to regain consciousness. If the doctor is proven guilty, he will pay or my name is not Sumika Luens."

"Auntie, can we approach Andrew with this? I am sure he can help," I say.

"I know for sure that he can help, but he won't do it and we won't ask him to."

"Why ever not? He *is* a doctor."

"Precisely. He won't do anything to hurt another doctor. All physicians stick together, they will never let one of their own fall, no matter what. That's why we won't ask Andrew, we like him too much to put him in such an embarrassing situation. But we can ask Walter. So, Arielle, if we have sufficient grounds, do you accept to take action?"

"If you'll be on board with me, then yes I accept. What should I do? I know close to nothing in this domain and may become a burden to you."

"All depends on what Simone tells you when she can talk again. We need to know the name of the medication first of all. Then I can ask Andrew what it is for. After that, things may develop quickly and we may have to brace ourselves if lawyers are to be involved, they can be venomous."

"Auntie, Mr. Rowlands knows many lawyers, maybe he can recommend one who will not bankrupt Arielle's mother."

"That's a thought, but we are not there yet. Don't worry, Ari, we are all in this with you," Aunt says.

"Thank you so very much, you are already making miracles, my morale is up a notch compared to where it was this morning. I should be going to the hospital now."

"I'll drive you, where is your car?"

"Simone's brother borrowed it for a few days. Nobody knew then that a catastrophe was about to hit us, it's hard not to have my car now that I need it most. Hopefully I'll have it back on Sunday."

On our way to the hospital Arielle cries silently, I see tears running down her cheeks. I open the glove compartment and point to the box of tissues.

"It's good to cry, Arielle, it cleanses your eyes, then the tissues will dry them and you'll look gorgeous again," I say.

"Sorry for this show of weakness. It's only that Mom and I are not prepared for such an ordeal; it's the uncertainty about Simone and about what we can or should do; it's about not having my car and imposing on you; it's about too many things crashing down on me. What do I do now?"

"You take a deep breath right now, I want to hear it in and out, twice please. You're not imposing on me, and Aunt and I are ready and more than willing to help you and your Mom. So, stop apologizing. I'll drive you every day to and from the hospital, and don't say No because I won't take it. That's what friends are for, we help each other, don't you forget it. What's the name of Simone's doctor?"

"It's Vivien Pronots, she is at the Vinell Walk-in Clinic; there are four other doctors practicing there."

"Was Simone ill that she needed to see a doctor?"

"No, she is in excellent health. She went to introduce herself to this new doctor because she wanted to have her own family physician. The doctor wanted to see her a second time for a routine consultation after the introduction. That's when she prescribed the goddam medication. Trusting her, Simone took one tablet the same afternoon. Later that evening she began to hurt all over her body, fainted a couple of times, her eyes had something like a veil covering them, she lost the ability to move and when the pain became unbearable, she moaned deep in her throat and sounded like a mortally wounded animal. We couldn't get a word or a reaction out of her. I think she was already drifting into a coma. That's when we called the ambulance. You know the rest. I am physically and mentally exhausted. It's the not-knowing that is gnawing at my sanity." Poor Arielle, I do feel for her.

"Ari, my Aunt and I will pray at our pagoda for you, your mother, and Simone. Already I have an imperceptible feeling that things will improve. And I always trust my feelings. Be brave, and sprinkle a little optimism around on your daily visits to Simone; you will feel better and so will she. Here's the hospital, you want me to go in with you?"

"You don't mind? Mom will like seeing you again, it's been a long time."

A surprise meets us as we enter the room: Simone is awake and whispering to Ari's mother ever so weakly. Ari and I look at each other and her eyes fill up again.

"Stop that, Ari, she must not see you cry. Did you forget the optimism outside? Dry your eyes and go to her, I'll wait my turn. Well, go on!" She hesitates a second or two and then walks towards the bed. I quietly exit and wait outside. The deepest of all sighs leaves my chest and I silently thank Lord Buddha for this miracle. She has come back from the coma, she will improve and recover.

While I wait outside Room 11, I look around me and have the leisure to stop at details otherwise unobserved. There is a vending machine way down the hallway; it probably sells lukewarm water smelling faintly of coffee, something reminiscent of the coffee served at a well-known coffee shop in town. There may also be cookies and donuts, peanuts and other nuts neatly packaged in clear cello paper. How long they have been in the machine is anybody's guess. Along the wall on one side of the hallway there are stretchers lined up waiting to receive patients. And two doors away from the vending machine I see a nurse's desk, unoccupied. I decide to walk around and what I see now alarms me. The walls are dirty, the desk is dusty, there are balls of paper on the floor near the vending machine, and not a basket or can in sight. The vision makes me shudder, I see dirt and filth in a place where the utmost cleanness is required; I am thinking of the patients who are exposed to this. People often say that you go to the hospital to die, not always of your own ailment but of what you catch from all the bacteria that thrive there. There are old bacteria, new bacteria, and lately super-resistant bacteria. It is a troubling thought that these germs may win over the most modern medicine and cost many lives. If such is the case, it would be best for Simone to be discharged quickly and go home.

The door of Room 11 opens and Arielle signals to me to come in. On the table I see two pink roses in a lovely vase. My eyes then turn to Simone. She smiles and I feel my eyes burn.

"How are you doing, Simone?" I ask.

"Not bad to be back with the living," she whispers.

"We are very happy. Mrs. Dowling, my Aunt sends you her warmest greetings, we have thought of you all and prayed for Simone's recovery."

"Very kind of you, thank you. The nurse said Simone can come home tomorrow but, because of the pain, she'll have to take a powerful pain-killer every four hours."

"More tablets or pills to swallow? I am sure she hates it," Ari says, and Simone nods her agreement.

"No, Ari, it is not OR, it is tablets AND pills," she whispers with a grimace of disgust.

"Right now Simone is under the soothing effects of the pill she took half an hour ago. The pains come back about an hour before the next pill is due. That's when she feels the most miserable and helpless and thinks of ending her life. We have to watch her very closely," Mrs. Dowling tells me in an undertone, her lips to my ear.

"Just think, Simone, tomorrow you'll be home in your own bedroom. I am sure you can hardly wait," I say.

"What's the point if I can't move, can't stand up, can't walk? Then a bedroom is a bedroom, is a bedroom here or at home. And why can't I speak normally instead of this whispering?"

"That's only temporary, the nurse said. So, don't worry about it. And we will help you stand up and walk, have no fear. The pains too will disappear gradually. It's only a matter of time, and we have plenty of it, don't we?"

"Thank you for the good pep talk."

"Wait till you see the new bed cover I got you," Arielle says.

"You did? What color?" asks the whispering voice.

"It's a surprise, just get well and come home tomorrow."

"I am very happy everything is better for you. I should go home now and tell my Aunt about it. See you soon and, Simone, keep up the good job," I say to all three.

On my way home I feel the urge to stop at the pagoda. Inside, there is a palpable peace and my heartbeats immediately adjust to the serene rhythm, I breathe in peace and breathe out contentment, tranquility and a deep feeling of gratitude. A life was saved today. Now we must focus on the punishment against the person responsible for Simone's ordeal. I can't do it on my own, we need doctors and lawyers on our side. Aunt Sumi and Mrs. Dowling need to work together, and Simone, Arielle and I will be ready to jump in the moment we are needed. I will contact Walter while Aunt consults with Andrew now that Mrs. Dowling has given her the name of the guilty medication prescribed by the bad doctor. This highly concerted effort will undoubtedly bring positive results. Doctors should never prescribe the wrong medication. If they do so accidentally, they have to pay. The title of physician gives them no right to hurt, indeed kill, anybody who has entrusted them with their health and lives. Doctors should not go unpunished for their mistakes, they are not above the law. We intend to severely punish this Doctor Vivien Pronots who almost caused Simone's death. I am talking to you, Lord Buddha, from my heart, this is how I feel, I am not hiding anything. I am asking you to assist us in this upcoming lawsuit, I don't much trust man's law but I sincerely hope the suit will bring Simone and her family the satisfaction they deserve. And I hope that the bad doctor will be made to pay to her last penny or go to jail, or lose her licence to practice medicine. Justice is needed and you can help bringing it to us. Thank you, Lord Buddha, I am your obedient servant.

I bow respectfully and leave the pagoda. A sense of accomplishment follows me to my car and all the way home.

NINETEEN

AUNT SUMI is on the patio with her breakfast and the newspaper open widely on the table. She looks very intent reading its contents, there must be an interesting article catching her full attention. She doesn't hear me opening the door and starts when she sees me.

"Good morning, Raffee. Did you sleep well, honey?"

"Good morning, Auntie. Sleep was all right, can I have half of your bagel? I'll go get coffee in a minute, do you want some more juice?"

"No, thank you, I am fine. Bring the jar of strawberry jam, please, it is on the dining table."

Our full breakfast is now on the table, nothing is missing. As usual, even before I have a chance to bite into a bagel or anything else, there are a few winged beggars approaching and chirping loudly. If I want to eat in peace I'll have to serve them first, the little rascals. It's done. Now I settle next to Aunt to enjoy the food and welcome a new day. Later I will call Walter and seek his advice. Aunt is back into the newspaper, she is turning to page four now. Curiosity eats me up.

"What's so fascinating in there, Auntie? Your coffee is getting cold."

"There is an incredible story about a Canadian man who left the country with his daughter and wherever he went he introduced her as his wife. The article is very long, I am sorry I've not paid much attention to you. How insensitive of me."

"Don't worry, I'm not quite awake yet. How old is the daughter that she can pass as his wife? What a weird situation. Is he mentally disturbed?"

"Absolutely not. He is a very successful businessman. When his wife divorced him, he took his teenage daughter with him and left on his yacht, destination unknown. They have been sailing around the world, stopping at various ports of call for a few days at a time, meeting people, dining out, living the good life as husband and wife."

"But that's not normal, how can she go along with such a stupid game?"

"It's not a game, honey, it's his way of getting back at the wife who divorced him."

"But isn't the daughter bored with it? Surely she must miss the company of people her age, what does she do all day?"

"The paper says that he has imposed his will on her and she'd better do

157

as told or else. That's why she goes along with the scheme and doesn't utter a word."

"That's not right. A daughter cannot be a wife to her own father, it's totally insane and against the law, isn't it Auntie? He should be institutionalized without further ado."

"You haven't heard the worst, honey. Are you ready? The paper says he has two children with her, his own daughter. It makes me want to vomit."

"I know it's against the law, the father must be prosecuted immediately unless we have reverted to ancient times when incest was an accepted fact of life. I hope they catch him soon."

"He is hiding on his yacht at the moment, anchored in a country that has no extradition law, he is safe."

"How did the newspapers come to know about this?"

"Apparently the daughter managed to escape one night. She took refuge in somebody's home on an island in the Pacific. These people protected her and kept her well hidden. When the father discovered she was gone, he did not loiter and left in a hurry, taking with him the two children. The daughter then contacted her parents in Canada. The police got involved, then the media. And today we have the story in our paper."

"I hope the police get to him before he can harm the children. A man must be mentally sick to do what he did. I mean, his own daughter, for crying out loud. How more bestial can it be? Do you know what penalty our judicial system has for such crime?"

"I don't know, it's the first time we've heard of something this revolting in our city. I hope the man rots in jail until he turns to maggots."

"And I hope the maggots start eating him while he is alive and there is nobody to help him in his cell. Are the children all right or were they born with congenital abnormalities due to inbreeding?"

"That will have to be determined by physicians if the culprit can be caught; nobody knows where he is at this time."

"I don't think he can play the invisible man much longer now that his picture is shown all over the world. What an ordeal for the two children, I feel for them, Auntie."

"He'll be caught, don't worry. The police in many countries are joining forces. He'll be in jail very quickly, I know it."

"And I know for a fact that he won't see the inside of a jail. He is rich and successful, if he pays what the court asks, he'll be free on bail and can just walk out of the courthouse, criminal or not. In other words he buys his freedom, it is part and parcel of our justice system. It makes me really mad when this happens, I feel that the criminal is insulting us and insulting all the police officers who have worked hard to catch him. I don't think it's fair, Auntie."

"No, it is not fair, but it is our system and has been for a very long time. We can really say here that money talks."

"Yes, it talks freedom for the criminals. I hope it will be different in Simone's case and lawyers won't act like sharks in a feeding frenzy. Are you going out today, Aunt?"

Before she can answer, the phone rings and I run inside to the living room to pick it up. It's still early morning, who could it be?

"Hello, Raffee, it's me Andrew. Did I wake you up?"

"Good morning, Andrew; no, you didn't wake me. What's up? Emergency?"

"Not medical. Marilla my receptionist can't come today and my appointment book is full. Do you have a friend who would be willing to step in just for the day? I'd be for ever grateful."

"I'll call Arielle. If she can't do it, I'll come myself. At what time do you start?"

"At nine and the last patient comes in at four thirty."

"I'll call you right back, don't go anywhere."

Aunt questions me with her eyes as I call Arielle. We talk for a few minutes and she agrees to take over Marilla's duties for the day. Andrew thanks me and I go back to the patio.

"That was Andrew. His receptionist can't come today, he needed someone to take over. Arielle will do it. Phew! Talk about quick action! My coffee must be icy cold, I'll get some more, do you want another cup, Auntie?"

"No, honey, no more coffee for me. Come back with yours and we'll talk about today's plans."

Aunt and I are loading her car with the bags of used clothing we have collected for the Women's Shelter. Walter showed us where the warehouse was and told us to ask for Meredith when we go there. Today is the day, we are taking six huge blue plastic bags filled with donations. Maria arrives and exclaims with both hands on her forehead.

"Dios mio! What you doing so early in morning? You work like men with boats at the jetty."

"We are taking the bags of clothing to the Women's Shelter, your donation is in there too, thank you, Maria. The women and their children will be happy."

"Not so sure, because many people are too proud and will be ashamed to wear used clothes. But, it's up to them, right? To wear clothes or go naked, especially in winter."

"Nobody goes naked, Maria, it's against the law."

"But exactly. If they don't obey the law, they go to jail and there, they wear same clothes as all the other inmates: the orange uniform! Ha, ha, ha." We join in her laughing. What a funny line of thought this early in the morning.

"I am sure there will be happy women at the shelter. Their children will have better clothes to wear to school."

"If the clothes ever go home with them. Maybe you don't know, but the women they prefer to sell these garments and get money to buy cigarettes and beer. Sometimes they buy bad drugs too, I see them many times at the open market on Sundays, they show the clothes and hide the drugs. Only the addicts they know which woman sells them."

"How sad if it is the case. We give and give out of kindness and the needy women do that? Why do we give then?"

"We give because we feel for these mothers and their children. And we feel because we have a heart that directs our actions. In your religion you say that to give is to receive, it is beautiful principle. Your god Buddha has very deep thinking."

"Buddha is not god, Maria. He is a creature of God. It is his wisdom and enlightenment that we seek and respect. By the way, we won't be home for lunch and we've already had breakfast."

"What's this? You give me holiday? Thank you very much, I prepare good dinner for tonight."

"Thank you, Maria."

We are off to the warehouse. Aunt is driving, we have to take her car because it has a large trunk to accommodate the huge bags. The warehouse is located a little away from the downtown core but not as far as the shelter. Above the front door a sign says 'Helping Hands'; there is a planter on either side of the door with yellow marigold growing profusely in each, giving the place a touch of cheerfulness. Aunt knocks and the door opens on contact. A woman is sitting at a small desk surrounded by three filing cabinets. We ask for Meredith.

"Hello, I am Meredith, What can I do for you? Did you bring your cards with you? We don't open till ten."

"We've come with bags of donated clothing. Walter, I mean Mr. Hausen, told us to bring them here and to ask for you. Shall we bring the bags in?"

"I am sorry, I thought you were customers and I asked for your cards. We don't open till ten for them. Thank you so much for the donations, let me call Steven, he'll help with the bags. It is so very kind of you, may I get you a cup of tea?"

"No, thank you, but if you don't mind, we'd like to chat with you before the crowds arrive. I am Mrs. Luens and this is my niece Raphaëlle." She shows us the only two other chairs by her desk and we sit down.

"Crowds is the right word. I would also say wave, a human wave taking over this little place. There are only Steven and myself holding the fort today and at times it looks like there is a war going on in here."

"Do you need extra staff?" Aunt asks.

"We are not staff, we are volunteers; we work in teams of two. Today and tomorrow it's Steven and me. Then another team comes in, and another. We close on Sundays. This place used to be a heavy machinery warehouse with a tiny office which we turned into a tiny kitchen; there is one small washroom in the back, we keep it locked on account of the crowds, you can well imagine." We both nod in full agreement. Then we hear voices and children shrieking; Meredith gets up abruptly from her chair and calls Steven.

"Steven, come quick, the tsunami has arrived." I look at the old clock on the wall, it says nine fifty-five. This then must be the first wave hitting the shore.

"Mrs. Luens, be my guest and watch the show, but stay behind my desk, it'll be safer," Meredith says. We waste no time and pin ourselves against the wall behind her desk. A barricade against bodily harm, maybe?

When the clock chimes ten times, Steven opens the door and we witness a stampede of humans of all sizes and colors rushing in as if Satan were on their heels. We can no longer talk, the noise they make is deafening; so we just look around from one person to the next, from one child to another. Clothes that were tidily placed on long tables before ten o'clock are now flying from hand to hand, "This one is too small," "Not my size," "That one does not have pockets, I want pockets for my keys," etc. Parents are too busy to supervise their offspring. Children are running everywhere, hiding behind winter coats that are dangling on hangers, shouting, falling, crying. I see Steven put something in his mouth; he blows his whistle and the strident sound stops the cacophony instantly. He wastes no time.

"If you don't handle the clothes with more care and if your kids don't stop running and knocking down everything, I'll give you two minutes to get out of here empty handed. Is that clear?"

The din resumes but I see less clothes flying around. A child who still wants to play catch-me-if-you-can gets smacked by his mother who pushes him down on the floor in one corner of the room and keeps him down with one hand on his head.

"You move from here and I will show your bottom to everybody before I make it turn red, you hear me?" Aunt and I want to laugh so badly, I have to look at my feet to nip the threatening giggles in the bud. Much as I think it would be funny to see a bare bottom in broad daylight, I am glad the child obeys orders and stays put. All the better for his bottom and his dignity. And I can at last control the stubborn giggles. One woman, half hidden under a mountain or garments walks towards the door. Steven stops her.

"Where do you think you are going with half of our stuff in your arms, Madam?" Meredith joins in.

"You must show me your registration card and stay within the limit assigned to each visitor. Right now you are already over the limit. Show me your card, please."

"Sorry, I forgot it at home, but I really do need these clothes."

"I am sorry, you can't take anything with you until I've seen your card and entered in details the items you are entitled to take this time. If you go home and come back with your card, you can shop again. We are open until six tonight."

"!#!* damn you! You're a bunch of !#!* mistreating us needy. You stink! Here's what you can do with your !#!* stuff." Clothes fly out of her arms and land on the floor, and she leaves fiercely angry. Aunt and I are stunned and speechless at such language and behavior. But the show goes on and Meredith explains,

"This is all in a day's work, our ears are now deaf to the various languages spoken here and we are no longer shocked. These people know full well they have to show us their cards before they leave the building with their bi-monthly selections."

"What type of card is it?" Aunt Sumi asks.

"It has their names and addresses, a registration number, the number of children living at home with them. We match this card with their personal files kept here and make sure they are not taking more than they are allotted every two months. In the winter they can each take a coat, a couple of sweaters, a jacket and boots according to availability. Mothers also shop in the children's department where we even have toys and strollers, it's that little room right after the umbrellas and raincoats."

"You must work really hard to keep this place in good order," I say, not envying her at all.

"We are here at eight-thirty in the morning to repair the previous day's damage. We don't do this at closing time because we would be here till well after nine p.m., very bad when you have a family at home waiting for dinner."

"Have you been physically harmed by some of these nuts?"

"No, thanks to the presence of a male worker or, in this case, Steven my team-mate. We work well together and he doesn't mind making coffee in our microscopic kitchen because I must at all times stay close to the personal files on my desk. We don't want any of them disappearing into thin air or transformed into paper airplanes."

"Your own desk? They wouldn't dare!"

"Oh yes. That's why one of us must be glued to this desk at all times, from ten till six, six days a week."

A little girl in a green dress comes, crying all the tears in her body, her blond curls shaking this way and that.

"What's wrong, young lady? Why the tears? Where's your mommy?" Meredith asks.

"I want a toy and she says No. She is mean, I don't like her."

"If you show me where she is, I'll go talk to her and maybe she'll say yes, all right?" Curls are bouncing again around the little head. Meredith follows the index pointed at an enormous woman who is busy selecting items of lingerie. After locking her desk, Meredith goes to talk with the woman and comes back within no more than two minutes.

"All right, honey, you can have one toy. Go to the room, choose one and bring it here to me, I'll look after it for you until your mom is ready to leave. This way nobody can steal it from you." Curls are saying yes in no uncertain way and the young lady marches proudly towards the children's department. Crisis defused. I shake my head in disbelief.

"How many times a day do you have to play police and referee, not to mention tear stopper!"

"All in a day's work, Mrs. Luens. They are not all bad people. Some cases are downright sad. There is a young woman with seven children whose husband committed suicide because he was let go by his employer when the company went into receivership a year ago. Seven mouths to feed and seven bodies to clothe, not counting herself. She is skinny as a rake, talks to nobody when she comes and the children look like shadows following their mother quietly, sometimes blindly because they don't look up around them at all. They are the picture of hurt, all of them."

"What can you do in a case like that?"

"I mentioned it to Mr. Hausen just the week before last. He is going to obtain a double ration card at the food bank for her and the children. They are all too thin and don't look healthy. I've tried to chat a little with the mother, but each time all I got was a look heavy with sorrow and suffering. She would come to the desk to sign her file after her shopping and they would all leave in silence, a silence that can break many hearts. It breaks mine each time. I would like to get to know her a little more than just 'Please sign here, thank you'."

When the clock chimes twelve, Steven comes to the desk and Meredith runs to the kitchen for a quick bite. We say goodbye and wish Steven a good afternoon.

At the little Vietnamese restaurant, Aunt Sumika and I remain silent for a long time before ordering our meal. I am sure Aunt is reliving our experience, as am I. It is difficult to admit that there is so much poverty and despair in this beautiful country. We are a rich country, we give millions to help other nations, why can't we give to our own people? Isn't charity supposed to begin at home? There is something here that I don't understand, I wish Walter were with us right now to answer my questions, he would know what to say and how to explain. Sighing deeply, I break the silence.

"Seven children! Auntie, have they never heard of contraception? Why did they do this to our pathetic world? Were they absolutely sure of the future? If so, they were taking life and fate for granted. Look at what fate decided to do to them. Seven children without a father, my heart breaks for them. What can we do, Auntie?"

"There is not much we can do, honey. As long as the mother refuses to open up to friendship, no one can tear down the wall, it would be tantamount to breaking and entering a private life and it may very well make things worse. It is sad for the little ones, at that age they are extremely sensitive and the experience may scar them for a long time, perhaps even harm their capacity to learn and grow up to be normal adults. These children will probably need psychological assistance."

"Life is too unfair and cruel choosing these innocent children to be its victims."

"What is worse is that we cannot punish or send life to jail... it has all powers and we have none. We cannot fight it, Raffee, it orders and we bow. Life is a mighty force to be reckoned with."

"I am also thinking of the mother, how tired, lonely and helpless she must feel. How long will her physical health hold?"

"And what about her emotional health? How long can she bear this burden alone? Unless she is wonder-woman, she is bound to snap. Then I fear for the children's well-

being. This entire ordeal can be traced back to one source: the bankruptcy of a company. It is all horribly unfair."

"On the other hand, let's congratulate Meredith and Steven and all the other volunteers, they are doing a magnificent job out of the kindness of their hearts. What patience and self-control they have handling such crowds of unruly and rude people. I could never do their job, my patience has the shortest of all fuses, don't you agree, Auntie?"

"It used to be so when you were a teenager, but with time the fuse has gotten longer, we have not seen a temper tantrum in years. You're an angel now, Raffee."

"So Mr. Kozell called me, remember?"

"And you told me that you were an angel of revenge…what does this mean?"

"All in due course, Auntie. Those were mere words, action is more valuable than words. A little more time and all will be cleared up. Did you enjoy your curried shrimps with white noodles?"

"I did. Are we ready for dessert?"

"Yes, let's have the durian ice cream, it tastes out of this world, I know you like it too."

We enjoy our ice cream silently, almost religiously, it is that good. Tea is served one more time and we are ready to leave.

"Where to, Raffee?"

"To the pagoda. I think we should talk to Lord Buddha and ask for his help."

At the pagoda we bow respectfully, sit down on the floor and each of us, in our own way, communicates with Buddha and the spirits. Soon earth fades away and we are one with the beyond, we taste the peace and serenity of a world that is kind and hospitable.

TWENTY

WHEN WALTER called last nigh it was like a confirmation of the existence of telepathy. No, it was telepathy pure and simple as I had wanted to talk to him about what Aunt Sumika and I saw at 'Helping Hands'. His call was more than welcome and we invited him to dinner tonight. After my work at the mansion today I will go to the Asian market to buy a dozen custard apples, I hope to find them at the right stage of ripeness or else it will have to be some other fruit because unripe custard apples are totally inedible. If Walter does not know this fruit, we will be happy to make the introduction and watch him fall in love with its sweetness; very few people can resist this fruit.

Aunt Sumi shakes her head and chuckles as I choose my lime-green smock for today's work.

"You couldn't have a gray or a blue one, you had to have a lime-green and a Halloween orange smocks! I wonder how your employer reacts to all this," Aunt says.

"No reaction whatsoever, Auntie. She may be color-blind after all. I'll be off now, see you later. Bye, Aunt Sumi."

"Drive carefully, don't let Spring intoxicate you, we have an important guest tonight."

"I'll stop at the market to buy fruits on my way home. Bye now."

Under a blue and cloudless sky it feels good to be in tune with Spring and in agreement with all the wild flowers that are adorning the road to St. Thomas. It is as if nature were forcing its beauty on us, spreading its miracle before our eyes; we cannot ignore it and deep down in our hearts we thank the Creator for his generosity, for the rebirth of everything beautiful, and for the promises this season unfailingly brings year after year. It's been two years since I've traveled this road for the first time. I've met Neil in the photo frame, had conversations with him and told him of Aunt Sumi's undying love for him. In his world beyond ours he must know of my intended mission and though I don't know his thoughts, I feel that I will be doing the right thing eliminating his killer, if only to bring back some happiness to my Aunt who loves him so deeply. Neil, Sir, she killed you; please help me to kill her. Soft tears run down my cheeks silently, and as silently I choose to ignore them. How did she elude man's law? She must be highly intelligent, how did she kill him? And to myself I ask, 'How am I going to kill her?' I am not extremely intelligent, I am more heart than brain, will I succeed in this difficult mission? I must, I must, by any means I must.

The outlines of the mansion loom ahead on a canvas of vanishing pink and whispering blue, an oil painting of high quality behind which the wicked witch of the west hides. I am going to clean the house of a witch. Nice going, Raffee! Oh but it's not for ever this cleaning job, it will end. So will she. I grind my teeth and knock on the door.

"Right, do come in, Raphaëlle, and good morning to you. What a gorgeous spring day, it makes everyone feel cheerful."

"Good morning, Madame. Yes, Spring is a lovely season."

As I walk towards the tools cabinet, the phone rings and the lady runs to it in the living-room, only a few feet away from the cabinet. I don my beautiful lime-green smock and psyche myself up for a whole morning of menial work. Standing by the cabinet's door I overhear her conversation. It stops me short and my eyes pop out of my head.

"Linda, calm down, breathe deeply and listen. If you are absolutely sure you can't stand your husband any longer, do what I did: dispatch him. It takes time and patience but in the end success will be guaranteed. Stop puffing and cursing around. Make up your mind and do it. I can help, I've been there, remember? And look at me now, not a worry in the world. Keep this between you and me, and let me know if you need me. Bye, Linda. Don't show your anger, stay calm."

My head is spinning, my rage wants to escape but I force it back inside where it is protesting by pounding viciously under my skull. My cheeks are burning and my hands are shaking. These are signs that I am enraged and out of control. Years ago this was the point where, as a teenager, I literally exploded and threw a formidable temper tantrum even my uncle could not stop. How dares the woman talk this way? Has she no shame, no remorse? She is even boasting! She is right, she can boast, didn't she fool everybody around here? She is intelligent and has planned for success. She is a first-class actor and has played her role to perfection. The perfect crime. Neil is one victim, my Aunt is the other. Oh Lord, how can you let this murder go unpunished for so long? Is she some super-human that nothing and nobody can touch? The untouchable killer. Well, we shall see, won't we? When intelligence is faced with sheer determination, it must yield and retreat. She is intelligent and I am determined. She will yield. All in due course, I tell myself. Now is not the time, not yet. Soon.

"Hello Raphaëlle, I have to go out, your money is on the kitchen table. Do you need anything?" One thought flashes through my head, 'Yes I need you dead' but my lips have more control.

"No, thank you Madame."

I will never understand how this woman can live so happily when she has taken the life of an innocent human being. Is it that easy? Happily ever after? I shut my eyes tight and shake my head in total disbelief.

With these thoughts and emotions still seething under my skull, I begin my work and go through my routine like a robot; downstairs first, then upstairs. I stop at the top of the stairs and look pensively at the hole in the carpet. What if this…what if that? Is this hole a friend? A helper? Can I rely on it? Can I do something to help it help me? I vacuum the bedrooms, dust the furniture and clean the washroom. Then I return to the bedroom with the photographs. Suddenly, like a total idiot, I cry looking at Neil and shaking my head. Why, oh why did you let her do that? You were too young to die, didn't you suspect anything? How cunning and malevolent she must have been. And you must have been in excruciating pain in the final stages of the pancreatic cancer that has been destroying you gradually. My Aunt Sumi told me about it. When you died, she died too in her heart and soul. That's why I want my mission to succeed and I want your killer dead. Then and only then will my Aunt be able to turn the last page of this tragic book and look ahead with inner peace until she is with you again. If in your world beyond ours you can assist me, I'll be for ever grateful. With the sleeves of my lime-green smock I dry my eyes and begin to gather my tools at the top of the stairs. Remembering my near fall of two weeks ago, I proceed with extreme caution. Midway down, I turn around and look back at the top where the carpet has had a tear for as long as I can remember. Now the tear is talking to me, offering ideas and suggestions, even a vision: her body sprawled on the floor near the last step, life gone out. I shudder as I continue on down the stairs. To be revisited, I tell myself. I will be patient and do it right the first time because there won't be a second time.

It took a good ten minutes to find a parking spot at the Asian market, but I am now walking towards the fruits and vegetables displays along Chong Street. Tables are overloaded and very colorful, vendors keep piling up more fruits of all sorts, rearranging this or that corner of their long tables. Busy ants in busy anthills where activity never stops. I am looking for custard apples but all I see are mangoes, lychees, rambutans and other fruits. Since I am determined to have custard apples for tonight's dinner, I keep walking from table to table, shop to shop, wondering if I'll be successful. At the end of Chong Street I turn into a small side street where there are less tables and less people. At the second table I sigh with relief, it is loaded with only one type of fruit: the glorious custard apples. Now begins the challenge. I must touch and gently squeeze each fruit to assess its ripeness; the softer, the riper. But we don't want the ripest one either because its taste has lost all freshness and the flesh has become too watery. What we want is a custard apple between green and over ripe. It is quite a talent to get it right. Aunt Sumi is very good at this, she has lived in Asia for so long. I am just a novice, proud that she is trusting me with choosing the perfect custard apple. Today it is a dozen that I have to choose, so help me god.

The vendor wants to assist, I accept with pleasure. She is an old woman with three and a half hairs on her head, hands with protruding veins, and teeth brown with betel stains. Her knowledge of the fruit is undeniable, I am happy with each one she presents to me. Soon the dozen is bagged, I pay her and thank her very much indeed; she gives me a broad and brown smile, and I leave the market. We will have delicious fruit for dessert tonight.

On my way home, I see before my eyes the tear in the carpet on top of the stairs at the mansion; it is staring back at me, throwing ideas, possibilities and questions left, right and center. Would this, could this be the way? If so, when? I have to succeed at the first attempt because I won't set foot there again after, regardless of the outcome. Why am I shivering at the thought? Isn't this what I want most of all? Isn't this my sacred mission? Am I scared now that it is so close?

"No, you are not scared, you are excited and anxious to act. You want a culmination, you want the end of your Aunt's sorrow and regrets." I am startled and speechless, there's no one else in the car with me. Am I going insane?

"Who are you? Where are you?" I ask aloud, feeling rather absurd.

"I am your partner and helper. I am your soul. Remember our talk under the stars? Remember I said Yes to you?"

"Oh yes, yes, I remember, thank you. If you are here with me now, it means the moment is very close, doesn't it?"

"Yes, it is at your finger tips, act fast and be extremely careful. I must leave now."

"Thank you, Soul." Time to act? So be it. My next workday is next Friday.

At home Aunt Sumi is about to sit down for lunch when I swing the door open and brandish my bag of custard apples.

"I got them, I got them, Auntie, they are ripe and smell like paradise. Sorry I am late. I'll just run to wash my hands and be right back."

We enjoy our good food and I tell Aunt about the kind vendor who helped me choose the fruits.

"I am surprised the other shops didn't have them yet, it is peak season in

Thailand. It's good you found them, we'll have a delicious dessert with Walter tonight. How was your morning?"

"It went fast because I was thinking of the market and the apples," I say with not an ounce of hesitation as if there wasn't a hurricane in my head. When did I learn to control myself so well? Is it the impending action that is giving me such self-assurance? Or is it the certainty that my Soul will be by my side until completion? Either way, I feel optimistic for the first time in a very long time. I want to ask Aunt one more question about Neil but at the last minute I decide to hold my tongue; we have a guest tonight, I don't want to cause her to sink back into sadness as would happen at the mere mention of his name. We're almost there, let's play it safe a little longer. Maria brings coffee and a small coconut pie, one of my favorite sins. I tell her so.

"You have sins, Raffee? How come I don't see them? Maybe I ask Mrs. Luens," she says, turning to Auntie who begins to chuckle.

"Oh, Maria, Raffee is an angel now. But you should have seen her when she was a young teenager, a real terror in our neighborhood; some people called her Bandit Raffee, do you remember, honey?" she asks me.

"I know who called me that. They moved away a long time ago, I wonder what became of Trisha their second daughter. Many people have many sins, big and small. I am no exception."

"But I never see your sins," Maria insists.

"That's because I am a good actress and I hide them well. I promise never to show you any of them, I like you too much."

"You're right, Mrs. Luens, she is an angel." Yeah, an angel of revenge, I think to myself. A cobra in angelic clothing, watch out you killer of Neil, you are next.

"To change the subject, Maria, have you decided with Roberto where he'll attend university? Does he have a particular one in mind?" I ask.

"He says he wants to become a veterinarian. If so, he'll have to go to Drelph to study. This means he will need to find a place to stay, pay rent, cook his meals, etc."

"With his full scholarship it won't be too hard on your wallet, Maria. But if necessary, we can help with food among other things. I would like to ask you something," I say.

"Anything, Raffee."

"I want you to explain to the other two boys the importance of obtaining a full scholarship. This means report cards with A or A- only, no B. Can you do this?"

"Oh yes, I will do and repeat often. Soon it will be Alejandro's turn. I am not sure, but I think he wants to be a science teacher, he is in love with science."

"That's excellent. Keep up the good job, Maria."

Aunt Sumika and I are relaxing on the patio. I am dying to tell her more about my morning but my brains tell me to shut up, and I obey. Why ruin a peaceful afternoon now and an evening with our dear friend Walter later. What I want to say must then never be told and I must swallow each and every word that my lips want to utter.

"I wonder what Raul wants to study when he starts university," I say.

"Maybe he'll want to be a language teacher, he is so good at it. I must say he impresses me with his poetry and haiku writing. What a talented little boy."

"He is not a little boy anymore, Auntie, he is in grade ten. University is not far away. And then Maria will be all alone, I am concerned about her."

"We'll always be there for her, honey. When she is all by herself, she will have less work to do at home and more time to rest, she deserves it. What a wonderful person she is. Did you notice that we've never heard a bad word from her in all the years she's been with us?"

"It's the same with her boys. Once Raul said the word "ass". The skies opened and punishment rained down on earth and on him. He never said it again, that was the only time. Unlike what we heard at the warehouse the other day; I was flabbergasted, to say the least."

"It was awful and very vulgar, but it takes all kinds to make a world and ours is far from perfect."

"I am sure we'll have a more pleasant time with Walter. Maybe we'll talk about the case of the widow with the seven children. For the life of me, Auntie, I don't understand why these people made so many children. They are not stupid people, they are educated, I am sure they know about contraception. I just don't comprehend."

"It could be their religion, their church, their priests. If they are devout Catholics, they reject contraception because their religion forbids it."

"Do you mean Catholicism promotes large families? In this day and age? It's rather primitive, wouldn't you say? Besides, what business does religion have with a woman's body and private life and the right to decide? It's none of its business."

"It's called blind obedience."

"And when something terrible happens and children are orphaned, where does this blind obedience take the woman and her children? To the food bank and the clothing warehouse. That's the help her church offers her? What a disgusting world, Auntie. I feel so bad for the woman we saw at 'Helping Hands'."

"That's a very sad case, I hope she'll get more and better help. If only she would open up a little and allow friendship to tiptoe into her life, I know it would make a big difference. But how to break that wall? We'll mention it to Walter tonight."

When Walter arrives, the clock says seven and we are ready to have a wonderful evening with a wonderful friend. Maria has prepared a duck à l'orange and for dessert we'll have the custard apples from Thailand. Walter lives alone and has to cook his own meals. I wonder what he can cook at ten p.m. when he gets home from work; I am willing to bet he opens a bag of chips and a can of pop. That's a bachelor's life. He needs to be pampered and, between Aunt and me, he'll be tonight.

"Hello Walter, come in," Aunt greets him and he gives her a bouquet of lovely thornless roses.

"Oh, no thorns? Where did you find these?"

"There is a small flower shop near my place, they have many interesting plants there. Nice people too."

"Thank you very much, I'll put these in water right away." She goes to the kitchen and I take over.

"Come to the living room, Walter. It's so good to see you. Be comfortable, remove your tie, you're family and this is an informal evening. Drinks?"

"Just two drops of rum in a soda, please, I am driving." Get that, Raffee? No hard liquor, he is driving.

"So, what kind of day did you have today? Or would you rather talk about something else?" I ask.

"I saw Andrew zip by in his car this morning. He looked in great hurry, his practice must be doing well. Life is funny and not funny. When he was in med school he worked inhuman hours. Now that he has his own practice, he works very human hours. It's the total opposite for me. In university I worked very easy hours; now I work outrageous hours. Of the two of us, he's got the better deal."

"How is that?"

"His practice closes at five p.m. and my work goes on till about ten p.m. And it's going to be this way until we retire."

"It doesn't have to be, Walter. You will get an assistant and be able to go home before ten p.m. Just holler at the head of Community Services, get your way. Then enjoy life a little more, it's normal."

Aunt calls us to the dining room. The table looks so inviting, hunger makes immediate demands. We sit down and enjoy Maria's cooking with gusto. Walter recovers first from the wonders of duck à l'orange.

"This is super delicious, I've never tasted anything this good." And turning to Aunt, he adds, "Mrs. Luens, this is paradise."

"Enjoy, Walter, enjoy, there is much more coming," Aunt says with a warm smile. I raise my glass of wine.

"To good health, good friends and especially to Walter," I say. We clink our glasses and return to the duck for more delights.

Then it's time to bring in the custard apples. Walter has never seen such fruit, we show him how to peel it bit by bit, how to eat the flesh and spit the little black seeds out; there are dozens of seeds in one fruit. When the custard apple is ripe, the taste is divine. Aunt can eat two for dessert and I can sometimes eat three; that's when I am pigging out.

Before we move back to the living room, Aunt dims the light in the dining room and offers after-dinner drinks.

"A coffee for me, please Mrs. Luens," Walter says.

"Tea for me, Auntie." Turning to Walter, I offer, "Would you like to freshen up? There's a little washroom in the hallway; be comfortable, Walter, you're home here."

As he returns to the living room, Aunt Sumi arrives from the kitchen with a tray. He takes it from her and places it on the coffee table. We settle comfortably to enjoy our warm drinks.

"Walter, if you liked the custard apples, I would like to introduce you to many other fruits from Asia; for you it will be like a trip to the Orient," I say.

"I would like that very much. How was your trip to the warehouse? Did it scare you?"

"We were not really scared, only surprised. Meredith and Steven were very nice and helpful with our bags of donations," I say.

"And we stayed until noon. What we saw showed us the other side of human behavior and it was incredible," adds Aunt Sumi.

"It is like that every day. Our volunteers do a marvelous job handling the hordes and keeping the place running. Anything you want to ask me?" Aunt and I look at each other. Who first?

"Walter, why doesn't the government give more assistance to these people, our people? It gives millions to help other countries and doesn't seem to see the rampant poverty right here at home?" I ask.

"The government does help, but chooses to keep its help to a minimum. Whereas helping other countries makes it look good and places it on a pedestal. That's the plain truth. We can't fight it, so we make do with what we're given."

"There was a woman who came with her seven children; they don't look healthy, they look like shadows of themselves. In them we saw three problems, physical, emotional and total dejection. They urgently need extra help.

Meredith says she has tried to befriend the mother but each time she found herself pushed back against the wall. This is a very serious problem, Walter. She needs professional help, can Community Services help?" Aunt asks.

"We are taking this very seriously, the woman will be helped, so will the children. Did you know – perhaps not – that they were living in one room, using a portable two-burner camping stove to cook their meals, and sleeping, all eight of them, on two mattresses thrown on the floor? When our inspector went to see them, he almost didn't believe his eyes, I mean the abject poverty, the sheer despair. He didn't wait to report to me at the office, he used his portable phone to call our emergency department. Believe me, help was immediate. The same evening the family slept in a new place, their new home. We found a one-bedroom apartment for them, for now. Yes, it is small for eight people but it was the only apartment available. It will get better soon. At least now they have a kitchen, a washroom, a bedroom and a living-dining room. The children can play on the huge balcony if they don't want to join the other children in the playground on the side of the building. I think the mother still clings to them and won't let them out of her sight, it's understandable in their situation."

"What about food, Walter? They are all so skinny," I add.

"I had to shout to obtain what I wanted: double ration for all eight of them at the food bank. And you know what? Two of my employees got together to provide fresh fruits and vegetables once a week, and our truck driver will do the home delivery. Doesn't this show that among the crowds of selfish humans there are still good hearts beating? Do you see why I like my job so much?"

Aunt and I are speechless and our eyes are burning hot.

"Walter, you are the best, the very best. We thank you on behalf of the mother and her seven children," Aunt says.

"And also on behalf of all the other mothers and children who come for help. Yes, even those who said !*!^! to Meredith!" I add.

Walter's resounding laughter is and will always be welcome in our home.

TWENTY-ONE

SHOTS were heard late last night and on the news this morning we hear that a man was killed and another is fighting for his life in the hospital. This happens so often, people have become blasé, 'Oh another one bites the dust' they say and shrug. Life goes on, temporarily disturbed by news of a death or two. Our city used to be called Windoaks The Beautiful. It has lost its beauty over the years, it is now often compared to some of the worst cities in the States where crime is a daily occurrence. The difference is that the States have the death penalty and murderers are removed for ever from society. Not so in our country. We protect the lives of murderers and ignore the pleas and needs of the victims' families. We are cold-hearted toward these families, perhaps it has to do with our cold climate, we don't have compassion.

I turn the radio off and ask Maria to fix breakfast, Aunt Sumi will come and join me in a minute. The day is gray, dark clouds are pushing away fragile pink clouds, a light wind arrives and our spring flowers bend their heads way down as if to protect their newborn petals. The sky is heavy with rains and our large trees can't wait to get drenched, they are strong, they don't bend easily.

"Good morning, honey, how did you sleep?" Aunt greets me.

"Not bad, Auntie, and you?"

"After such a good evening with Walter, I slept well until I heard some shots. What were they?"

"The usual, one dead, one in the hospital. It's so easy to obtain firearms, why not use them to settle your scores?"

"And we no longer have capital punishment, so it's free for all. Let's have breakfast and plan our day."

Midway into waffles and coffee, the phone rings. Is it Andrew's receptionist again?

"Hello, Raffee, it's Arielle, sorry to wake you up."

"You're not waking me up, Ari, how are you and what's up?"

"Good news for a change. The lawyer we've consulted about Simone has accepted to represent us. We have strong grounds for a suit he calls 'substandard medical care'. It's a new term for me but I've learned to say it correctly without closing my eyes. So it is now All Go, the bad doctor will get it where it hurts her the most: her bank account."

"And serve her right. How is Simone?"

"She is improving a little each day. She uses crutches to move around and no longer whispers. But because of all the horrible medication she was prescribed, her digestive system is totally berserk. She has appetite and wants to eat, but doesn't dare eat because she is afraid of how her stomach will react. My friend the nurse says it will get better and to eat very little at a time."

"How was your day at Andrew's office?"

"It was hectic, but he is so nice; well organized too, I must say, each file in alphabetical order and good magazines in the waiting room. All in all it was a pleasant day for me. But I am keeping you from breakfast, I am sure. Go back to your coffee, say a huge hello to your Aunt, and let's get together soon." We hang up together. I turn around and scream my head off "Hello!" to Aunt who jumps and looks at me with raised eyebrows.

"Arielle told me to give you a huge hello. It's done. How do you like it?"

"My goodness! You still have your loud teenage voice. Say thanks to Arielle when you see her."

I fill her in on Ari's news, she keeps nodding in agreement, everything is going the right way.

"What are your plans for today?" I ask.

"I would like to take some offerings to the pagoda if you'd like to come."

"Absolutely. That's exactly what I've had in mind for a while. We always think alike, don't we, Auntie?"

"And it's wonderful to have an alter ego; it's the same way between your Uncle Chris and me."

"He's been away too long, we miss him, he should come home now."

"If he does, he'll find out what kind of work you're doing and he won't be happy."

"Oops! Oh well, my job won't last for ever, you know."

"Are you tired of it?"

"A little. Maybe it's time to move on to something more serious."

"That's music to my ears. So, shall we go to the pagoda?"

Aunt takes fresh fruits, boxes of incense sticks and matches to give to the monks. I add two packets of cakes made of rice flour with a sweet mung bean center.

At the pagoda we place our offerings on the table near the main entrance and walk up to the base of the altar where we will sit and pray. At this time of day silence greets us and peace invites us to converse with Lord Buddha. My mind is filled with suppositions, visions, fear of failure, uncertainties and a million questions. My brain is trying to sort things out for me in order to show me the right path to follow in my mission. Culmination is near, I need your assistance, Lord. You already know that I am not very intelligent but soon I will face an extremely intelligent foe: she who killed Neil and broke my Aunt's heart. I want retribution, payment. The long overdue payment must be made now. You have directed my soul to become my partner and my helper, I thank you. Knowing that I have on my side you, my soul, and all the spirits who live near you in the other world gives me great encouragement. My next work day is Friday, day after tomorrow, I will be cautious and act quickly.

"No, not Friday, wait for Monday," a voice whispers distinctly in my ear and I freeze on the spot. Who is this?

"I am your soul, follow my advice, Monday and I will be with you."

Little by little I am beginning to understand why Monday and not Friday. It is all clear now and I will do as I am told. Thank you, Lord Buddha, I am your obedient servant. After bowing respectfully, I get up and walk toward the door. Aunt Sumi follows right behind me.

Although it is still wet outside with the morning rain, we decide to go to Chinatown and spend a few dollars before heading home for lunch. This decision soon becomes an excellent idea when we see tables loaded with custard apples among many other fruits. I also see some huge jack fruits and prickly durians. Aunt told me a long time ago that in Thailand people eat durian with sticky rice and the combination had a taste that would appease the gods on stormy days. I wish Walter were with us, he would find all this very interesting. We buy bags of various fruits and walk back to our car looking like two overloaded donkeys on a Mexican country road.

The next day brings us more rain and Maria says she feels like a duck learning to swim, there is so much water on the ground.

"Rain is good for all plants, Maria," I say.

"But I am not a plant, I no need so much water. In my country we have severe flooding and each year people drown. I cannot forget the vision, it was nightmare."

"Won't happen here, we are on a hill and rain water runs down toward the lake."

The phone rings, I pick it up in the living room.

"Sumika?" a far-away voice asks.

"Just a moment please." I run to the master bedroom calling Auntie, "Phone for you". She takes the call in her room and I leave discreetly, closing the door behind me.

By early afternoon the rain finally stops and there are two or three patches of light blue in the sky trying hard to wash away the gray. Soon a glorious sun smiles at Earth and turns the rain droplets into little diamonds on the leaves of all plants. Pity Maria is not a plant.

Evening finds Aunt and me on the patio with a glass of cool rum-soda, enjoying the garden's freshness after the rain. I like the smell of earth after a downpour as much as I like the smell of freshly cut grass. It has a scent that inspires peaceful thoughts and makes me feel I belong to this earth.

"The phone call was from my friend Arlene in Pennsylvania. Her father passed away, he was one hundred and four years old," Aunt Sumi says.

"I am so sorry, I hope he did not suffer and went peacefully."

"He was in very good health, physically and mentally, he did crossword puzzles every day. It was a minor cold that turned into pneumonia and took him. Arlene and the whole family are very distressed. Even Adam, the retarded boy, knew something was going on and kept asking over and over what happened. He does not understand death and thinks that his grandpa will still play with him every afternoon in the backyard."

"How old is the boy?"

"He is Arlene's nephew and will turn eighteen in two months. Needs around-the-clock help and supervision; he cannot change his clothes and has difficulty handling a fork or a spoon, they don't give him a knife, it would be too dangerous."

"Did the parents know the baby was retarded before he was born?"

"Yes, the mother went through several medical tests and was told the truth by her doctor when the baby was just a tiny little thing in her womb."

"Ant the parents still wanted the child? Incredible, selfish and cruel! What kind of life are they giving this child? Have they given it one speck of thought? No, they did not think of him, they thought of themselves. Selfish. They wanted someone they could control for life, someone who would have no freedom, no privacy, no independence. This is not love because to love is to give; what they are doing is take, they are taking and owning his life under the disguise of providing twenty-four-hour care."

"What else could they have done, honey?"

"In-utero euthanasia, termination of pregnancy at an early stage, a medically safe procedure. Instead, there is now a child, a young man, who can't read or write, play sports, date or dance. He is not an asset to society, he is by his parents' will a burden. When his parents die, who will look after him? Where will he go? He doesn't deserve any of this, he didn't do anything to deserve this. The parents are totally to blame for their selfishness and thoughtlessness. To bring into the world a being who can never love and enjoy his world is the worst of all sins. And his parents have willingly condemned him to this."

"But the mother loved her child and had established a bond very early on, it's called maternal instinct."

"So, it's maternal instinct that pushed that poor boy out of the womb and into a world he will never understand, enjoy and love? I don't like what you call maternal instinct, Auntie, it is very wrong and in this particular case it stinks of selfishness, especially on the mother's part."

"There are things and feelings we do not understand, we certainly cannot blame the mother for wanting to keep her retarded child."

"Society *is* keeping her child, and when he becomes an orphan, it is society that will continue to keep him. He is a ward of society because his mother did not have enough courage to end her pregnancy when it was still safe to do so and prevent the hell that is her son's life now. Maternal instinct misplaced."

"It's really a difficult situation, I wonder how Arlene copes with it. She didn't say much on the phone but I am sure it weighs heavily on her heart. Are you working tomorrow, honey?"

"Yes, I am. The lady entertains every Friday night and wants the place sparkling clean to welcome her guests. Then the following Monday I come and clean up the jumble from Friday. It's beginning to be boring."

"Then you should tell her you're quitting."

"Yes, soon. What shall I do next?"

"You can teach school or college, you can travel for a while, you.."

"And leave you here all alone? Never."

"What a sweetheart you are. You could approach Stephie's father or Walter. Who knows? There may be something interesting for you. There is no hurry at all, you can take your time and try anything you want, barring another cleaning job." This makes me chuckle.

"On account of tomorrow's work, I shall bid you good night, Lady, and head to my bedroom. Happy dreams, Auntie."

"Sleep tight, honey. What color smock tomorrow?"

"The Halloween orange."

"You're crazy!"

"Thank you for the compliment. Good night." I blow her a kiss as I tiptoe to my bedroom.

In the middle of the night I woke up and saw standing before my eyes Adam, the retarded young man. Tears were running down his cheeks, he was sobbing and didn't know how to wipe his face; he was just standing there motionless and speechless. I had to rub my eyes to make sure I wasn't dreaming. When I opened my eyes and he was still there, I began to doubt my sanity. I took my courage in both hands and decided to speak to him.

"What are you doing here, Adam? And why are you crying?"

To my greatest surprise, he stopped crying, blew his nose with a tissue he took from his breast pocket and looked directly at me. There was life and high intelligence in his deep blue eyes. For some reason I began to shiver. And then Adam spoke.

"I am here to tell you that I am deeply unhappy with my life. I am crying because people around me think I am a bucket of shit and treat me as such. I never asked to be born, she forced me to be born. I am considered a mentally retarded person and they won't stop treating me as such until I die. Or until they and I die." He looked intently into my eyes and then continued.

"My mother thinks she is a saint, a martyr, because she looks after me day and night. Because she feeds me and bathes me, she thinks she is giving me the best of life. She thinks she is GIVING but in fact she has taken everything from me the moment she decided that this retarded fetus would be allowed to be born. I had no say, the doctors had no powers, they could only recommend, not command. And so, for the past eighteen years I have been a burden to society, a whipping boy, a good-for-nothing. I have recently made a decision: they, my parents, and I will die the same day, soon. I wanted to tell you this because, though we are strangers, I know that deep down in your heart you are on my side. Your thinking is right, your feelings are right. Keep walking on the right path, Raphaëlle. Farewell for now."

Adam leaves. I remain motionless for a long while. My face is wet with my own tears but I have no idea when they began their journey down my cheeks. My heart is torn apart, I am sad and I feel totally helpless. So much unhappiness in so young a person. Oh how I hate the parents who caused this to be. Well, Adam, when you have accomplished your deed and moved on to the world beyond, know that I was on your side and agreed with every word you uttered. Go in peace, my friend.

The rest of the night was, surprisingly, calm and peaceful enough to allow me a few hours of good sleep until it was time to get up and go to work.

I feel very light this morning, as if somebody had removed a heavy burden from my shoulders. I didn't say a word to Adam last night, I let him speak out and empty his heavy heart of all the bitterness that had accumulated there for the past eighteen years. It did him good to talk as it did me good to listen. Now we are on the same wavelength, he knows I am on his side, I am his friend.

After the last left turn off the highway, I see the massive form of the mansion on the horizon. My work begins now in my head, not when I am inside the house. This reminds me of what my mother used to say, 'When you are expected to work at nine o'clock, you arrive ten minutes earlier so that at nine sharp you start working. You don't arrive at nine because you are not expected to arrive at nine but to start work at nine. Remember this always, Raffee.' May she enjoy the peace of her resting place with my father by her side. The lady of the house is in the front yard when I pull into the driveway. She is watering invisible plants in a brown planter.

"Right. Hello Raphaëlle, beautiful day isn't it. I am trying to make these seedlings grow fast, I am told the flowers are beautiful but the plant requires lots of TLC," she says as I step out of my car.

"Good morning, Madame. What's the name of the flower?" I ask.

"It's called Twelve o'clock rose because it blooms at noon and stays open till six in the evening."

"I know the variety, the flowers have no fragrance, but they come in many gorgeous colors."

As I head toward the entrance, she adds, "I have a dentist appointment this morning, your money will be on the kitchen table."

"Thank you, Madame," and I close the door behind me. Phew! No more talking. It's time for the grand ballet to begin, broom, rags, gloves, feather duster and company, a great corps de ballet ready to perform for a mean killer. The show will be called Danse Macabre and there will be only two performances: today and Monday. I fly from room to room, sometimes on points, sometimes in a pirouette, all the while hoping she wouldn't see me. Then I hear her car's engine, she is leaving. I resume my chores and once the downstairs is done, I climb the stairs to go clean the bedrooms, all beautiful three of them. I must give her credit, she has a keen sense of artistry, each room is exquisitely decorated. There is even a tree in the washroom, it is made of imperial jade and must have cost a small fortune. To have this kind of money and not call somebody to repair the tear in the carpet is beyond my comprehension.

In the room with the photographs, I stop cleaning and start a silent conversation with Neil. It won't be long now, Sir, I promise. Soon your killer will be made to pay for what she did to you. The day of payment is fast approaching, the day of your liberation from your present jail. I will make sure you get your freedom back. Better yet, I will make sure you are with Aunt Sumika again. I am not sure yet how it will all be accomplished, but I know it will be; trust me, Mr. Jahe. And remember, I am your friend and ally because I am the niece of the woman you love so much and who loves you so deeply. There is a time for everything, and everything will be done in its own time. I will see you next Monday. Good bye, Sir.

With all my tools now gathered at the top of the stairs, I begin to go down step by step, avoiding the gaping tear at the very top. Thoughts, and because of them, questions are now invading my mind. My Soul said Monday but not *how* on Monday. Will I be intelligent enough to pull it off? One thing is certain: I will not change my mind. At this very moment I wish I had someone near me to talk to me and lighten up the invisible heavy blanket that is threatening to bury me under the magnitude of what will take place next Monday. I am frightened all of a sudden and it is with shivers that I close the front door and hurry to my car.

The pagoda is where I must go before heading home. I had no one to talk to all morning at the mansion. I need to share my feelings of uncertainty and seek reassurance and encouragement. I also need peace in my heart and on my face so Aunt Sumi won't be suspicious, she can read faces so well, it's uncanny.

The coolness and silence inside the pagoda is a balm on a rather agitated mind, I feel its blessings even before I reach my usual spot to sit down and converse with Lord Buddha. I do not waste a minute and confide in him immediately, telling him all that is on my mind, everything mixed together, fear, uncertainty, doubts, hopes, begging for help and promises to do as I am told. So much concentration and fervor causes me to shake and close my eyes. In this very moment I see in vivid details with eyes closed how my mission will be accomplished, what I will do before I leave the mansion for ever, and who will accompany me until I reach home. Opening my eyes, I look intently at the altar and deep down in my heart I thank Lord Buddha for allowing me to see things not yet materialized.

With gratitude and respect, I leave the pagoda to go home and have lunch with my beloved Aunt Sumika. I feel safe now that I know what will take place next Monday and it is with a light heart that I enter our house, almost skipping with relief.

TWENTY-TWO

YESTERDAY Maria brought us three large egg plants from her garden and today she will cook them for our lunch. I can't wait, I've never eaten egg plants before. She promised us, 'You will like them I am sure.' There is a vegetable Aunt introduced once, it is called chayotte and it grows on a vine in tropical climates. It has a pleasant taste and is very easy to cook. Aunt says I am easy to please, I eat everything; it is true with the exception of raw fish and raw meat. You put these on the table and I fly to Timbuktu.

Yesterday was my last day of work at the mansion. Nobody else knew it was my last day. I did my usual thorough job of cleaning the house. The lady went out to see a friend of hers around ten and left my money on the kitchen table as usual. "In case I am not back before you leave," she said. "Thank you, Madame," I replied and she was off. I pretended it was a day like any other day, there was nothing special, I would just clean the downstairs first, then the upstairs. I even hummed a tune or two, all the while telling myself 'everything will be all right, no need to get excited, anxious or afraid'. I kept reminding myself that I was not alone, that my helper was near me and would help and direct me when the time came.

Upstairs in the room with the photographs, I lingered on after each frame had been gently dusted off. Then I looked at Neil in his prison, I envisioned Aunt Sumi and him together, and my eyes began to burn. In one instant, one lightning instant, I removed his photo from the frame, placed the empty frame in one of the drawers, rearranged the other photographs around so as not to show the empty space left by Neil's photo. "You will be free today, Sir. Never again in jail," I whispered to him in the left pocket of my smock, and I went on to finish my work.

On my way home I felt a strong, almost physical push to drive directly to the pagoda, someone invisible was giving me the order. I did what I was told, without questioning. Inside the pagoda, surrounded by silence and peace, I bowed deeply to the altar and began a dialogue with Lord Buddha. "You know why I had to do it. It was not for pleasure, it was not even for me. I don't know what the outcome will be, I just obeyed instructions and did what I was told to do. And I am grateful that you sent me a helper because on my own I wouldn't have achieved a single thing; I do not have the superior intelligence of Neil's killer. If my mission has met with success, I'll know how to present the results to my dear Aunt Sumi. From then on I would hope to see happiness tiptoe back into her life. All this I owe to your kindness, understanding and compassion. From the bottom of my heart I thank you. I am your obedient servant."

Today, although I am breathing a little more easily than yesterday, one question remains stubbornly in my mind: did I succeed? Until I know for certain, nothing should show on my face, not a single spark of the fierce fire that is burning inside me, Aunt must suspect nothing of the ongoing battle between me and the yet unknown result. Will I be able to keep cool in her presence? Or will I fall apart? Not wanting to take a chance, I decide to call Arielle to plan something together for the day. This decision is also known as the ostrich game, head in the sand.

"Hello, Ari, did I wake you up?"

"Hi, Raffee, no you didn't, I was up at six this morning. What's new?"

"I was wondering if you would like to spend some time with me downtown today."

"Oh yes! That'll be nice, I like downtown but not on my own. What time? You pick me up or I you?"

"I'll come in about half an hour, we can have breakfast in Chinatown. See you soon."

I scribble a note for Auntie, don my jeans and a blue shirt, grab my handbag, and take off. On my way to Arielle's place I keep repeating to myself, 'everything is all right, don't fret, you had a good helper with you'.

The fence around Ari's house is covered with blue Morning Glory blooming profusely. What a beautiful sight. I ring the bell and she comes running.

"I am very hungry, let's eat first, shall we?" she says.

"Right on. We are going to that small eatery with the funny name "Potbelly", they serve delicious Chinese things for breakfast, are you game?"

"I am so hungry, you could take me to Dracula's place, I'd be game. How is your Aunt?"

"She is very well. How are Simone and your Mom?"

"Mom is fine, Simone is getting better. She hates the crutches but still needs them to move around."

The little restaurant is packed and we have to wait for a table. When the waitress points one to us, we run to it before someone else snatches it. Quickly we order and the waitress brings us a pot of coffee and two cups as a start. The rest follows within five minutes and Arielle and I fall silent, we are both very hungry; talking comes second to eating. Arielle is not eating, she is swallowing.

"Take it easy, Ari, show some respect to your stomach," I say.

"Phew! I was starving, too lazy this morning to fix breakfast, I just had a glass of milk. This stuff is really good, I mean the fried 'chia wai'."

"How is the lawsuit going? Do you have a good lawyer, not a shark?"

"He is not a shark, he is an old gentleman who called Mom 'kid' the other day. It made her smile to heavens. I didn't know these things could take years, and I still wonder why. I always thought it would be something like Get In, Fight, and Get Out. But that's only me talking. Mom and Simone have more patience. What's new aboard your ship?"

"We had a very nice evening with Walter last week. He works so hard, I told him to hire an assistant. Did you enjoy being Andrew's receptionist for a day?"

"I was glad I could help, he is so busy I wonder if he ever has time to breathe deeply in and out now and then. His practice looks very successful and he is a nice man. Remember in Grade Seven when that bad guy Matthew wanted a fight with him?"

"Oh yes, it was something else and we all liked the way Andrew handled it. Do you remember every word of the exchange?"

"Sure, it went like this: Matthew told Andrew to 'go to hell'. Andrew answered, 'No I won't, I don't like the way your mother runs it.' It was grand! We applauded. Fortunately there was no teacher around, especially the Math teacher who was always generous with detentions, I never liked him."

After another cup of coffee each, we leave the 'Potbelly'.

"You know, Raffee, Simone's brother is home with us for a few days. Come and meet him, he always has interesting stories to tell. And Mom and Simone will be delighted to see you again."

"Simone's brother who borrowed your car when the catastrophe hit you? What's his name?"

"It's Eric, he is really a good guy. Shall we go?"

"All right, let's go, I have all the time in the world."

I drive us back to her place. She can't wait to show me her small herb garden and tell me with pride that she has planted all the herbs from seeds. It is quite an achievement and I congratulate her. We remove our shoes and enter by the side door.

"Well, hello Raphaëlle," her Mom greets me.

"Hello to you, Mrs. Dowling. How are you?" I hear a klip klop sound and Simone arrives on her crutches.

"Good to see you up and around, Simone," I say.

"Better when I can throw the crutches away," she rolls her eyes in disgust.

"And this is my cousin Eric, he travels a lot and has many stories to tell." Turning to him, she adds, "Eric, this is our good friend Raphaëlle."

We settle in the living room, Simone places the crutches by the side of the sofa, and Mrs. Dowling goes to the kitchen to get drinks and treats.

"Eric, tell us again what you saw on the road between Montial and Windoaks," Arielle asks.

"It was on a country road, not the highway. A woman and three children covered in rags, holding a small cardboard box close to their chests and walking in single file with the mother at the back."

"What were they doing?" I ask.

"They were going to the market place to beg for their food for the day. I followed to see who would give and how people would treat them. What I saw made me sick and ashamed. I saw humans treating humans like animals, even spitting on the sidewalk where the family was standing. I couldn't hear what the people said because the car's windows were closed but I could easily see what was going on. I didn't know what to do or who to call for help. On impulse I parked the car, walked to the mother, and we spoke.

"I am not asking for much, Sir, just enough food for the four of us for the day. We beg every day and we get insulted every day. I told the boys to bite their tongues and keep quiet, except to say Thank you if somebody gives us something," she said.

"I don't have food with me, but if you'll accept money, I would like to help," I offered. In an instant I saw her eyes fill up, it almost made mine follow suit. I gave her fifty dollars and a piece of paper with a phone number to call."

"Whose number?" I ask.

"Community Services where my friend Frank works. The mother and her boys thanked me and I left, hating the well-to-do humans who spit on the have-nots."

I keep shaking my head in disbelief and in anger. Life repeating itself, life unable to think of something new, and repeating itself over and over. First it was the widow with seven children and now this. I will mention this to Walter.

"You did the right thing, Eric, bless you," I say.

Mrs. Dowling serves us tea, we chat a while longer, have lunch and around four o'clock I leave my friends to go home, I've been out all day. I needed this diversion, I didn't want the company of my other thoughts. But now I'll have to face them and not show Aunt Sumi that I am preoccupied. As I enter the living room, she hears me and runs to me from the kitchen.

"Raffee, you had a call from somebody named Francesca, she asked you to call her back today. Sounded rather urgent."

"It's the employment agency, maybe she has something new for me, I'll call her in a minute." And to myself I say, 'not another cleaning job, please, I am done with cleaning'. I go to my bedroom to change and freshen up. Back in the living room, I call her.

"Hello Francesca, my Aunt says you called me? Sorry, I was out with friends. What's up?"

"Bad news, Raphaëlle, I learned this morning that your boss is dead."

"Boss? Who's my boss?" I am beginning to shake.

"I mean Mrs. Betty-Ann Jahe died Monday night in her home. Her friend Linda called to let me know, I am calling to let you know. Your job at the mansion has ended. If you need another job, please let me know. Mrs. Jahe left excellent references for you."

"How awful, I can't believe it. Thank you for letting me know, I'll talk to you soon. Thanks again."

I need to sit down immediately, my head has been replaced by a machine gone berserk, I don't see the living room or the furniture in it for the wild spinning that has taken over my entire body. My brain tries to throw visions of death by staircase before my eyes but I strongly push them away. "Why?" the brain asks, "you deserve to know, you have accomplished your mission. Now you take three deep breaths, that's right, in and out. Again. Composure, take back your composure. BREATHE for heaven's sake! That a girl. Go to your room, splash cold water on your face until it is close to freezing. Towel dry. Leave your room, return to the world outside. The storm has passed. You will finish your job later."

Suddenly I am hungry, famished. In the kitchen Aunt Sumi is still very engrossed in the new recipe for stuffed portobello mushrooms; I don't want to disturb her, so I just grab a plastic bag full of mini croissants. There are glasses and good bottles in the dining room, red wine, rosé and white. With food and drink comforting me, my composure happily returns. It is time to plan the finish of the mission and present to my dearest Aunt the fait accompli. It is high time for me to erase from memory the mansion, the witch and everything connected to both. It is also urgent that I go to the little pagoda and have a long talk with Lord Buddha and the spirits. But it is almost six o'clock and evening is in a hurry to come. Since I don't drive after sun down, I must wait till tomorrow to go to the pagoda. One night to spend in earthly limbo before I can talk to the master in his home.

In today's newspaper there was an obituary about Mrs. Jahe which I hastened to cut out and take to my bedroom. Tonight when Aunt and I are on the patio, I will bring my mission to a close and present to her the results. From then on I want the words happy and happiness to sound and resound everywhere in our home. I myself will breathe out all the worries and concerns, the doubts and uncertainties that have kept me hostage for so long. The past will truly be past, I'll have nothing to do anymore with the witch, she is gone for good, my horizon is clear. Aunt and I will now concentrate on praying for Uncle Chris's return. There is like a veil of peace covering me, this feeling has been with me since I woke up this morning. It gives me the impression that I have just come home from a very long trip far away, a pleasant and soothing feeling.

"Good morning, Raffee, how are you this morning?" Aunt asks as she enters the kitchen.

"Everything fine, Auntie, how about you?"

"I slept like a log, this April weather is delightful, you leave your window open at night and sleep moves right in the moment the light is out."

"I'll fix breakfast, Auntie. Toast or waffles? Coffee first, of course."

"Of course. Make it toast, honey."

We feed our winged beggars first, then we settle comfortably to enjoy breakfast.

"Maria told me Roberto was accepted at the University to start his studies to become a veterinarian. He is in for several years, I hope he doesn't drop out," Aunt says.

"I don't think he will, Auntie, he is such a serious boy, sometimes too serious for his age."

"He needs to be a model for his younger brothers. Since their father's death he has assumed the role of head of the household. I know Maria relies on him to keep discipline at home when she is not there."

"It's hard to believe that all three of them are now young men, little boys no more. I can't help admiring Maria."

"The sum of her efforts and sacrifices, three magnificent successes. She can rest on her laurels, she deserves the gold medal. What are your plans for the day, honey?"

"The day belongs to you, Auntie, but tonight I invite you for dinner at the Golden Lotus."

"Oh, lovely surprise, what's the occasion?"

"Nothing very special, just a good meal for the two of us."

"Tonight? This means I'll do the driving, right?"

"You don't mind, Auntie? It's my stupid reduced night vision condition."

"I don't mind at all, and it is not a stupid condition, I know many people who have it and they are far from stupid. None of them are lucky enough to have your gorgeous eyes though."

"It's the Luens color, isn't it! Dad and Uncle, Peter and me."

The Golden Lotus is very busy as usual and we have to wait to be seated. But the wait is worth it because the food is divine. We place our order and take a first sip of the hot jasmine tea served the moment we sat down.

"The place looks different at night," Aunt says.

"Yes it does, but it is a lovely difference, look at the oil lamps on every table, each one rests on a golden lotus leaf and the light reflects on the leaf. Quite a nice sight I must say."

"It's beautiful. So, again, what's the occasion for this treat, honey?"

"Well, er.. Let's eat first, I'll tell you later, it's a bit too noisy here. Deal?"

"All right. Here come the evening delights, let's enjoy."

We eat our succulent seafood with gusto and for dessert we order sour sop ice cream, it's to die for. But then with the Luenses, all ice creams are to die for, it must be genetic. Uncle Chris's favorite is the durian ice cream. At the pagoda this morning, Uncle was mentioned and spirits told me to expect his return shortly. This made me very happy indeed, he has been gone too long, life at home was not normal, he was missing and we didn't feel whole without him; we need to be three, not two, in this family. So, he is coming back finally. I was elated at the news and thanked the spirits for bringing it to me. Life looks good, Neil's killer gone for good, Uncle coming back, I can now turn a certain page away, the page with an illustration of a witch in a beautiful mansion. I am rid of the past, Aunt will know the truth soon, and happiness will, at long last, reside in our home again. I may go away for a few days to allow Uncle and Aunt to rekindle their love and renew their marriage vows. Their happiness is dearer to me than my own, that's the measure of my love for them. Not to mention my deep gratitude.

The night is gentle and so inviting, Aunt and I decide to take our glasses of Curaçao out to the patio. It is winding down time, a time for relaxation, contemplation and reflection; it is day's end and the birth of night, we behold this in our own way, acknowledging the divine superiority of the Creator. As discreetly and silently as I can, I go to my bedroom and bring back with me a brown envelope.

"It's for you, Auntie, all for you, open it," I say.

She opens it and finds first the obituary. I brace myself. She gasps, shivers, and then looks at me. I simply nod.

"Go on, Auntie, there is something else inside."

With Neil's photo in her hands, she screams, places the photo on her cheek, shakes her head, and then finally the tears come. She sobs, her shoulders move up and down, she chokes and it scares me a bit, but I let the reaction follow its course. She has suffered for too long, she needs time to wash the suffering out of her system. If it takes one hour or ten, I will keep quiet and allow her memories to calm down to a point where she can finally look up and physically see me, her niece Raphaëlle.

"Oh Raffee, oh my sweetheart, when did this happen?"

"A long time ago and recently. I had known the truth shortly after I started to work at the mansion and I've made it my mission to one day present you with these papers." As she raises her eyebrows in horror, I hasten to add, "Have no fear, Auntie. It's all done now and in the past, the killer has gone for good. You need to look ahead, never again back. I've had many conversations with Neil at the mansion, I called him 'the prisoner in a photo frame' and I promised him freedom and a reunion with you, albeit a yet intangible one. You have to concentrate on the future and on the good news."

"What good news?"

"Hold on to your chair, Auntie. Uncle Chris will be here in a matter of days."

"No! Impossible! How on earth do you know that?"

"Not on earth, Auntie. From the beyond the news came to me while I was praying at the pagoda. Let me tell you this: I will always trust the word of one spirit against that of a thousand homo sapiens. Uncle will be with us soon. And Neil is now with you on earth waiting to be with you again in the other world where he lives. It is happiness wherever you look. Let's raise our glasses and call it a day, shall we, favorite Aunt?"

How quickly a week goes by when you are busy getting yourself and your home ready for a great joy. Auntie is now truly believing that Uncle Chris will be here soon; she has been to the Asian market several times to buy his favorite food and fruits, and cakes. "Making up for lost time," she said because for two days after the revelation, she thought it was too good to be true and had doubts about his return. She hasn't asked me for details of my mission, at least not yet. I know some day she will. I hope she won't, but I am ready.

I myself have certainly erased that part of my life, those days are gone for ever. In the end, I didn't have to buy any products or gadgets to do my job, the tear in the carpet did it for me, I only needed to enlarge it a wee bit before I left the mansion that Monday. It is now fait accompli and I am moving on.

I hear Maria picking up the mail from the box at the front of our house, she usually brings it inside before getting herself busy in the kitchen.

"Hello, Maria, gorgeous morning, how are the boys today?" I ask.

"They are in a hurry for Easter break to come and Roberto is already getting ready for University, six months ahead!"

"He is eager, that's good. What kind of mail do we have today?" She hands me a half dozen envelopes, one of them a brown thing sticking out of the pile. It is addressed to me from – who on earth? – and it comes from Belke, Langford & McMahon LLP, Barristers and Solicitors. Bells start ringing in my head, my eyes cloud over, not with tears, but with fear. "The thing" is coming back to haunt me, I'll end up in jail for sure. Poor Aunt and Uncle, I have failed you, I am going to jail, I am so sorry. There is no forgiving, you should disown me totally.

"Open the envelope, you idiot," an inner voice tells me. I obey. Inside, accompanied by a letter full of legal jargon, there is a certified cheque for five hundred thousand dollars payable to Raphaëlle Luens from the estate of the late Mrs. Betty-Ann Jahe. I want to vomit on the spot but somehow anger conquers my stomach, I don't vomit, I silently lash out at her, the witch. I don't want your money, not a penny of it; it makes me sick, you make me sick. Stay where you are, out of my life for ever, you are not welcome in my world. The money is going straight to Wat Phanri, the Buddhist pagoda where my Uncle has lived and prayed for so many months. You have killed, you are now dead. Retribution, justice.

Payment in full.

Raised in the Far East, the author has traveled extensively around the world on numerous teaching contracts and has become an expert at living out of a suitcase.

Now retired from teaching, the author enjoys reading, writing and getting together with friends for conversations and hearty debates on linguistics, poetry and world events.

Buddhism holds an important place in the author's life.